SPELLBOUND

SPELLBOUND

THE CHARMED CITY™
BOOK ONE

KELLI ROBYNS

MICHAEL ANDERLE

DON'T MISS OUR NEW RELEASES

Join the Florid Romance email list to be notified of new releases and special promotions (which happen often) by following this link:

https://floridromance.lmbpn.com/about/sign-up-for-our-newsletter/

Published by Florid Romance
an imprint of LMBPN Publishing
2375 E. Tropicana Avenue, Suite 8-305
Las Vegas, Nevada 89119 USA

Version 1.01, May 2025
eBook ISBN: 979-8-89354-808-2
Print ISBN: 979-8-89354-809-9

ONE

Lila Matthews groaned as she shouldered open the door of The Daily Grind and juggled two cardboard boxes of lids and napkins. The morning sun had hardly peeked over the rooftops, yet a stiff warmth clung to the Manhattan air. It was the kind of humid, sticky summer day that made bending over an espresso machine feel like working inside a sauna. She grumbled under her breath, frustration already carving lines into her usually cheerful face.

She set the boxes on the front counter with a soft thump. An ivory envelope—grimly official and sealed— slipped from the top box, fluttering to the floor near her scuffed canvas sneakers. Lila recognized the rent notice immediately. Just seeing the envelope's return address sent a spike of anxiety through her chest. She scooped it up and shoved it deeper into her purse, trying not to let the swirl of dread ruin her entire morning. Of course, her rent would be overdue now, and part of her paycheck had vanished into repairing the flickering old neon sign outside the café.

Why did she ever think opening a coffee shop in one of the most expensive rental properties in the world was a great idea? Oh, yeah, she loved Manhattan and decided to stay after graduating from NYU seven years ago. At first, she worked here as a barista while a student but then coffee seeped into her DNA. When the owner decided he'd had enough of Northern winters, he pulled up stakes, moved to Florida, and fronted Lila the money to take over the shop. At the time, it seemed too good of a deal to pass up.

She exhaled sharply. There was also her overdue phone bill to consider. The red font had screamed PAST DUE, and the zero in her bank account glared at her each time she checked it. It had become a daily weigh-in of which crisis was more pressing: rent or phone service. Both threatened to unravel her precarious balance, but there was no time for that now. She flicked on the lights, then the main switch on the coffee machines, preparing to open in thirty minutes.

The Daily Grind had an unassuming exterior, a worn brick façade squeezed between a flamboyantly painted nail salon and a discount electronics store. Above the entrance, the café's neon sign sputtered with the letters D-A-I-L-Y flickering more often than not. She had spent money she didn't have trying to fix it last week, but the repair job seemed to have lasted only a few days. She clenched her jaw, forcing herself to smile. Customers would show up any minute, and if there was any skill she had truly mastered, it was pretending everything was under control.

She nudged a button on the register to check if it would wake from its usual morning grogginess. As she waited for the system to blink to life, she noticed her reflection in the glass pastry display that was now overflowing with expensive treats she sourced from a team of local stay-at-home moms. That was also part of this place's charm, homemade pastries, but she was wondering if this was also something she'd have to soon cut.

Her wavy auburn hair was pulled into a messy ponytail that kept threatening to escape, and faint shadows marred the skin under her bright green eyes, courtesy of yet another sleepless night. She tugged the collar of her shirt to let in a bit of air. The overhead lights caught a subtle scattering of freckles across her cheeks, an inheritance from her mother. She swallowed down a twinge of homesickness and flicked her gaze away.

"Hey, morning," came a cheerful voice from behind her. Maya Chen, best friend and co-worker extraordinaire, strode in. She wore a loose black T-shirt and jeans stained from weeks of spilled coffee grounds, and her short, stylish hair sat in neat waves around her face. Her chipped black nail polish provided a hint of rebellion beneath her otherwise glowing smile. "Wondering where you were. You look stressed."

Lila gave an offhand grunt, not trusting her voice to hide her problems. "Bills," she said, hearing how flat and tired she sounded. "And this ancient place is basically on life support." She jerked her head toward the espresso machine. "Who knows if it'll work today."

Maya let out a sympathetic hum. "We should get hazard pay," she joked. "I bet half the folks who come here have no clue how close we are to meltdown daily."

It was a typical brand of gallows humor for them. The café was known for its unassuming charm, a far cry from the sleek chain coffee shops scattered across Manhattan. People came to The Daily Grind for the softly piped music and the promise of personal attention—Lila liked that. Despite the old machines and flickering sign, or maybe because of them, regulars found it had more soul than those big-name franchises. Not that intangible "soul" did anything to fix Lila's bills.

As soon as Maya helped prop open the front door, the first wave of customers trickled in. Half of them wore impeccable business attire, the other half wore bleary-eyed expressions that pinpointed them as either students or night-shift survivors. Lila forced a grin. She and Maya settled into their well-rehearsed dance: Maya took orders, and Lila manned the espresso station, pulling shots, texturing milk, and sliding lattes across the counter with practiced efficiency.

Time blurred for the next thirty minutes, a nonstop churn of cappuccinos, caramel macchiatos, and double shots for the caffeine-starved. Somehow, Lila managed to keep her head above water, though each time she had to refill the milk steamer, her arms burned in reminder of how physically demanding the job was. During a lull, she braced her palms on the counter, letting out a low sigh.

"You okay, Lil?" Maya asked softly as she popped the top on a stack of pastry boxes. She glanced around to ensure no customer was in earshot.

"Fine, yeah. Just...money stresses. You know, the usual." Guilt twinged in Lila's heart for letting everything get to her. She had never enjoyed complaining, but Maya saw through her bravado anyway. Thankfully, her best friend knew when to nudge and when to let it go.

As if on cue, the door chimed again, announcing a second rush of patrons. Lila planted a pleasant smile on her face and dived back into the fray. She poured an iced vanilla latte for a woman in a crisp linen blazer while double-checking the bakery inventory on her phone. Then she turned around just as someone shouted, "Extra foam, please," and realized the espresso machine's gauge lights were flickering ominously. She scolded the contraption under her breath to behave.

The air in the shop began to feel thick, or maybe that was just her tension clogging her chest. She needed a breeze, a break, anything. The café's door was open, but no real breeze drifted inside. Once she'd finished topping off the cappuccino, she picked up the milk frother to prepare the next latte. Its metal surface was warm from repeated use. Yet something about the warmth felt... different. The handle seemed to vibrate in her grip, as if tiny pulses were throbbing through it.

She paused, blinking. Maybe she was just exhausted. She took a breath and tried to center herself—like her grandmother used to say about controlling stress: "Inhale for three seconds, exhale for three seconds." Lila had always scoffed at such advice, but right now, her body trembled with tension.

A sudden jolt flashed through her fingertips, seizing her muscles. It felt like an electric spark, except it wasn't painful—just alarmingly hot, like static electricity that crackled through her veins at lightning speed. Before she could even cry out, a brilliant green spark arced from the tip of the frother, dancing across the stainless-steel wand as if it had a mind of its own.

Lila sucked in a sharp breath. A strangled "What the hell?" slipped from between her lips. The milk frother clattered against the machine, narrowly missing the steaming pitcher as she jerked back. Her heart hammered. Around her, the entire café seemed to pause: the steam subsided, customers fell silent, and Maya looked up in alarm.

Time clenched for a split second. Lila stared at the frother in her grip, certain she had just imagined the spark. But she could see the bright afterimage imprinted on her vision, the color etched behind her eyelids like a ghostly green swirl.

It hadn't been a reflection or a trick of the overhead lights. A surge of hot panic rose in her chest.

"That was—did you see that, too?" asked a middle-aged woman with a worried frown, drawing back from the counter. Her purse strap slipped from her shoulder, an unspoken sign of how uneasy the sight had made her.

Lila's throat went dry. She opened her mouth but found no coherent explanation. Instinct screamed at her to say something normal, something to dismiss it as a glitch. But her mind felt scrambled.

Maya, usually quick-thinking in bizarre moments, leaned forward and pasted on her best "nothing to see here" smile. "Looks like a little power surge," she said, far too brightly. "Our wiring is ancient. No worries, folks. Happens sometimes in older buildings." A ripple of uneasy murmurs passed through the small crowd, but after a beat, they seemed to accept the excuse. Conversations resumed, more subdued than before. A few people eyed Lila like she might spontaneously blow a fuse again.

Lila swallowed hard and dropped the frother onto its station. Her heart hammered so loud that she half-expected the customers to notice. Maya nudged her gently. "Go check the fuse box or something," she whispered, trying to sound casual. Lila nodded stiffly, relief flickering in her eyes. She wiped her clammy palms on her apron, stepping away from the espresso station as Maya took over, voice bright with forced confidence.

But Lila never made it to the fuse box. Curiosity and dread propelled her glance toward the café's entrance, drawn by an odd awareness prickling along the back of her neck. That was when she saw him.

A tall man leaned against the threshold, arms folded. His hair was dark and neat, though a little tousled in the front. The overhead light caught in his eyes, intensifying their deep shade of blue, almost unnaturally vivid. Even from across the room, Lila felt pinned by the intensity of his gaze—as if he had singled her out the moment she touched the frother. Her pulse stumbled.

He wore a fitted gray jacket and dark jeans, standing out in the sea of corporate suits and bleary-eyed students.

His posture radiated a calm, self-assured energy that made the hair on Lila's arms rise. Something about him felt out of place in this ordinary morning rush, like a piece of a puzzle inserted from a different box. He still hadn't moved from the doorway, so he must have witnessed the mysterious spark. Did he think her some kind of walking hazard?

A small beep from the register startled her enough that she tore her eyes away from the stranger. She cleared her throat and tried to regain her composure. The overhead fluorescent bulbs flickered ominously, as if the power surge was still bouncing around the wiring. She prayed it was just an electrical coincidence.

Returning to the counter, Lila plastered on a polite smile for the next customer, an elderly man who wanted his usual black coffee. Her hands shook slightly as she rung up his order. She poured the coffee slowly, deliberately. Her entire body buzzed with leftover adrenaline. Even the air around her felt charged, as though microscopic sparks leaped from her fingertips where the frother had touched her. She couldn't remember ever feeling this alive yet unnerved, as if some dormant nerve in her body had awakened.

Maya's voice drifted into her thoughts. "You sure you're all right?" Her tone was light, but her gaze showed genuine concern. She had finished helping the line of customers, and most people had now settled at tables or retreated with to-go cups.

"I think so," Lila said softly, though every inch of her doubted it. "Could've been static from the machine, or the wiring...maybe I'm just short-circuiting from stress." Nervous laughter bubbled in her throat.

Maya must have sensed her panic because she snuck a supportive touch to Lila's elbow. "You've been tense for days. We'll figure out your money problems, okay? Just... take a minute. Breathe." She jerked her head toward the narrow hallway leading to the back room. "I'll cover the counter and Mary, in the kitchen can cover me. We'll be fine."

Before Lila could acknowledge that generous offer, the bell above the door jingled again. More customers. The earlier tension all but vanished into the usual symphony of clinking mugs and low chatter, though Lila felt anything but normal. She dried her sweaty palms on her apron. She wanted to blurt everything to Maya: how that spark felt more than just electrical, how for a heartbeat she'd felt some primal warmth surging inside her. But the café was busy, and the last thing she needed was to spook customers with wild talk of "weird green sparks."

She slid another iced latte across the counter, forcing a professional smile, when she noticed the neon sign outside flicker. The D in "Daily Grind" nearly winked out, then gave a bright shimmer that somehow pulsed with her own heartbeat. Or was that her imagination, fueled by frantic anxiety? She tried to ignore it. The next two customers left happily with their drinks. Lila exhaled slowly.

Once the mini-rush subsided, she busied herself restocking the front display, all too aware that the tall stranger with the piercing eyes hadn't approached the counter. He was still there, lingering by the entrance as though waiting for someone. A prickle of unease wove through Lila's stomach. She couldn't dismiss the creeping sense that he had his focus locked onto her.

Moving stiffly, she returned to the espresso station for a short small-batch brew. She needed some caffeine to settle her rattled nerves. She tried to measure the grounds meticulously, but her hand trembled, sending a scattering of coffee beans onto the countertop. She cursed softly, sweeping them up. Get it together, she scolded herself.

She pressed the button to begin brewing, but the traction was off. The coffee spurted in fits, dripping unevenly. At the same time, she spotted an odd reflection in the machine's stainless-steel panel. The reflection revealed the stranger turning his face slightly, as though he might approach at last. Her pulse spiked with unsettled curiosity. She whipped around, anticipating him at the counter —only to find him perfectly still, arms still crossed, gaze unwavering.

"Okay, that's it," Lila mumbled under her breath, half to reassure herself. She marched over to where Maya was double-checking inventory. "That guy is definitely creeping me out," she said softly, jerking her chin toward the door.

Maya snuck a quick look. "Who, Mr. Mysterious? Maybe he's waiting for someone?" But the uncertain edge in Maya's tone suggested she found the entire situation unsettling, too.

Lila pressed a hand to her chest. "He's just...watching."

She lowered her voice. "It's weird. Especially after that spark."

Maya's brow furrowed. "Want me to go ask if he needs help?"

Lila hesitated. She hated the idea of letting fear chase away a paying customer—especially when money was so tight. But there was something in the man's stance that exuded neither anger nor friendly curiosity. It reminded her of the measured patience of a predator waiting. Her heart hammered at her own melodramatic thoughts. Maybe she was imagining everything.

Forcing a breath, she ventured over to the café entrance, carefully stepping around two chairs. She schooled her face into what she hoped was a polite expression. "Hi," she greeted, voice only slightly shaky. "Can I...get you something? A coffee, pastry...um, anything?"

He swept his gaze over her, inch by inch, and she could swear the air in front of her crackled. After what felt like an eternity, he spoke softly. "Not yet." Those two words carried a quiet confidence that made her breath catch. Then he tilted his head, and a faint smile—the barest twitch at one corner of his mouth—appeared before he turned and strode out the door.

Lila stood there, rooted to the spot, fighting the urge to chase him and demand an explanation. The sudden absence of his presence left the café feeling hollow. Maya sidled up beside her, eyes wide. "Seriously, what was that about?"

"I have no clue," Lila managed, adrenaline still flaring

in her veins. Her head swam with too many questions. The entire morning had shifted—some invisible line had been crossed, some boundary she hadn't realized existed until now. The unsettled feeling made her want to pinch herself, just to confirm she was awake.

Behind her, the espresso machine hissed, a reminder that real life demanded her attention. She cleared her throat and went back to the counter, mind spinning. More orders arrived, but she handled them on autopilot, her customer-service smile plastered in place while a swirl of panic churned inside her chest. What sorts of "power surges" produced green sparks that fired from a milk frother like tiny lightning bolts?

By ten-thirty, the morning rush dwindled to a handful of loyal regulars tapping on laptops or reading newspapers at small wooden tables. A few sat at round café tables on the sidewalk, soaking in the rising warmth. Lila seized the chance to catch her breath. She grabbed a damp cloth and began wiping down the counter, trying to calm her racing thoughts. Her reflection in the glossy wood looked as startled as she felt.

Maya busied herself at the pastry case, humming a soft tune. "So, we do not talk about that little...incident?" She tried to keep it playful, but Lila saw the genuine worry carved in her expression.

"I have no explanation," Lila admitted. She patted the cloth between her hands. "It was more than a glitch. It felt...alive." Her confession brought a fresh wave of dread. That strange jolt had flooded her blood like a spark that refused to fully extinguish.

Maya opened her mouth to respond, probably with a reassuring "It's fine," but she was cut off by the abrupt sputter of the neon sign outside. Everyone inside the café turned their heads. The flickering sign danced in a rhythmic pattern—like Morse code blinking from another world. Then, as suddenly as it started, the flicker steadied, the sign returning to its half-working glow.

A nervous gasp escaped Lila before she could stifle it. She pressed a hand to her chest, feeling the rapid thud of her heart. Another horrifying thought crawled through her mind: was her body doing this? Each time fear spiked or confusion swelled, the sign acted up. She had never believed in coincidences. Something was happening, and she stood at the center of it.

She turned back to watch the remaining customers resume their reading or their phone calls, oblivious again. Her gaze drifted to Maya, who was wringing the edge of her apron, eyes darting from the sign to Lila. "That's new," Maya whispered.

"Yeah," Lila managed. She swallowed a lump in her throat. "Let's just hope it stops."

But deep inside, she suspected it wouldn't. Closing her eyes, she tried to conjure the memory of the spark, half expecting it to return at will. Though nothing sprang forth this time, a faint warmth lingered in her fingertips, a subdued current that both thrilled and unnerved her. Determined not to scare the remaining customers, she rubbed her hands down her apron in small, firm strokes, as if that could ground this unexpected energy.

The sliding door to the kitchen swung open as Maya

took a tray of fresh muffins out of the warming oven, placing them on the countertop. Lila inhaled the comforting scent—blueberry, sugar, a reminder of normalcy. She latched onto that scent with relief. By now, she had been rattled so deeply that even a fresh muffin felt like a lifeline, a tether to her usual routine of coffee and pastries.

Outside, the day brightened, and the city bustle continued as always. Traffic rumbled, distant sirens wailed. Inside the narrow walls of The Daily Grind, Lila felt the air hum with a subtle, crackling promise of more. Another wave of trepidation curled around her chest. She had no idea what might happen next—only that whatever it was, her life had already taken a turn she wasn't prepared for.

For one last moment, she let her gaze flick to the door, picturing the tall stranger. The vivid memory of his curiosity settled on her shoulders like a weight. She felt a pulse of involuntary warmth surge through her, then vanish. She couldn't ignore the tingling of energy that lingered in her veins, the sign that her mundane morning had careened into something far beyond her control.

She was left breathless, heart pounding, and terribly aware that something big had awakened in her—or around her—and there would be no going back to normal.

TWO

Lila Matthews exhaled her tension into the still air of The Daily Grind as she wiped down the last table ready to close. Dusk had settled outside, gilding the café windows with a faint glow from the streetlamps. Inside, all felt oddly quiet, and she would have welcomed that soothing quiet if not for the way her heart insisted on pounding at every little sound. She tried to push back the day's strangeness: flickering green sparks dancing off the milk frother, that unsettling sensation in her veins, the jolt of warmth still sparking across her fingertips whenever she remembered the moment. The memory refused to leave her alone.

She paused and glanced around the interior. Usually, the café drew her comfort with its well-worn booths and the smell of roasted beans that clung to every surface. Tonight, the cluster of empty tables and the echo of the humming espresso machine felt unnerving, like a stage missing all its actors. The vinyl seats showed scuffs from countless customers. Crumbs from the day's pastries had been swept away, but the ghost of cinnamon lingered in the air. She set the rag aside and massaged the back of her neck.

Her reflection in the large front window caught her eye. She looked more tired than she cared to admit. A loose strand of auburn hair worked free from her ponytail, framing her face in a way that made the dark circles under her green eyes more obvious. She thought about heading home, burying herself under blankets. But she had promised Maya that she would finish stocking napkins and scrubbing the counters before she left so the play would be ready for the morning.

"You're just overtired," she whispered to herself, her voice echoing off the empty chairs. The closed sign on the door faced out to the street, and she was certain she had flipped the lock.

A gentle clang caused her to spin around. The espresso machine had rattled another tray as its automated wash cycle ended. She inhaled, telling herself to calm down, reminding herself that an empty café naturally made every little noise feel important. She busied herself by sliding a new stack of lids and cardboard to-go sleeves into the display next to the register, hoping to keep her mind too occupied to dwell on possible reasons behind that green spark.

At last, she shut the machine off, letting the last of the steam fade into the overhead lights, then hopped over to tidy the condiment station. Outside, a distant rumble of traffic reminded her that the rest of Manhattan continued swirling with life, though she felt contained in a private bubble of tension. She was about to dump a few stray sugar packets in the trash when she heard the faintest scrape of footsteps near the door.

Her muscles seized. That had not been the espresso machine. She thought she was alone. Slowly, she placed the packets down, her heart hammering so loudly she was sure it might echo through the café. Could it be Maya coming back? No—Maya always called out a greeting before stepping inside. The lock was engaged, right? The possibility of a burglar or random stranger lingered in her head, dredging up every worst-case scenario she had ever worried over.

She slid behind the counter, telling herself to remain calm. If someone had somehow gotten in, she could always grab the phone and call the police. She even considered the small can of pepper spray stashed in her bag near the coat hooks. A new surge of adrenaline spiked in her, raising goose bumps along her arm.

She heard the unmistakable ding of the door chime. The café door nudged open. A figure in a gray jacket entered, movements unhurried, as if he belonged there. The overhead lights cast shadows across the floor, picking up dark hair and broad shoulders. Lila's pulse stuttered.

"Sorry, but we're closed," she managed, voice wavering despite her best attempt at composure. Her hand hovered near the countertop phone. "I'm about to leave."

The man took another deliberate step forward. He was tall, definitely taller than most, with neat dark hair that brushed his forehead. His posture exuded confidence, and he kept his hands at his sides in a way that did not scream threat so much as certainty. Something about the way he carried himself startled her. She recognized him from earlier that morning. He was the man who had lingered near the doorway, watching her with those unsettling blue eyes. The same man who had walked out without ordering.

At the memory of that encounter, her thoughts twisted with fresh alarm. Nobody else had seen him earlier except a few idle customers, and she had not caught his name. She scrambled through her mind for a rational reason he could be standing in her locked café now.

He paused near a table, turning to face her fully. A faint swirl of city light seeped through the window, illuminating his face. His eyes were indeed a remarkable shade of blue, intense enough to make her breath hitch. He inclined his head, offering a polite smile. "Lila Matthews," he said, voice low and steady. "I think we need to talk."

Her gut reacted to his voice. There was something inherently calm in its rich timbre, as if he had said these words countless times before. The confidence in that greeting did not reassure her. Her heart slammed against her ribs, and she looked at the door, verifying that it was indeed closed behind him. How did he know her name? She had not worn a name tag. Something tugged at the edge of her memory—the unnatural flicker outside the café that morning, that odd moment she had locked eyes with him. Cold sweat prickled along her spine.

She swallowed. "How did you get in here?" she demanded, praying she sounded braver than she felt. "I'm sure—I locked everything."

He gestured toward the lock, though he made no move to approach the counter. "The door is secure. I promise I haven't damaged anything."

She clenched her fists, feeling the outline of the counter's edge dig into her palm. She wanted to believe this was all some weird misunderstanding—a glitch in the automatic door or a trick of an old building that let him wander in. Yet she could not ignore how every nerve in her body insisted something was off. "Who are you?" she asked. "And how do you know my name?"

He studied her for a moment before responding, as though measuring how honest he wanted to be. "I'm Caleb Blackwood," he said quietly. "I sensed... something unusual this morning. At first, I assumed it was a simple anomaly, a power surge or a stray bit of magic. Then I realized it was you." He paused. "I needed to see if you were all right."

Her heart stuttered again. Something about the word magic snagged her attention in the worst possible way. She almost burst out laughing at the absurdity, but her mouth went dry instead. This was no dream—he was talking about that bizarre spark as if it were real. "Magic," she echoed, voice hollow. "You're joking." She snuck a glance at the phone, half-considering hitting 9-1-1. Every rational cell in her body urged her to call for help.

Caleb shifted his stance. A subtle motion brought his hand up, and she saw a flicker near his fingertips—like pale light dancing across his skin. She gasped, eyes widening. It was not a reflection from the overhead bulbs. It looked like a shimmer, real as the green glow she had seen from the frother. He let it fade before speaking again, as if to confirm she believed it.

Shock tumbled through her, fueling her next demand. "What did you do? Is that some trick? Because if it is, it isn't funny." She hated how her voice trembled.

"I promise, this is no parlor trick. I need you to hear me." He spoke softly. "You felt something at your station earlier, correct? Like a surge beneath your skin, maybe sparks you couldn't explain?"

Her stomach flipped. She tried to lace her words with defiance, but they came out quietly. "You were watching me."

He inclined his head. "Not in the way you think. But while I was here this morning, I saw enough to suspect someone had awakened power—wild magic." He paused, giving her a moment to process. "I've been looking for you all day. Well," he added gently, "I found you."

Wild magic. It sounded ridiculous, a phrase plucked out of a low-budget fantasy movie. She stared at him, dangerously close to letting hysterical laughter bubble out. Had she lost her mind, or was he truly claiming the spark she felt was supernatural?

She realized she was shaking. The edges of her vision felt too bright, like the overhead lights had grown intense. A prickle of fear danced across her arms. "What do you want?" she managed. "Are you poking fun at me?" She struggled to keep her fury and panic in check.

Caleb took a slow breath, and she glimpsed a hint of compassion in his expression. "It must be unsettling," he said, choosing each word with care. "I understand your hesitation. But I'm here to help you. I think you may have tapped into something you can't fully control yet."

She pressed her lips together, uncertain whether to trust even a single syllable. But her curiosity flared, despite every warning bell going off in her head. "Explain," she challenged. "Convince me."

He nodded as if satisfied with that request. "Magic is real, and it's hidden in plain sight," he said. "Most people never sense it. But once in a while, someone awakens with abilities that defy normal logic. Imagine living your entire life with a sleeping storm inside you, and one day it flickers awake." His words felt calm, as though he had rehearsed them. "I suspect that's what happened to you this morning."

She wanted to protest. Still, she recalled the jolt across her palms, the bright green spark that danced around metal. Her pulse did a strange skitter. She swallowed. "This is insane," she whispered. She licked her dry lips, forcing her voice to stay steady. "You have no proof. Maybe you messed with the café's wiring."

His lips curved in the faintest smile. "I understand your doubts. Honestly, I would be more worried if you just believed me without question." Then he slipped his hand into his jacket pocket, pulling out a small, pristine white card. An intricate, gold-foil scrawl glinted on its surface.

The café's fluorescent lighting hit it in a way that made the letters glimmer.

He stepped forward until the tip of the counter separated them, then offered her the card. She hesitated, heart pounding as she glanced from his face to the glossy edges. Finally, she took it. Her fingertips brushed the embossed lettering that read:

Caleb Blackwood

481-U 8th Ave

A swirl of confusion flooded her. "Why are you giving me this?" she asked, tilting the card to observe how the address glowed weakly, especially on the uppercase U. It looked almost as if it shimmered on its own.

He hooked his thumbs in his pockets, posture relaxed yet undeniably watchful. "I live in an apartment at that address. If you join me tomorrow evening at seven, I promise I'll explain everything properly. You and I both know your life shifted the moment that spark appeared. I can help you figure out why."

Everything about him set her entire being on edge—his unwavering confidence, the quiet surety in his tone, and the strange shimmer of light that had danced near his hand. She should have thrown him out, maybe threatened to call the police. Yet a reluctant, undeniable pull made her hesitate. Something in his gaze promised that he held answers to the questions that plagued her thoughts all day. Her rational mind warred with the lingering sense of absolute strangeness.

She glanced at the white card again. "You want me to come to an address I've never heard of to talk about magic." She wanted to laugh at how bizarre it sounded. "And you want me to just... trust you?"

"In the end, your choice is yours," he said. "Maybe you'll decide none of this is worth pursuing, and our paths won't cross again. But if you feel that spark once more, or if anything strange happens, come to 481-U 8th Ave. I'll be waiting."

The finality in his tone tightened her chest. This was a man who did not ramble or bargain. He wanted her to step into his world, no matter how insane that sounded. She scraped her nails over the counter's surface, torn between wanting to hurl the card back at him and wanting him to stay.

She settled for exhaling a shaky breath. "You show up again in my locked café at night, and you expect me to just... what, pretend this is normal? You're claiming I have magic, but I'm not in a Children's Fairy Tales 101 class, you know."

He almost grinned. "We don't have fairy tales, as far as I'm aware, but there is a hidden community that understands awakened power. You're not alone in this. That's why I want you to meet me. I'd prefer we talk away from prying eyes."

Her wrecked thoughts tumbled in circles. She clutched the card, reading the address again as if the letters might rearrange themselves into a more logical explanation. Silence pressed in, broken only by the faint buzz of the overhead lights. Finally, she forced herself to look him in the eye. "If I show up," she said, hardly believing the words leaving her own mouth, "you'd better have real explanations."

His expression softened in relief, and he inclined his head graciously. "I promise. Tomorrow at seven." Then he turned. Her heart lurched in panic that he might disappear without another word. But as he moved to the exit, he paused. He looked over his shoulder just long enough to say, "Lock the door after I leave. Seriously this time." With that, he stepped outside.

The door clicked shut behind him, and the interior fell deathly quiet. Lila's pulse kept a rapid staccato, and she raced to twist the lock again. She gave it a few savage tugs, verifying it was indeed secure. A flare of annoyance and confusion mingled in her mind—how had he bypassed it so easily in the first place?

Trembling, she stared down at the white card. 481-U 8th Ave, in elegant gold embossed letters. The U cast a faint flicker in the dim overhead lighting, like a miniature star winking at her. Her entire body felt overheated, and her thoughts zinged from the day's fiasco to the impossible details Caleb Blackwood had whispered.

It felt as if her entire sense of reality had cracked. She tried to gather her wits, stepping away from the door to lean on the newly cleaned table. The smell of stale coffee clung to her clothes, grounding her in something familiar, but a new current buzzed in her veins.

THREE

The next day, Lila stood among the clatter of dishes in The Daily Grind's small back kitchen, wondering if her nerves would ever settle. She had nearly caused a scene that afternoon when her foot caught on a stray mat near the sink. The entire tray she was carrying—laden with mugs and plates—should have crashed to the floor. She felt it slip from her fingers, her breath lodging in her throat. Yet in the dizzy heartbeat between her stumble and her frantic lunge to catch the tray, the air seemed to hold it in place, as though time had paused so she could regain her balance. When she finally got hold of the tray, it felt heavier than a busted cinder block, and her hands shook so badly that Mary had to take it from her. Embarrassed, she muttered something about being overtired and hurried out of the kitchen.

That incident replayed in her mind all day, an echo of strangeness that only compounded the memory of the green sparks and the mysterious man, Caleb Blackwood. A single question kept pounding inside her skull: How was any of this possible? Each time she peered at her hands in the café's fluorescent light, she half-expected to see them glowing. They did not glow, but unease simmered in her veins. By the end of her shift, sweat beaded her neck despite the café's air conditioner. She could not suppress the knowledge that something monumental had changed in her life.

After closing, she counted tips with unsteady fingers, tossed her apron in the laundry hamper, and left. She made a quick detour by her apartment, grabbing the small canister of pepper spray from a kitchen drawer. Then she set off down a muggy Manhattan sidewalk toward the address on the crisp white card he had given her. He had said 481-U 8th Ave, though she had not known what "U" could mean at an address. She clenched the pepper spray tightly in her palm, both a reminder of ordinary safety measures and a flimsy guard against impossibilities. If the man who had conjured shimmering sparks with his fingertips was any kind of threat, she doubted pepper spray would stop him, but she brought it anyway.

The sticky warmth of the evening pressed around her, the city's summer heat rising up from the asphalt. The bustle of traffic and neon lights grounded her anxiety just enough to keep her feet moving. The trek took her about seven blocks, weaving among tourists and late-shift workers. Too many times, she considered turning back, but each memory of that floating tray and the morning spark spurred her forward. She had to know what she was capable of—or what dangerous new reality had latched onto her life.

Eventually, she reached the imposing facade of the New Yorker Hotel. She paused under the bold neon sign, drawn to the splendor of a building that seemed caught between old-world elegance and modern hustle. People streamed in and out through the main doors. She wondered if she should simply stride through the lobby and ask for Caleb, but that plan dissolved into bafflement as she scanned the entrance for any sign of 481-U. A regal doorman greeted arriving guests. Lila took a single step toward him but stopped. Nothing about that short conversation at the café, nor his quiet command that she meet him here, suggested he was waiting in the standard guest suites.

She circled a half block the base of the building, heart pounding. At first, she sensed only the usual swirl of city life. Then a faint prickle crawled up her neck—as if her pulse recognized some hidden magic. Under the glow of a flickering streetlamp near a side entrance, she saw it: a subdued letter "U" carved into a discreet wooden panel by a door leading away from the grand foyer. For a moment, it looked like just a scratch in the varnish. Then a beam from the streetlight glinted off the letter, and a soft shimmer teased her vision.

She approached slowly, checking over her shoulder. The sidewalk behind her was busy enough, though nobody seemed to notice the hidden door. She tested the handle, but the panel clicked open on its own. Her heartbeat thudded as a small corridor revealed itself. She did not see any occupant or employee. She swallowed her fear and reminded herself that she had come this far, so she followed the corridor's shallow steps downward. A faint glow threaded along each step, guiding her feet.

At the bottom, a dimly lit hallway stretched in both directions. The walls were unremarkable, just plain plaster in need of fresh paint. Doors lined the hall on each side, blank and identical except for one, which displayed a second shimmering "U." Lila's mouth felt dry. A small doorbell button glowed faintly next to the handle. She double-checked that the pepper spray was still in her bag, and then she pressed the buzzer.

A short static hiss filled the hallway, followed by a click. The unadorned door rippled. She stared as wood morphed into intricate carvings, vines and runes swirling across the surface in an ornate pattern of gold filigree. Her mouth fell open. It was as though she was watching an illusion conjure itself from the plain door. She scraped her palm across her jeans, trying to ground her nerves.

The door's panel abruptly shaped itself into a man's face, complete with carved eyes and a neat carved mustache. Lila nearly yelped but clamped a hand over her mouth instead. The carved face inclined in a small bow.

"Good evening, Miss Matthews," the door said in a perfectly cordial voice. "Mr. Blackwood awaits you in the library."

Her breath jammed in her throat. She had no idea how it knew her name. Before she recovered enough to respond, the door swung inward, beckoning her. She stepped through, the carved face watching with polite detachment. She heard a whisper of something closing behind her, and when she glanced back, she saw only polished wood. No trace of a face remained.

Now she found herself in a more elaborately decorated entry: polished floors, sconces along each wall flickering with gentle white light, and beyond them, an arched doorway leading into a wide room lined from floor to vaulted ceiling with bookshelves. She forced herself to keep moving forward, adrenaline pumping. She tried to quell the urge to run back outside. But the memory of that impossible tray in the café kitchen demanded that she find answers. She stepped under the arch and arrived in what looked like the heart of Caleb's domain.

The library took her breath away. Rows of shelves rose two stories high, each shelf brimming with volumes in rich, jewel-toned bindings. A spiral staircase at the far side connected the lower floor to an upper gallery that circled the room. Along the left wall, tall windows revealed only the dim glow of night. The place smelled of old parchment, polished wood, and something faintly herbal, like rosemary or sage.

As she stepped further in, movement caught her eye on the second level. A familiar figure—Caleb—leaned over the railing, watching her with the same calm intensity she remembered. He wore a charcoal shirt that showed the outline of lean muscle in his arms, and his dark hair brushed forward along his forehead. Relief and wariness mixed in Lila's stomach as she recognized the man who had arrived at her café two nights earlier and who had intruded on her locked premises after closing time.

He lifted a hand in greeting. "You found the place," he called, voice echoing softly through the library. Then, in one fluid motion, he vanished from her view. Lila gasped, unsure what she had seen—did he leap off the balcony? Before she could blink, he stood just a few feet in front of her, near a polished table stacked with books. There was no displacement of air, no rush of footsteps, just a faint drift of displaced energy that made the hair on her arms prickle.

He gestured toward her, a polite invitation to step deeper into the space. "Welcome, Lila." His voice remained low and warm, with that measured quality she remembered.

Too many questions fought to burst free from her lips. She pressed them down, heart racing. "You... did you just teleport or something?" she managed, her voice flat with astonishment.

A hint of a smile crossed his mouth, as though this was the simplest question in the world. "Let's call it a short-range illusion trick. Not full teleportation, but close." He paused, then looked at her gently. "I appreciate you coming. I suspect you have quite a few questions."

She wanted to bark out that yes, obviously she did. Instead, she swallowed the dryness in her throat. "It's better if someone explains... what the hell is going on with me," she admitted.

The tension in her posture must have shown, because Caleb stepped aside and inclined his head toward an inviting nook by the fireplace. "We should talk where you'll be comfortable."

Numbly, she let him guide her along. At the far side of the library, a wide stone hearth dominated the wall, flames dancing eagerly behind ornate ironwork. Oddly, though, the heat did not radiate outward in the heavy summer air. Instead, a cool breeze seemed to emanate from a hidden fan or an enchantment. She stared at the dancing flames, mystified that they were not warming the room.

Caleb guided her toward two overstuffed armchairs covered in dark green velvet. The soft lamplight overhead made the upholstery glow with a subtle sheen. Lila lowered herself into one, still gripping her bag strap so tightly that her knuckles whitened. She nearly placed the pepper spray on her lap, but decided that would make her look either paranoid or rude. "So," she began, voice shaky, "this is... an interesting place."

"That's one word for it," he said, seating himself in the adjacent chair. His movements were graceful, easy. She noticed he seemed comfortable here, in a realm of runes and wards. As though he had lived in this magical space his entire life. "I have shaped some of the wards in this residence myself. It is safer this way."

"Wards, what's that?" She looked around, scanning the elaborate shelves. Countless books, each one a potential clue.

He flushed for a moment realizing what a novice she was. "After we have a chat I'll tell you about many things including wards."

She had thought about the cost of rent for a space like this, but that question was woefully mundane compared to what she wanted to demand: Who are you, really? What is happening to me? Instead, her gaze landed on the miraculous cold fire. She pointed at the flames, unable to hide her astonishment. "How... no heat?"

His eyes followed hers to the hearth. "It is a shielded fireplace. I prefer the light of fire, but not the heat during the summer." He glanced back at her, the corner of his mouth lifting. "Magic makes such things possible, Lila."

Her name on his lips sent a soft ripple of familiarity through her, recalling how he had walked into her café that morning, introducing himself in the most disorienting moment of her life. She opened her mouth to speak, but he stood smoothly, cutting off her next question.

"How about some refreshments," he said, crossing to a low table centered between the armchairs. "Then I will explain."

She hesitated, unable to decide if she should leap up and insist on details immediately, or if she should simply let him proceed. Some part of her recognized that he was giving her time to process. In her chest, her heart hammered a rhythm of anxiety and undeniable curiosity.

He lifted his right hand. She caught a glimpse of a slim silver ring on one finger, etched with symbols she could not read. He murmured something under his breath, too low for her to catch. At once, the table's surface shifted. She watched in stunned fascination as a wide tray appeared, bearing two slender glasses, a bottle of champagne, and a dish of small pastries. She blinked, momentarily speechless.

Caleb offered her a reassuring nod. "You have stepped into a different realm of possibility, Lila. Think of it as a new world behind the one you have always known. It is my duty—my privilege, in fact—to help you navigate it."

Her stomach flipped as she realized how bizarre it all was, yet she could not deny the surge of relief that someone might actually have answers about her freakish experiences. Realizing she had been gawking, she cleared her throat. "Okay," she said softly. "I'll... I'll hear you out."

He reached for the champagne, uncorking it with a practiced motion. No pop, no fizz spilled. It slid open with a whispered hush, as if even the sound was subdued by magic. The sweet tang of grapes mingled with the sharper scent of something floral. He poured two glasses, the liquid glinting in the gentle light, bubbles swirling.

Watching the pale gold fill the glasses left Lila feeling as though she stood at the edge of a precipice. Caleb turned back to her with both champagne flutes in hand. She forced herself to breathe. One foot tapped anxiously on the polished floor, betraying her nerves. Despite her lingering fear, a spark of excitement glowed in her chest. If she could learn why trays suspended themselves and milk frothers spat green sparks, maybe she would reclaim some sense of control.

He paused in front of her, gaze quietly assessing the tension in her face. She sensed no ill will in that silent study, only a cautious sincerity. "You can trust me," he said, though he did not push it. His voice was gentle. "I want to help you make sense of everything."

She nodded, though her heart still pounded. Reaching

up, she brushed stray hair from her forehead. "Just don't blow up the floorboards, or my mind, or... anything else," she said. It was an attempt at humor, but her voice trembled with the truth that maybe either outcome was possible.

His lips curved slightly. "No blowing anything up tonight." Setting one glass on the side table near her chair, he offered the other into her hand. The champagne felt oddly solid, as though she was giving weight to her choice by accepting it. She closed her fingers around the stem with care, the chill of the glass matching the trembling in her palm.

He retained his hold on his own glass, swirling the liquid gently. "Drink this," he said, meeting her eyes. "We will talk."

FOUR

"Being as you're a total stranger, I'd prefer we switch glasses," Lila pointed to his glass.

"Of course," Caleb nodded as he took her glass and passed his over to her. Lila smiled and took a sip of her champagne. The armchair's plush cushions pressed against her shoulders, yet no comfort reached her knotted muscles. Her gaze flicked toward the fireplace, where cool flames danced without radiating heat. She wondered if the quiet hum in the room was another trick of magic. Part of her wanted to jump out of her seat and run, but curiosity anchored her in place.

Caleb set his glass on a side table with deliberate grace. He headed toward the library's door, each step silent on the polished floor. Lila watched his profile, noticing the concentration etched into the small lines at his temples. Then, in one smooth motion, he closed the door and tested the lock. She swallowed, catching the faint click of brass, a sound that felt final.

He turned, meeting her eyes from across the library. Awareness rippled under her skin, and a new hint of nervousness tickled the back of her neck. She tightened her grip on the woven arms of the chair.

"Lesson 1," Caleb said softly. His voice carried an authority that simultaneously intrigued and unsettled her. Without another word, he moved toward the tall windows on either side of the fireplace. Two sets of heavy velvet drapes hung there, drawn aside to reveal the moonlit cityscape. He placed a firm hand on the wall near the first window and murmured, "Claudeta noctum, audi silentum."

The words flowed like water in a language she did not recognize. Tiny sparks flickered around his fingertips, and the drapes glided shut on their own. At the same time, a faint vibration traveled through the room. Somewhere in the corners, the room's ambient light softened. The hum she had sensed earlier became muted. He repeated the incantation at the second window, and that set of drapes slid closed just as elegantly.

Lila shivered despite the mild temperature. She had seen him conjure that swirling shimmer of magic in the café, but she still struggled to believe any of this could be real. The glass in her hand rattled against her knuckles, so she placed it down before she dropped it. Every nerve felt taut. Why did she feel so exposed by a few drawn shades?

She forced a shaky laugh. "Okay, what in the actual hell was that? Are you drawing the curtains, or something else?"

He cast her a steady look. "Remember when you asked

about wards? It is a warding spell, shaped with illusions. Basic but effective. It blocks noise and dims stray lights from this space, so nothing escapes. No one outside sees or hears us."

Lila's stomach churned at the stark reminder that she was sealed in here with him. Alarm flared in her chest, though she tried to quash it. "You can seal an entire room with a fancy phrase. Of course."

Caleb stepped away from the window, the lamplight giving him a subtle glow. "It is precisely what it looks like," he said. "I prefer privacy when discussing topics that most people would never believe. I thought you might appreciate that."

She clenched her hands on the arms of the chair. Her heart pounded. "WTF—who are you, and what is all of this about?" Her voice cracked. She let out a breath, willing her courage not to fail. "I'm completely freaked out right now."

His expression softened with what looked like genuine concern. "I understand. Truly." He raised one palm, an invitation to calm. "I told you: my name is Caleb Blackwood. I am a guardian warlock whose job is to find and guide people like you."

She wanted to scoff. Part of her craved a normal explanation, something that would chalk all these weird sparks up to a broken fuse. Yet that rational lie would not hold anymore. "And people like me are...?"

"New witches," Caleb said. His voice fell a degree quieter, as if the label itself could shake the pillars of her reality. "Those who have awakened to magic they never knew they possessed."

Lila twisted in her seat, cheeks hot. A swirl of memory flickered inside her, from that day in the café to the moment she nearly dropped a tray only to have the air hold it for her. "Magic," she repeated. She almost let out a hollow laugh. "You sound so sure. I can't wrap my head around this."

He nodded. "I know it can be frightening." He took a step closer, though he kept a respectful distance. "It is real, and it can be dangerous if you do not learn to control it."

Her pulse fluttered. A jolt of warmth rushed across her hands, and she glanced down. A faint green glow pulsed beneath her skin. She gasped. "No, no, not again." She bolted upright, stumbling away from the chair, her fingers trembling and lit with an eerie emerald color.

Like a living thing, the glow spread across her palms, trailing to her fingertips. She felt it charge and collect in her chest. Panic spiked in her throat. "It's happening," she whispered, breath ragged.

She shrieked as a flash of green light burst from her hands. There was a thrum of energy, and she felt the library shiver as if swept by an invisible gust. The floor quivered under her feet. Her vision blurred for an instant, and she might have fallen if not for the strong arms that caught her.

Caleb pulled her against him, his arms braced around her waist. The scent of his cologne—something woodsy— filled her senses. Her pulse hammered so hard that her ears rang. "Breathe," he murmured near her ear. "Stay calm. If your magic flares while you are uncentered, this entire building is at risk."

The words were so calmly spoken that her panic dimmed under shock. She clung to his shirt, her legs nearly giving way. The spark in her hands flickered, then subsided, leaving only a faint glow resting on her skin. She felt dizzy, as if every part of her was trembling. "This is crazy. I can't—I can't control it."

He eased her down to sit on the arm of the chair. His touch lingered against her waist. The contact sent a flush along her spine, and she realized how close they were. She fought the sudden swirl of conflicting sensations: fear, embarrassment, and an odd jolt of awareness at his nearness.

"You can," Caleb said. "You just have not learned how. You are a new witch discovering her powers, Lila. The magic is emerging faster than you realize, and it is raw. Like a wildfire, it will burn through anything if you do not focus."

She swallowed hard. Her gaze darted to her still-glowing hands. The color had lessened, but a faint shimmer remained just below the surface. "So I'm," she muttered, "a witch." The phrase made her stomach flip, a bizarre cocktail of wonder and fear.

He released her waist and stepped back, giving her space. "Yes. In this city, many witches and warlocks exist in secret. We have a system to keep mortals safe from magical harm and to prevent widespread chaos. The Council of Magical Guardians is at the core of that system."

She rubbed her eyes, brain spinning. "Council of Magical Guardians." She tried the words on her tongue. "This sounds like a shitty B-movie script. Are you all wearing cloaks and chanting in basements, or something?" She gave a short, humorless laugh. Real tears threatened to spring up behind her eyelids, so she forced them away.

Caleb let out a soft breath, and the lamplight cast subtle shadows at his jaw. "I know how it must sound. We do not exactly wear cloaks or gather in musty castles, but the secrecy is real enough. The Council watches for new witches who appear, for large magical surges, or for reckless magic that could endanger innocent people."

Her emotions churned, half disbelieving, half enthralled by the logic he offered. His explanation would at least make sense of the bizarre things happening around her. "So, you're telling me that I caused that weird spark at the café, and I almost caused some shockwave in here? Because this... this magic woke up?"

"That is it, in simplest terms," he confirmed. "Magic can skyrocket when it first awakens in someone with a strong affinity. We are taught from childhood how to harness it. You grew up with no training, so your abilities manifested unexpectedly."

She fell silent, chewing on that. Her tension had not faded, but it shifted into a bristling curiosity. "Then what do I do now? I have to fix this. This is too dangerous. If I can accidentally blow things up, who's to say I won't burn down my apartment by sneezing?"

A faint smile touched the corners of his mouth. "You

are not the first person to worry about accidental destruction. It is exactly why the Council steps in. We train novices in controlled spells, wards, and ways to handle sudden surges." He paused, scanning her expression. "I have been assigned as your mentor. It is my responsibility to teach you and keep you safe until you can manage your abilities on your own."

The word "mentor" rattled her, and she shifted her weight, crossing her arms. She did not like feeling so unmoored. "So you... watch me full-time, or something?"

He seemed to sense her unease. "Not in a literal sense. I will help you gain control, teach you the basics of magic, and report your progress to the Council. In time, you will decide how deeply you wish to be involved in our world."

Lila tried to form a coherent thought, but confusion tumbled inside her. She also felt a surge of indignation, though she was not entirely sure why. Maybe it was the idea that her normal life had cracked wide open. "You keep saying 'our world.' That's not my world. I'm just a barista who can't pay her rent on time. I don't do wands and potions or whatever."

His gaze roamed her face, a flicker of sympathy softening his posture. "You say that now, but the power inside you is real. Whether you choose to embrace it or not, it is part of who you are. I am simply giving you the chance to understand it."

She pushed out a shaky exhale. The green glow had finally ebbed, leaving her fingers normal again, if still tingling. She could not deny that the memory of that pulse in her veins was too strong to dismiss. It felt as though she had touched a live wire. "What if I say no?" she asked. "What if I don't want any part of this?"

Caleb lowered his eyes momentarily. "Then the Council would still keep an eye on you. Untamed magic can flare at any time, especially under stress. But you can't be forced to train. We do not imprison people. We offer a path to control."

She noticed the solemn lines in his face, the sincerity behind his words. "So, either I ignore it and live in fear of blowing things up, or I let you... tutor me in magic." She paused, still hearing how ridiculous it sounded in her own ears. "Those are my choices?"

He lifted a shoulder in a gentle shrug. "Essentially, yes. My advice is to let me help. Otherwise, every day will bring fresh surprises, and not the pleasant kind."

The library felt smaller than ever, as though the drawn curtains had trapped both the candlelit shadows and her roiling emotions within these walls. She rubbed her arms, trying not to focus on how his voice resonated in her chest. "You said the entire city is involved in this, in some secret capacity. How big is the Council, and why do they care about me specifically? Like, what if I'm too small to matter?"

He raised an eyebrow, stepping closer again. Though he kept his hands at his sides, Lila could almost sense a protective aura radiating off him. "You are not too small," he said. "The Council keeps our existence hidden, but it is vast. Warlocks and witches come from all backgrounds. The difference is that you awakened unexpectedly, strong enough to spark illusions and energy surges. That catches their attention."

She felt her breath catch on the word illusions, recalling the flickers of green sparks and the floating tray. "But why me? I didn't sign up for this."

He frowned, losing a bit of that stone-like composure. "We do not always know why certain people awaken at a given time. It could be hereditary, triggered by strong emotion, or due to external forces we have yet to understand. Regardless, you must learn to harness it. Our city has enough hidden dangers without uncontrolled magic complicating things."

Lila's head spun. Caleb's admission that her awakening did not have a neat explanation left her more uneasy. Still, she recognized the honesty in it. "So, you've been doing this for a while?" she asked, trying to center herself.

"Many years," he replied. "I joined the Council young, trained under older guardians, and eventually took on the role of mentoring. My specialty is illusions and wards, so I usually handle novices who display a strong raw spark."

She tried to gather some sense of humor, though her pulse still pounded. "So, I'm just a raw spark?"

He almost smiled at that. "Raw but also potent. You will discover new capabilities once you stop fearing them."

She let her shoulders slump, feeling the weight of acceptance. Maybe she did not fully believe everything, but the memory of the green spark made denial impossible. Her eyes flicked to the windows, where the blocked-out city sighed in darkness. "Then... what comes next? I assume you have some kind of plan?"

Caleb offered her his hand, a quiet invitation that sent a flutter through her stomach. "We begin with a promise that you will not ignore this. You do not have to decide everything right now, but I want you to trust me enough to let me teach you. Will you at least consider it?"

She glanced at his palm, then the lines of his face. Part of her remained guarded, but another part, the reckless one that had always yearned for something bigger, felt drawn to him. Slowly, she placed her hand in his. "I'll consider it," she said softly.

His fingers folded around hers in a reassuring squeeze. "Thank you. Come, I will walk you out. It is late, and you have had enough shocks for one night. Tomorrow, we can talk more."

She rose, uneasy but determined to see this through—whatever "this" turned out to be. They crossed the library together, her nerves still jangling. At the threshold, Caleb muttered something else, and the wards around the room released with a subtle shift in air pressure. Suddenly, the distant hum of city traffic slipped into her awareness.

FIVE

Lila stared at the pale glow of her laptop long past midnight, eyes burning with exhaustion as she scrolled through yet another forum. Her tiny apartment was stifling and far too quiet. Each click of her touchpad felt like a drumbeat in the stillness. She had tried half a dozen search terms—"mysterious green sparks," "random static discharges," "freak electrical accidents"—but nothing quite resembled the bizarre jolts she had experienced. Every mundane explanation, from faulty wiring to electromagnetic pulses, fell short of capturing the impossible phenomena she kept replaying in her mind.

She rubbed her temples, wincing when her fingertips brushed the faint warmth in her skin, a lingering echo of the strange magic that had flickered from her hands only a day before. The memory of that terrifying moment still made her heart pound. Caleb, this unnervingly calm warlock, had insisted it was magic, called her a "new witch," and then vanished back into his hidden domain.

Yet here she sat, a regular barista with a pile of unpaid bills, trying to rationalize something that defied all logic she knew.

A new forum thread loaded—someone claimed to have witnessed little sparks while using a faulty karaoke machine. The user blamed cheap electronics. Lila scanned the post, hopeful and desperate, but quickly saw it was just another run-of-the-mill mechanical glitch. She exhaled and leaned back in her rickety chair, feeling her spine protest from too many hours spent hunched over the laptop. This was pointless. Whatever was happening to her wasn't the typical flicker of static from a faulty appliance.

Turning off the browser, she stared at the dark reflection on the screen. Wind rattled the flimsy window frame near her kitchenette. She thought about calling Maya, but it was nearly two in the morning, and she couldn't bear to worry her friend without any hard answers. Talk about just finding new ways to freak her out.

Her mind drifted toward old bedtime stories. Growing up, she had spent long weekends at her grandmother Evelyn's house not far in Connecticut, lulled to sleep by fireside tales. Once upon a time, they had been just that— stories. But now the words returned with an eerie relevance:

Some in our family, her grandmother used to say, come from an ancient line that holds the gift of earth, a power that can mend or shatter if not grounded in the caster's heart. As a child, Lila had pictured it as a fairy-tale ability—making flowers bloom at will, twisting vines into shapes. She had never thought to question whether it might be real.

. Her grandmother's voice, gentle yet steady, used to warn that fledgling magic lashed out like a storm, swirling unpredictably until it was claimed and steadied by the witch who bore it. At the time, absurd or not, those fables were comforting snippets of her grandmother's mysterious background. Now, with her mind frazzled from half-sleepless nights, Lila couldn't decide if those stories were nonsense or if they might be the only threads of truth she had left.

Whenever she would ask her parents about her grand mother, they would look at each other and just say, "she was eccentric." They would also say not to take her too seriously.

She sighed, glancing at the digital clock glowing from her bedside table. Another hour or two of restless tossing awaited her, but the idea of sleep felt impossible.

Eventually, fatigue tethered her to bed. She left her laptop half-open, gave the macabre hum of the heating vent one last suspicious glare, then slid under her thin covers. Her thoughts remained a chaotic swirl—her grandmother's tales, the memory of green sparks dancing across her fingertips, and the echo of Caleb's low, measured voice telling her she was a new witch. It was madness. Yet she drifted into a fitful sleep haunted by fragments of shimmering illusions and muffled voices whispering that the world was not at all as she had believed.

When her alarm blared at dawn, it felt as if she had

only shut her eyes for minutes. She slammed a palm against the off button, ignoring the dryness in her throat. Her entire body felt heavy, like she was dragging sandbags. Bracing herself on her dresser, she glimpsed her reflection in the mirror—dark circles under her eyes, hair a tangled, coppery mess. She would have to fake normalcy at The Daily Grind somehow. Her boss wasn't known for mercy, and missing work could spell doom for her rent next month.

She hurried through a lukewarm shower, letting the water rouse her enough to function. The scalding pressure on her tired muscles at least shoved away the last threads of sleep. She threw on her jeans and a simple brown sweater, then rummaged for her battered sneakers. The laptop still glowed on the table, open to those fruitless searches. She clenched her jaw and snapped it shut. No part of her wanted to rehash that heartbreak of dead-end websites again. Not until she had something more tangible to go on—like actual answers from the man calling himself Caleb Blackwood.

Outside, the sky was flat gray, hinting at possible drizzle by midmorning. She hurried along the sidewalk, hugging her arms around herself as she navigated the throng of New Yorkers pushing through their routines. She could almost pretend this was any other day, that the scalding sense of magic she'd felt was just a one-time hallucination.

At The Daily Grind, she paused under the awning before stepping inside. This café had always been her sanctuary—a place of grounded routine where the sweet aroma of fresh espresso mingled with the hum of chatter. But the moment she pushed through the glass door, her shoulders tensed. Last time she'd walked in feeling weird, she almost blew the power circuits with her freakish spark.

Maya was already behind the counter, fiddling with the cappuccino machine and scowling at the persistent drip from one of the nozzles. She greeted Lila with a small wave and a wrinkle of concern across her brow. "You look like you slept in a dumpster," she teased, though her eyes flicked over Lila's face in genuine worry.

"Feel that way too." Lila forced a half-grin. "Cheap coffee's not doing it for me anymore."

Maya's expression softened. "You okay? You were kinda jumpy yesterday."

Jumpy was an understatement, but Lila shrugged. "Couldn't sleep. I'll be fine." She attempted a breezy wave of dismissal, hoping Maya wouldn't push. She cared deeply for her friend, but any conversation about green sparks or illusions would dig a hole she couldn't climb out of.

The morning rush pounced almost immediately. Familiar faces tumbled in, demanding lattes, soy cappuccinos, and double espressos with extra foam. Lila tossed on her apron, praying the mechanical hum of the espresso machine would ground her. For a while, it worked. The motions—scooping coffee grounds, tamping them down, steaming milk—felt as routine as breathing. She slipped into her barista autopilot, offering fleeting smiles to regulars. Her arms still tingled with exhaustion, but at least she could focus on something normal.

Until, much too soon, she spotted him.

Seated at a small table near the front window was Caleb. The morning light touched his dark hair, revealing faint highlights of brown. He wore a fitted coat, and a harmless paper cup of latte rested between his hands. He didn't look sinister or outwardly magical—just a man quietly sipping coffee. But the instant Lila's gaze locked with his, her heart lurched.

She quickly busied herself with a new order, though her thoughts whirled. She hadn't expected to see him again so soon. Was he following her? Did he just like the coffee? She forced her attention to the cappuccino she was preparing, but awareness of his presence threaded through her every thought. Heat coiled in her stomach. Now that she knew he possessed unearthly powers, she couldn't see him as just another customer.

After a few tense minutes, she sensed him approaching the bar. He moved with a certain smoothness, his steps silent on the tile. Her pulse jumped. She felt pinned under the weight of his gaze.

"Hello, Lila." His voice was calm, as though they were casual acquaintances.

Maya flitted by, and Lila quietly prayed Maya wouldn't pay too much attention. She cleared her throat. "H-hey," she managed. She wished she didn't sound so startled, but her tone betrayed her nerves.

He set his paper cup down gently. "I was hoping we could speak outside for a moment."

Her grip on the milk pitcher tightened. She glanced around—customers milled about, some tapping away on phones, others lost in conversation. No one seemed aware of their exchange. Lila glanced at Maya, who was busy punching in orders on the register. She exhaled. She had little choice. Maybe he had answers. Or maybe he'd confirm she was losing her mind. Either way, she couldn't keep ignoring him.

"Give me a sec," she said, tension winding through her shoulders.

Caleb nodded, stepping back to give her space. She quickly passed responsibilities to Maya, mumbling something about needing a break. Maya shot her a curious look but nodded. The last thing Lila wanted was a scene in the middle of the café.

Outside, the city bustle assaulted her senses immediately. Horns blared, pedestrians jostled one another for space, and sidewalk vendors called out from their carts. Amid that chaotic dance, Caleb seemed almost untouched by the noise. He waited near a newspaper stand, dark coat catching the swirl of morning air. When he saw Lila, he lifted a hand in a small gesture of greeting.

"You're persistent," Lila said warily.

He met her gaze, eyes flickering with that calm intensity she remembered from the library. "I'm worried about you," he answered, voice low. "New witches often need guidance. It's normal to feel overwhelmed by the surge of magic when it first appears."

Lila swallowed. "Can we not use that word so casually?" she muttered. "People can hear you, you know."

His mouth curved—but whether in amusement or understanding, she wasn't sure. "Relax," he said softly. "We're lost in this city's noise. No one will pay attention unless I want them to."

The subtle self-assuredness in his tone sent a reactive bristle along her nerves. She tried to push down her flutter of anxiety. "So that's how it is?" she challenged, crossing her arms. "You step into people's lives, wave your magic around, and act like it's normal?"

He hesitated, studying her expression with a hint of sympathy. "In a way, yes. Our world is woven through the everyday fabric of this city. We slip in and out quietly. People rarely suspect a thing, especially those who lack any magical sense."

Lila scanned the bustling sidewalk. Men and women hurried by, chattering on phones, clutching briefcases, sipping coffee. Not a single person spared them more than a glance. She realized this conversation, bizarre as it was, would likely blend seamlessly into the background. That realization rankled her, as if the city's obliviousness felt like a betrayal.

Caleb took a small step closer, his voice dropping so only she could hear. "There are centuries-old lineages walking these streets. They ride the subway to work, brew cappuccinos at local cafés, attend yoga classes—just like anyone else." He paused, letting the weight of his words sink in. "We aren't living in some distant, hidden fortress. We're right here, among everyone else."

Her heart pounded. "That's insane," she whispered. "A week ago, my biggest worry was paying my rent. Now you're telling me there are witches and warlocks scattered through Manhattan, casually performing spells while the rest of us order lattes?"

He offered a quiet chuckle, one that rippled with unexpected kindness, and that annoyed her somehow. He was far too calm. "It can be hard to grasp," he admitted. "But it's real. You've seen it yourself, even if you can't fully explain it yet."

She folded her arms protectively over her chest, glancing at a passing taxi. "And so I'm...one of these witches? I'm part of some centuries-old tradition I've never heard of?"

Caleb's eyes softened. "It happens sometimes, if a family keeps magic hidden or if the lineage appears dormant. Perhaps your parents never awakened, so your grandmother didn't share everything with you. These things can skip generations." His tone remained gentle, as though coaxing her away from panic.

Lila's pulse buzzed in her ears. She remembered that fleeting moment last night—pawing through the internet for explanations, stumbling on nothing but nonsense. Then the memory of childhood bedtime stories drifted in her mind again. Could it really be that those legends about someone with the gift of earth, someone who could steady storms, were real? She forced a humorless laugh, running a tense hand through her hair. "I feel like I'm losing my mind," she said, voice tight. "None of this is normal."

A flicker of compassion crossed his face. "I don't blame you for feeling that way. But you're not losing your mind.

You're crossing a threshold you never knew existed, that's all."

Another wave of commotion rolled down the sidewalk as a group of office workers bustled past, jostling them closer to the newspaper stand. The air smelled of roasted almonds from a nearby vendor's cart. For a beat, Lila felt as though she were on the edge of two worlds: the mundane rush of a random Tuesday in Manhattan, and the surreal realm of conjured sparks and hidden powers.

She exhaled shakily. "I'm not sure I believe you. But I don't...disbelieve you either. Does that make sense?"

"It does," he said gently. "Doubt is part of the process. In time, you'll see the signs more clearly."

She bit the inside of her cheek. "And if I don't want this?" she asked, voice quiet. "If I'd prefer to go on ignoring it?"

His jaw tightened almost imperceptibly, though his eyes remained kind. "Pretending won't make the surges go away. They can grow dangerous, not just for you but for those around you. You have a friend inside, correct? Maya?" When Lila nodded, he said, "If something flares out in your café again...you can guess how complicated that might get."

She felt her stomach clench. A stray memory flickered —toppled mugs rattling on the counter, the green spark dancing along the milk frother. If that surge had been worse, if her magic had lashed out in front of customers... Fear twisted her insides.

He read the concern on her face and laid a hand lightly on her arm. "That's why I came," he murmured. "I'm not forcing you to believe. But I'd like to help you understand enough to keep yourself safe. Keep your friend safe. The city safe, in fact."

She wanted to snap that Manhattan's safety was a bit bigger than her shaky, untrained sparks, but she held her tongue. Some part of her recognized the gravity beneath his words. If she really did have some deep well of power, ignorance wasn't an option. Being unprepared could spark chaos.

Pedestrians jostled past them, oblivious to the life-altering conversation happening just feet away. Lila's gaze slid across the flow of strangers. It felt surreal, as though the entire city was continuing on autopilot while her reality cracked open. She shifted her weight, hugging her arms around herself again. "I'm not ready to just...jump into this creepy world of yours," she said quietly.

"You don't have to decide everything right now," Caleb assured her. "But I'd like you to keep an open mind, and maybe tomorrow, we can talk again. Perhaps somewhere you feel more comfortable."

He nodded, then offered her a small, reassuring smile. "I'll stop by soon," he said. "Until then, if anything odd happens, try not to panic. Focus on breathing, keep your mind calm. Sometimes that's enough to suppress a surge in the early stages."

She gave a shaky exhale. "Duly noted," she managed.

A moment passed in charged silence. People on the sidewalk surged around them in a wave of suits and coffee cups, but Lila felt oddly anchored by Caleb's quiet steadiness. She wanted to resent him for messing up her normal life, but the truth was that his presence, however unnerving, also brought a strange solace. It was as though, in admitting these hidden truths, he offered her permission to question everything.

"All right," she muttered. "I should get back to work before my friend wonders if I've done a runner."

Caleb inclined his head in a polite gesture, stepping aside to let her pass. "Take care, Lila," he said gently.

Leaving him there on the busy sidewalk felt like stepping out of a dream. Part of her wondered if, the second she walked inside, he'd vanish in the swirl of city traffic, taking his unimaginable world with him. But she suspected he'd be back, as persistent as ever. She wasn't sure yet if that was comforting or terrifying.

She pulled the café door open, letting the warmth of roasted beans wash over her. Maya threw her a questioning glance, clearly waiting for an explanation, but Lila only offered a tight smile and reclaimed her station behind the counter. The semi-familiar hiss of steam calmed her nerves in small increments.

Despite the routine, her mind spun with each latte she prepared. That presence outside, that quiet acceptance in his eyes, kindled an odd reassurance. Maybe she wasn't crazy after all. Or maybe she was, and Caleb was just the first person who didn't label her insane.

She wondered if her grandmother's bedtime tales would have frightened her less if she'd known they contained grains of truth. Maybe she would have paid closer attention. Her stomach knotted at the thought that someone in her family might have known exactly what she would face.

She shook her head, trying to focus on the choreography of espresso, milk, and foam. But with each moment, her mind crept back to the sidewalk conversation—centuries-old lineages living in plain sight, illusions hidden in broad daylight, and a jarring reality that might link her to an unknown heritage. She could practically hear the city's heartbeat pulsing around her, weaving the everyday with the impossible.

She replayed his final words—keep calm, focus on breathing—like a tiny shield against the raw confusion swirling in her thoughts. If she didn't hold on to that advice, she risked slipping into full-blown panic. Yet she couldn't deny that a tiny spark of curiosity smoldered within her. If magic was real, if she truly possessed it, then all of her grandmother's cryptic lullabies might be more than old fables.

As the last rush customer left, Lila allowed herself a single look through the café windows. She half expected Caleb to be gone, whisked away by the crowd. Instead, she caught sight of him through the glass, weaving gently into pedestrian traffic, a faint tilt to his head as if he sensed her eyes on him. He gave a subtle wave without turning fully around, then merged with the throng. Her heart did a strange little flip.

She set aside the milk frother, feeling unsteady. She inhaled deeply, forcing air into her lungs as the city's clamor echoed outside. She still thought she might be slipping into some fantasy or losing every sense of normal she had, but she also felt a trickle of relief, as if that one conversation lifted an invisible weight.

A strong sense of two diverging worlds tugged at her chest: the normal job she knew and the swirling magic that hovered just behind the curtain. And despite her anxiety, something about Caleb's quiet self-assurance told her she might not have to face it alone.

In that realization was an inkling of hope, a stubborn candle's flame in a dark corridor of confusion. She wiped her hands on a damp towel, trying to chase away the tremor in her fingers. Even if he unnerved her, even if she doubted her own sanity, she felt oddly less isolated. Somehow, this stranger's presence made her feel less alone in her confusion.

SIX

Lila adjusted her green apron for what felt like the hundredth time that morning and tried to smile at the throng across the counter. The Daily Grind was packed, buzzing with coffee orders, clinking spoons, and the relentless hiss of steaming milk. On any other day, she would have thrived on this lively chaos. She prided herself on cheerfully juggling orders and real-time banter with customers. Lately, though, her stomach knotted at every small surprise, terrified another spark of inexplicable magic would flare without warning.

She needed this shift to be normal. She needed the world to remain the simple place it used to be. No illusions. No weird green lights dancing at her fingertips. Just coffee, foam, and easy conversation.

A tall man wearing a tasseled hat waved her over to the register. His coffee order was complicated—pumpkin spice with a hint of hazelnut, extra hot, no whip—but she nodded politely, punching it into the old cash register. The machine's keys clicked louder than usual, or maybe that was her nerves. She forced a grin.

"That will be five seventy-five," Lila said, voice only slightly shaking.

The man fished out exact change from a worn leather wallet and dropped the coins into her palm. She murmured a quick "Thanks," passing on the order to Maya, who stood behind the espresso machine. Maya offered Lila a curious glance as she took the slip, but Lila just shrugged, trying to convey that all was fine. Except her heart thudded a little too fast, and her apron strings felt too tight. She yearned for the day to end before something unraveled.

Next in line was a fidgety woman reeking of impatience. Lila mustered her best customer service voice. "Morning. How can I help you?"

"Plain cappuccino. Extra foam," the woman said, tapping her nails on the counter. "Please tell me you actually know how to froth it properly."

Forcing politeness, Lila nodded. "I'll do my best," she said.

The woman snorted, casting a glance around the bustling space. Lila sensed incoming complaints, so she prepared her mental shield: a pleasant smile, a quick nod, nothing more. But the woman turned away without further comment, leaving only a mild tension in her wake. At least that small interaction ended quietly.

A few minutes later, the dynamic of the morning took a sharp turn. A new customer—middle-aged, short-tempered, tie askew—marched up to the counter with a half-finished latte in hand. He pointed at the swirl of foam on top as though it were a personal insult.

"This is wrong," he snapped. "I asked for sugar-free vanilla, and I'm tasting hazelnut. Hazelnut! I can't even stand the smell of it."

"Oh, I'm so sorry." Lila's throat constricted. She wiped sweaty palms on her apron and tried to keep her tone calm. "Let me fix that right away. I can remake your drink at no charge."

"That's not the point," he huffed, cheeks flushing red. "I asked specifically for sugar-free vanilla. Now I have to wait in line again because you messed up? Are you not paying attention or something?"

Lila glanced over her shoulder, spotting Maya's tense frown as she pressed a new filter into the espresso machine. They were both used to impatient customers, but something about this scene unsettled Lila more than it should have. Her nerves tingled. She released a small breath.

"We'll do a fresh drink, no waiting," she promised, raising her hands in what she hoped was a soothing gesture. "I'll handle it personally. No line."

His voice rose a notch. "You better. I don't have time for mistakes."

She tried to hold her composure. A handful of customers nearby paused their conversations, sensing the confrontation. Pressure built in Lila's chest. Her pulse pounded. She reminded herself to keep it together, to not let that unusual warmth spread through her fingertips.

But the man wouldn't let it go. "Are you new here? Because the baristas here used to be decent."

She dug her nails into her palm. "I've actually been here a while," she said, injecting forced brightness into her tone. "I'm sorry for the inconvenience. Let me just remake that for you."

He slammed the paper cup on the counter, foam sloshing over the rim. "Fine. Do it quickly."

Tension spiked around them. Nearby patrons started glancing their way. Maya called Lila's name softly, handing over a fresh cup. Too many eyes were watching. A cold sweat prickled at the back of Lila's neck. She hated how her heart hammered double-time, as if her own body expected a magical outburst. She had no reason to lose control. It was only a rude customer. She could handle this. She always could.

Yet despite her internal pep talk, her nerves soared. The man stood stiffly on the other side of the counter, complaining under his breath about incompetent staff and wasted money. Lila blinked back a surge of panic. Her nails pressed deeper against her palm.

"Here you go," she said, gently placing the new latte on the counter. Her voice shook. "Sugar-free vanilla. Extra hot."

He seized the cup, took a loud sip, and barked, "Let's hope it's not too sweet," before turning to go. She exhaled shakily. Maybe that was the end of it. Maybe—

He coughed as though discovering something in the foam, spinning around. "You know what, this still tastes off. You call this sugar-free? Let me guess, you used the same pitcher. That means there's cross-contamination. Unbelievable."

Blood rushed to Lila's ears. The café seemed to hush, only the clang of mugs and hiss of steam in the background. She tried to reason with him, words stumbling. "Sir, I used a clean pitcher. I promise. Maybe it tastes different because the foam—"

"No!" He rattled the cup's lid. "You're incompetent. Where is your manager?"

At that moment, three things happened in rapid succession: her stomach twisted with dread, her frustration skyrocketed, and the overhead fan made a strange clicking sound. A sudden swirl of air rippled along the display shelf next to the register, a breeze far cooler than the normal ventilation. Lila stiffened—her newly awakened magic crackled unexpectedly at the edges of her awareness.

Sure enough, mugs displayed on a nearby shelf rattled ominously. The movement was slight at first. Then the wind gusted harder, clanging ceramic against ceramic. Before Lila could react, two mugs wobbled to the shelf's edge, tipping off and smashing to the floor with resounding crashes.

Coffee drinkers froze in their seats. Someone at a table let out a startled yelp. A new hush fell, so profound it made Lila's heart pound faster. The rude customer jumped back as shards of blue ceramic scattered near his shoes.

"What was that?" he barked, eyes wide. "Is there a window open in here? That was practically a gale."

Lila's face burned. She stared at the broken shards, pulse in her throat, unsure how to explain. Her mind whirred with excuses: Maybe an air conditioning glitch. Maybe an unexpected draft from outside. Anything but the real explanation. She saw Maya's worried expression, then realized half the café had turned to watch.

"I—I'm so sorry," Lila stammered, crouching to retrieve the largest pieces. Her cheeks flamed red. In that instant, the adrenaline made her hands tremble. She couldn't make sense of how, exactly, the wind had swooped through all at once. But she knew deep inside that her emotions had slipped free again, unleashing something bigger than a meltdown.

"She dropped them on purpose," the man said, pointing at Lila as though she were the cause of everything from clumsy bartending to bad weather. "You're telling me I have to trust my drink to this? I want somebody else to fix my coffee."

Maya hastily set down a rag. "I can fix you a new one, sir," she offered, voice tight. "Free of charge, as many times as you want. Let's step away from the broken glass."

He mumbled complaints as Maya guided him to the side. Lila swallowed back panic and kept gathering broken bits. Her breath came in short, sharp bursts that did nothing to calm the racing in her chest. She knew she had caused that gust of wind. She felt it almost sigh through her veins an instant before the mugs tumbled.

Someone cursed from a nearby table. A middle-aged woman began whispering to her friend, speculating why the shelves had rattled so wildly. Lila's eyes misted with embarrassment, but she refused to crumble on the spot. She just needed to hide in the back room, toss the shards, and calm down.

She placed the fragments on the counter behind her, willing her shaking fingers to behave. She tried for an apologetic smile at onlookers, but her lips quivered. A swirling sense of dread churned in her stomach. It was happening again—this creeping, potent energy that liked to surge with her anxiety.

Her gaze flicked across the room. She locked eyes with Caleb. He had been seated at the far corner table, sipping a black coffee. At her realization, he rose slowly, every movement deliberate, as if ready to intervene. When she met his gaze, her pulse gave a traitorous flutter. His posture was tense, and in that moment, she felt his silent support, though she also sensed concern in the slight furrow of his brow.

An older gentleman in the next seat had stood up, evidently planning to investigate the cause of those fallen mugs. Caleb pivoted, drawing a faint pattern near his sleeve—a small motion that looked like he was adjusting his cuff. Lila saw a shimmer in the air, almost invisible unless one knew where to look. She recognized that shimmer from the night in the library, the subtle wave of illusory calm that he was so adept at weaving. In the space of a few breaths, the café's tension smoothed over, as if the entire room had collectively decided nothing unusual was happening.

A young woman who had frozen with her mouth open slowly returned to sipping her latte, brow no longer knotted with suspicion. A cluster of college students near the door resumed chatting about their assignments, seemingly forgetting the outburst they had witnessed. Even the rude customer stared down at his new latte in mild confusion, as though the memory of broken mugs and swirling wind had slipped away.

Feeling lightheaded, Lila pressed a hand to the back of her neck. She didn't know whether to feel relief or guilt. Caleb had just disguised the truth again, giving everyone a mental nudge to carry on unbothered. The hush lifted, replaced by a low murmur of returning chatter. The crisis was over in a blink. Yet Lila's heart hammered so loudly she swore the entire café could hear it.

She turned back to the shards, ignoring how her hands shook. Maya hovered behind her, mouth parted as if wanting to ask if she was okay. Lila waved her off gently, willing herself to appear calm. She needed a moment alone, but the café offered no such privacy. The best she could do was straighten her spine and pretend the quake in her legs was from kneeling too long.

When she finally stood, the rude customer remained at the side station, blowing on his latte. He didn't look upset anymore, but he also didn't look particularly grateful. He grunted something about "finally tasting fine," then ambled off to a table near the windows. Lila doubted he recalled how tense he had been moments earlier.

Maya whispered, "You alright?" She pressed a sympathetic look upon Lila when a lull in orders allowed them a second to talk. "You looked freaked out."

"I'm fine." Lila managed a numb nod. "Just... I'll go get the mop." She grabbed the broom and dustpan first, sweeping up stray shards with shaking hands, trying to ignore the heat rising in her cheeks again.

Her mind spun. She had made zero progress controlling this bizarre, growing magic. Apparently, some part of her decided to fling gusts of wind whenever she felt cornered. She couldn't keep explaining these incidents away. People would ask questions next time. And the time after that. She couldn't expect Caleb to keep covering for her, not if these surges grew stronger.

She shifted her gaze to find Caleb again. He was near the far side of the café, smoothing the hem of his coat. She sensed his illusions settling over the room like a gentle hush. Although he tried to appear casual, his eyes were locked on her, watchful and intent. There was no anger there. Instead, she caught a flicker of concern, maybe even a hint of admiration for how she was holding it together.

Her chest tightened with a mix of gratitude and raw embarrassment. He had seen everything. He had witnessed her losing control, again. And while he had shielded her from suspicion one more time, how long could that protection last? All of the warnings he had delivered about untrained magic were suddenly undeniable. She had shattered the thin veneer of normalcy she clung to in moments like this.

One more day of near-disaster. One more sign that she was in over her head.

She emptied shards into the trash, stashed the broom behind the counter, and forced herself to greet the next customer—a timid older lady wanting a simple American coffee—while her heart still beat irregularly. The entire interaction felt surreal. The lady might as well have been speaking through water for how distant her voice sounded. Lila's own voice wobbled but she faked a smile, letting Maya fill the cup so she wouldn't risk messing up again.

Eventually, the line thinned, and the commotion died down. A few employees swept the floor and wiped tables. The normal hum of the café stuttered back into place, but Lila couldn't shake the tension from her spine. She found herself sneaking glances across the room. She spotted Caleb sitting at his table, apparently content to nurse a second black coffee. He caught her looking, and she swore a small, crooked smile played at his mouth. Maybe amuse-ment. Maybe empathy. Either way, heat flared in her cheeks.

Finally, the last determined wave of customers departed, leaving only two students hunched over their laptops. Maya, noticing Lila's trembling hands, silently offered to hold down the fort. It was the friend's version of an unspoken break suggestion. Lila nodded in thanks, removing her apron. She stepped outside for some air, but paused near the door, reconsidering the swirl of uneasy thoughts in her head.

No, she told herself, running wasn't the answer. It

never had been. She pressed her palm to the glass door, battling the urge to flee. The city outside was loud and unpredictable, but in here, illusions and magic threatened her normal life. Either direction felt hazardous. She swallowed, squared her shoulders, and turned back to the café. Caleb's gaze found her again.

He made a small gesture, an invitation to come over. For the briefest moment, she hesitated. Did she want to face him right now? The wave of embarrassment still clung to her like a cold sweat. But curiosity and need outmatched her discomfort. Heart pounding, she walked between the tables until she stood by his side. His presence was steady as ever—like a pillar in a storm, even if that storm was of her own making.

Caleb's eyes flicked to the newly cleaned floor, and then to the blossoming pink across her cheeks. "That was quite a commotion," he said in a gentle murmur that no one else would overhear. "Are you hurt?"

Her cheeks burned. "No, I'm okay. I just... lost my grip on my temper, I guess. These bursts keep happening." She swallowed and stared down at his coffee cup. "Thank you for stepping in."

He inclined his head. "Glad to help." His tone was neutral, but the concern beneath it was unmistakable. "We can leave it at that for the moment, if you want."

She let out a breath she didn't realize she was holding. "I'm scared," she admitted quietly. "Every time I think it'll be fine, something sets me off. This place—my job—my friends... everything's in danger if I can't handle it."

Caleb's hand shifted, as if he were tempted to reach for

hers, but he kept it flat on the table. The small restraint made her stomach flip in a mix of gratitude and regret that she needed so much caution.

"We'll talk soon," he said. "You won't be alone in this."

She gave a tense nod, accepting a solace she didn't quite trust herself to keep. She half-expected him to mention the Council, or the training he had strongly suggested before, but he stayed silent, letting her gather her composure. The hum of the café's AC returned to a gentle whir.

A few minutes later, she had to get back behind the counter. Her shift was far from over, but she kept stealing glances in his direction. He, in turn, looked ready to respond to the slightest ripple of magic. It was both comforting and unnerving to have him watching her so closely.

Time dragged on until the last of the midday rush trickled out. The lights flickered once—the building's old wiring protesting the strain—but nothing catastrophic occurred. Lila wiped a bit of spilled espresso off the bar, telling herself to breathe easy. The worst was over.

At last, she turned away from the bin and caught Caleb's gaze again. Even from across the counter, she sensed the question in his eyes: Are you ready to accept that your life has changed? A flush of heat crawled up her neck. Everything in her wanted to say no, to keep pretending, but that ship had sailed the second green sparks had popped from her hands. She was out of time for denial.

Caleb stood, slipping a bill under his empty coffee cup in a polite gesture. Then he inclined his head once more, that faint sense of unspoken understanding passing between them. Lila's heart pounded, realizing the little bubble of her normal life had burst wide open. She couldn't hide behind the daily grind forever. If she refused to learn how to control these surges, the next accident might be worse than a few broken mugs.

SEVEN

Lila's feet dragged over the last few blocks to her building, and every step felt like trudging through thick sand. A light drizzle slicked the sidewalk, staining her sneakers and seeping cold through her worn-out socks. Her thoughts spun with lingering panic over the strange incidents earlier that day. She had forced herself through a closing shift at The Daily Grind, jabbering hollow reassurances to customers who noticed the odd electrical flickers whenever she passed too close to a light fixture. Even Maya, usually quick to tease, had seemed worried enough to press Lila for answers. Lila gave half-truths and deflections, too drained to cope with real explanations.

When she finally reached her apartment building, she paused beneath the chipped overhang. A single bulb illuminated the metallic directory on the side wall, reflecting her tired features as she fished for her key. The faint sound of traffic at the corner felt unnaturally distant. A new heaviness pressed between her ribs, and she shivered at a flicker of movement in the alley across the street. No one was there, but her nerves screamed otherwise. Magic, illusions, warding, all of it seemed to loom in every dark corner now.

Her building's door squeaked in protest when she pushed it open. She climbed the stairs, two flights that felt like an eternity, until she stood in the narrow hallway where mismatched bulbs cast odd shadows along the dingy walls. Her cramped apartment was at the end. Normally, she would hurry inside, fling herself onto her solitary futon, and let the chatter of nearby televisions lull her to a restless sleep. Tonight, her senses were too on edge.

The hallway smelled of stale onions, as though somebody's dinner had gone tragically wrong hours ago. The faint odor made her queasy. She fumbled with her key, fighting the door's stubborn lock. Her fingers trembled more than she cared to admit. Exhaustion nipped at her from every angle, yet a jangling pulse kept adrenaline trickling through her bloodstream. The lock clicked at last, but her relief was short-lived.

A soft rustle drifted from the stairwell behind her. She froze mid-turn, heart slamming into her ribs like a trapped bird. When she glanced over her shoulder, a tall figure moved in the dim light, coat catching a fractured glimmer. Her throat went dry until she recognized the face.

"Caleb?" Her voice emerged far more breathless than she intended.

He paused on the landing, the single overhead bulb reflecting in his dark hair. There was a moment of quiet before he moved closer. Everything about him radiated an odd mixture of concern and urgency. He wore the same fitted coat she had seen at the café days before, hands half-hidden in the pockets. "I'm sorry," he said in a low tone. "I realize this isn't a casual hour to drop by."

Her brain scrambled for a response, but it stuck on one alarming detail: she had never given him her address. The next beat of her heart thundered in her ears. She tightened her grip on the doorknob, mind flicking to everything he had told her about hidden watchers, illusions, and the so-called Council that policed the magical community. Was this how closely they monitored novices?

"How did you find me?" She realized she was practically whispering. The hallway seemed too enclosed, every door silent as if the other tenants had retreated behind thick walls.

Caleb's expression flickered with something like regret. "The Council keeps a registry of newly awakened witches. Every time your aura spikes, the records update. I sensed a surge from you earlier tonight." He stopped, hesitating as though he wanted to check her reaction before continuing. "I'm not here to corner you. I just needed to be sure you got home safely."

She swallowed, a thread of anger mixing with her fear. It was unnerving knowing total strangers could track her aura, as if she were pinned on some magical map. She squared her shoulders a fraction. "Well, I'm—fine," she said, though her voice trembled on that last word. "Or as fine as I can be after the day I've had."

His eyes, bright even in the dim hallway, studied her face. She couldn't tell if he was about to offer reassurance or a lecture. Finally, he spoke quietly. "Lila, there's something you need to know. The Council will expect you to attend a formal meeting soon. They value secrecy, so novices who display public surges—like the ones you're having—draw attention. We have to talk."

"All right," she said, keeping her voice hushed. "But not out here."

She pushed the door open and nodded for him to step inside. It felt surreal, inviting him into her personal space. The hallway's harsh lighting gave way to the gloom of her tiny apartment, still faintly smelling of coffee grounds from her breakfast mug. Her first instinct was to apologize for the clutter—a half-folded blanket on the futon, a few scattered magazines, an empty pizza box on the counter— and then she remembered he was hardly a normal guest. Right now, her sloppiness didn't seem like the biggest issue.

He entered with cautious steps, pausing near the threshold. In the faint glow of a single lamp on her side table, his coat looked darker, and a faint weariness shadowed his face. The door clicked shut behind her, leaving the two of them alone in the confined space. She willed her pulse to settle, but it only jumped higher.

"Please," she said, nodding at the small kitchen corner. "We can talk here. I'd offer you coffee, but I'm—" She trailed off, remembering that touching the coffee machine after hours of chaos might not be the safest plan. The last thing she needed was to inadvertently set off a new surge that knocked out the power. Besides, the thought of more caffeine made her stomach churn.

He dismissed the concern with a slow shake of his head. "I'm good." He leaned gently against the edge of the counter, arms crossing in front of his chest. "Sorry if I startled you. I know it feels intrusive, but the Council can sense these fluctuations. They track your aura more closely when it's new and unpredictable."

She let out a ragged breath, stepping cautiously into her own living space, as if she'd become a stranger to it. The overhead light flickered ominously, so she flipped on the light over the sink instead. Warm, yellowish light fell across his face, amplifying the quiet tension in his features.

"So," she said, trying to keep her voice steady. "Give me the short version. Why is my aura surging so much?"

His gaze held steady on her, and she felt a tiny jolt at the intensity behind those eyes. "Because your magic is fully awakening. Stress and fear cause spikes. And from what I can tell, you've had plenty of both."

She wrapped her arms around herself for comfort, leaning against her rickety dining chair. "No argument there," she muttered.

He took a small step forward, letting his posture soften. "Lila, I need you to understand that this attention from the Council isn't necessarily about punishing you. It's about making sure illusions or surges don't blow your cover and cause panic among mortals."

She pursed her lips. "I'm guessing they're not exactly a tolerant bunch if I keep losing control in public."

His jaw flexed. "They're more wary than cruel. But the secrecy they maintain is what keeps innocent people safe—and keeps witches from being hunted. Not everyone in the world is ready to accept our existence."

She absorbed that, spotting a flicker of genuine concern in his calm composure. "You mentioned they'll want to meet me soon. What does that look like?"

He frowned slightly. "Likely they'll request a formal interview, with an oath about secrecy. They'll want to see how stable you are, gauge your potential. And they might assign additional training beyond what I've offered." The corners of his mouth tightened, as if the responsibility weighed on him personally.

"You're my teacher, right?" She realized how thin that label sounded in the confines of her cramped apartment. She remembered the swirl of sparks in the café and how his illusions had steadied the chaos. "Do you get in trouble, too, if I keep messing up?"

Caleb let out a breath. "My job is to keep you and everyone else safe. If illusions escalate, the Council might question whether I'm guiding you properly. But I'm less worried about them disciplining me and more concerned about you getting overwhelmed or exposed."

A silent pause stretched between them, broken only by the faint hum of her refrigerator. Her exhaustion stabbed at her temples, yet she felt more awake than ever.

"You talk like you've been through this before," she ventured. "Mentoring new witches, I mean."

He nodded, gaze flicking to a stray mug on the counter, as if searching for a new focal point. "Yes, I've helped novices adapt. But not many awaken with aura spikes like yours. You have a...unique signature. It's strong." Something in his tone hinted that there was more he wasn't saying.

"So I'm special," she said, a hollow laugh escaping. "Funny how I don't feel that way. Mostly I feel tired and freaked out."

His expression softened. "It's a lot, I know. That's why I'm here." He unfolded his arms, edging a little closer, though he didn't reach out to touch her. "You shouldn't handle it alone. The Council can sometimes be unclear in their expectations, but secrecy is absolute. If people outside our world see too many magical mishaps, it puts everyone at risk."

She realized how easily this new life might swallow her. One misstep, and she could jeopardize Maya, her own job, and any normal future. She forced down a surge of desperation. "It would help if I knew more about what I'm getting into. Can you tell me—about the Council, about illusions that...that I keep half-accidentally making?"

His shoulders relaxed just a fraction, and he inclined his head in agreement. "Yes. I can explain more than I've managed to so far." He gestured at the small table. "Mind if we sit?"

She tugged a second chair away from the wall, and they both settled at the table, knees almost touching in the cramped space. For a moment, Lila noticed the subtle signs of fatigue in him too, the faint smudge beneath his eyes, the tension in his mouth. A hint of unspoken warmth punctured the air. Despite the swirl of fear in her gut, she felt drawn to the quiet strength he radiated. She could only wonder if he sensed it as well.

They talked for what felt like hours, voices soft. He told her that illusions were among the most delicate yet dangerous forms of magic, able to warp perceptions if not carefully controlled. She admitted how the smallest anxiety at the café had led to broken mugs or flickering green sparks dancing over the espresso machine. He explained that the Council's watchers, scattered throughout the city, were adept at containing or masking these accidents so mortals never truly grasped the truth. She trembled at the idea of an unseen network always hovering.

At times, their conversation sidetracked to personal details. She confessed she had trouble sleeping, that nightmares of swirling lights plagued her whenever she closed her eyes. He listened closely, nodding in empathy. He shared glimpses of his own introduction to the Council, how mentors had guided him through illusions that threatened to spiral. Now, he believed novices needed even more support, especially with modern city life providing constant stressors.

She told him about her time at NYU where both her parents were professors of European history. For the past several years they had taken visiting professorships in international programs so they could continue research for a new book on the fall of the Roman empire. Before she had the coffee shop they would travel all over Europe together. She talked to them often but hadn't seen them in months but wanted to catch up to them in Rome soon.

He asked if she had siblings or any relatives who might have magical powers. And she said she was an only child. Then she stopped for a moment thinking about her Grandmother Evelyn who lived in Connecticut. "I love her but my parents always kept our distance from her. She's always been a mystery to me."

A subtle shift occurred the longer they spoke. The tension between them changed flavor—no less intense, but threaded by an unspoken magnetism that made her pulse skip. She would realize how close their arms were and move away, only to find him leaning nearer at her next question. Once, her hand brushed his by accident, and neither pulled away immediately.

Her cheeks warmed at every unintentional touch. She wondered if he noticed the color rising in her face, or the slight tremor that raced through her fingertips. The words between them alternated between softly spoken facts and quiet confessions. Each minute chipped away at her initial wariness, though the undercurrent of danger remained. There was no way to banish it. If the Council was indeed tracking her aura, there was no telling how soon they might summon her.

Eventually, exhaustion coiled around them both. Caleb's voice grew quieter, and Lila felt her eyelids growing heavy, every question blending into the next. He glanced around, noticing how her small lamp cast faint shadows across the cluttered table.

He cleared his throat. "It's late. You should rest."

She offered a small nod. Though her body ached for sleep, part of her wanted to cling to his presence. The moment he left, she would be alone again with a thousand thoughts gnawing at her. But she couldn't keep him here indefinitely.

Rising, she walked him to the door, feeling the drag of weariness in her limbs. He turned to face her, expression solemn. "I wish I could give you simpler answers," he said. "We're both navigating unsteady ground. But I promise you're not alone in this."

Her heart thudded at his earnest tone. She saw a glimpse of vulnerability in him, that same regretful guilt she'd glimpsed once or twice before. He hesitated, as if weighing whether to say something more. Finally, he just dipped his head.

"Thank you," she managed, throat tight. "I appreciate it. Even if everything sounds scary, it's...better not being in the dark."

He inclined his head one last time, eyes flicking to the shadows along the hallway. For a breath, he looked as though he might step closer again, but he instead turned and she opened the door for him, half wishing he'd stay, half terrified by the mess her life had become.

Hallway light spilled into her apartment as he exited. In that faint glow, their eyes met for a final heartbeat. She caught the subtle shape of his lips in a near-smile, then he was gone. Alone in the silent aftermath, she exhaled unsteadily.

Her door clicked shut.

Sighing, she tossed the pizza box into the trash and

rubbed at her tired eyes. The lamp still burned, washing the cramped apartment with a pale glow that suddenly felt emptier without Caleb's presence. She replayed his warning about secrecy. She couldn't even involve Maya. Staying quiet about the illusions might protect her best friend, but guilt settled in her stomach like a stone.

With swollen eyes, she sank onto her futon, picking at the worn edge of her blanket. Caleb had left her marginally calmer, but also adrift in new uncertainties.

She let out a tired laugh, no humor in it at all. Her gaze lingered on the faint ring of light cast by the lamp, imagining illusions slyly creeping just out of view. The night's conversation hammered one fact home: the deeper she waded into magic, the more the Council would demand her compliance. And the more she felt a dangerous pull toward the man who had appeared so abruptly in her life.

CHAPTER

EIGHT

Lila woke to the metallic jangle of her phone alarm and the leftover tightness in her chest. The anxiety that had kept her from sleeping now crawled through her veins, pulsing with each beep of the alarm. She blinked at the dim light of her apartment, where the curtains hung crooked and a leftover pizza box teetered on her kitchen counter. The normal routine—throw on jeans, grab a quick cup of coffee—felt like climbing a mountain this morning. She wondered if her magic had multiplied overnight, the energy in her fingertips tingling as she flexed them. That possibility made her stomach clench. She had no time for any new incidents before work.

She managed to shower and pull on her barista uniform, a simple black T-shirt and the signature apron of The Daily Grind. The floorboards creaked under her feet as she crossed to her tiny kitchen, ignoring the bright green sparks that flickered when she touched the light switch.

She mumbled a curse of frustration. Each reminder of her shaky control felt like a fresh bruise.

Her phone buzzed again, this time a text from Maya: Good opening. Already dreading a busy morning. Lila sighed. At least Maya was thinking ahead and pulling more than her weight. Their typical banter might have brought a smile to Lila's face on any other day, but right now, those small comforts only amplified the hollowness in her chest.

At the café, the usual morning rush came on fast. Customers piled in for espresso shots, cold brews, and sugary lattes. Lila tried to greet the regulars with a warm smile, but her cheeks felt stiff. The steaming milk sent her heart jumping, as though any second, she might let slip a surge of magic. She kept her eyes trained on her hands, praying nothing outwardly glowed or rattled. It was only a matter of time before stress pulled the strings.

"Hey," Maya called cheerfully over the roar of the espresso machine. "I need that large Americano up front. Customer asked twice."

Lila wiped her brow with the back of her hand. "Coming right up," she said, forcing a note of brightness into her voice. She hoped it didn't sound as frayed as she felt. She made the drink hastily and set it on the pickup counter, nearly knocking over the cup of the previous order. The customer frowned but said nothing. Lila swallowed hard.

Maya bustled to her side once the customer departed. "You alright? You look exhausted," she said in a low voice that still managed to convey her worry. "I can handle things if you need a quick break."

Lila forced a tight laugh. "I'm fine," she lied. She should have accepted the offer to go sit in the back, yet she could almost hear the rustle of invisible watchers. She feared being alone even for a moment, as if breathing in private might conjure a fresh outburst. "It's just crowded," she added. "I'll make the next latte. Then I can breathe."

Maya gave her a lingering, concerned look before nodding. "Alright. But holler if you need me."

Unfortunately, the morning rush only got busier. The line stretched to the door as impatient customers muttered under their breath, complaining about anything from the toasted bagels to the temperature of the café. Lila did her best to keep a polite smile, but she felt cracks splitting her composure. A portion of her thoughts drifted to what little she knew about "Council watchers." She had begun to suspect that half the city might be judging her from the shadows. Even during small talk, she found herself scanning the crowd, worrying that any stranger in line might be part of some secret network.

A short, wiry man stepped forward, complaining about how his macchiato tasted off. Lila clenched her jaw and assured him they would make it correctly this time. While she rang him up, her fingertips tingled with a flicker of that unsteady power. She gripped the register so hard her knuckles turned white. In her peripheral vision, she saw Maya peering at her curiously.

"I'll remake the drink, absolutely," Lila told the man,

though her voice trembled slightly. A bead of perspiration trickled down her temple. She turned to Maya, hoping her friend would not notice how pale she felt. "Extra drizzle, right?" she asked, stalling. He nodded, muttering something about incompetent staff. Lila fought to swallow a retort. Her magic thrummed, ready to lash out.

She stepped away from the register to prepare the drink. Maya joined her, calibrating the espresso machine's settings. "Seriously," Maya said in a hushed tone. "Are you sure everything's alright?"

The gentle concern in Maya's voice cracked Lila's remaining patience more than any rude customer could. Lila could not stand the pity. Anxiety churned in her stomach, and she snapped, "I said I'm fine. Drop it, okay?" She nearly slammed the milk steamer into place. Her heart pounded with immediate guilt, but frustration coated her words. "Please, just... let me handle this."

Maya's eyes widened, then narrowed in hurt. Without another word, she stepped back to handle a separate order at the other end of the counter. Lila bit the inside of her cheek, struggling not to let guilt override her. She wanted to reach out, to say sorry, but her throat felt raw. The harshness had slipped out, an unfiltered product of her crumbling composure.

Silence stretched between her and Maya for the next half-hour. The relentless line of customers forced them to keep working, side by side but not speaking unless it was about toppings or the number of shots in a latte. Lila found herself longing for an easy joke, anything to wash away the tension. The reality that she had wounded

Maya, her closest friend, made her want to sink into the floor.

By the time noon neared, the surge slowed. Lila massaged her temples, wanting to vanish for at least five minutes of solitude. In the lull, the door opened again. She looked over, heart jolting at the sight of Caleb stepping inside. He wore a dark coat, shoulders tense as though ever-prepared for trouble, and the moment he spotted her, his gaze softened. That fleeting look made heat rise in Lila's cheeks despite her anger and confusion. Part of her wanted to run to him, demand an explanation for how he kept reappearing in her life. Another part resented him for dragging her into this swirling madness.

Caleb approached the counter, nodding a quick greeting to Maya. Her lips tightened politely as she took his order for a black coffee, but Lila noticed the worried flicker in her friend's eyes as she handed him the change. He took his cup, stepping aside to let the next customer order, but the moment was enough. Lila's chest squeezed at the swirl of relief and annoyance festering inside her. She couldn't decide whether she blamed him or needed him right now.

Maya's gaze flicked between Lila and Caleb for a second, but Lila avoided her eyes. Instead, she faced the espresso machine, fighting the urge to fling her apron down and flee into the back room.

Minutes later, she saw Caleb move to a small table near the wall, sipping his coffee and observing the café with that calm watchfulness she once found comforting. Now it only ignited her restlessness. A wave of tension passed through her shoulders, and she muttered to Maya that she would take a short break. Her friend nodded silently, prompting a pang of renewed guilt in Lila's chest. She had no idea how to mend the rift she had caused earlier. For now, she just needed to breathe.

In the back room office, Lila slumped against the wall, her hands trembling. Her phone vibrated in her apron pocket with a new message—likely something mundane, but she felt too frayed to check it. Instead, she picked up her laptop from the tiny desk. Maybe searching for more information on "Council watchers" or any clue about these illusions would give her a sense of control.

She opened the laptop. Her reflection on the black screen stared back, circles under her eyes. She powered it on. The slow boot-up gave her time to scold herself for lashing out at Maya. She should have apologized immediately, but she felt pinned between secrets and shame, unsure if she could stand another question she couldn't answer with honesty.

Eventually, her laptop connected to the café's Wi-Fi. She typed a few keywords and hit enter. At first, the results seemed to revolve around historical references or conspiracy theories. "Council watchers." "Magical guardians." She clicked link after link.

She squinted at a half-baked website that claimed an "Arcane Circle" protected major cities, complete with forum posts citing second-hand accounts. One mention struck her: "Some families rumored to hold relics passed down for centuries" was quoted under a poorly formatted paragraph. The speculation made her heart tumble. It felt closer to the bizarre truth of her own recent experiences than any standard myth. She ran her fingertips across the trackpad, lips trembling. Could her grandmother's bedtime stories about a line of witches in their ancestry be real all along? Of course, that possibility no longer felt far-fetched. She had seen too many flickers of green sparks in her own hands.

A chill breezed over her shoulders, and she realized she had been sitting in the stuffy back room so long that sweat had cooled on her skin. Her next click led to a cryptic mention: "Council watchers maintain illusions to keep normal folk unaware. If you see strange lights or illusions, you may have glimpsed their wards." The text that followed included a half-baked explanation that watchers belonged to a sanctioned group that wiped memories or performed illusions to obscure magical slip-ups.

Lila let out an unsteady breath. She exhaled, shutting the laptop carefully. There was no place for denial anymore. She would call grandmother Evelyn tonight. No, as soon as she left work. The sudden resolution steadied her nerves. All those old stories about ancestors who supposedly harnessed the essence of earth might not be nonsense. Her grandmother had once mentioned a line of witches. Maybe the woman could give her answers or direct her to a better resource than half-baked internet forums.

Tucking her laptop away, she forced herself to stand. Another wave of guilt over Maya hit her. If she told her friend even a fraction of this madness, would Maya think she was losing her mind? That threat of betrayal pressed on Lila's lungs. She pictured Maya's wounded eyes from earlier and cursed the circumstances that demanded silence. She had to keep pushing forward in secrecy, at least for now.

When she returned to the main floor, she found Maya restocking the pastry display with a forced efficiency. Lila approached carefully, the tension humming between them.

"I'm… sorry about before," Lila managed, voice low enough that customers at the far tables would not over-hear. "I'm a wreck. I really appreciate you covering."

Maya glanced at her, pushing a plate of croissants into place. "You don't have to pretend with me," she said, sounding more hurt than angry. "Something's obviously going on. But if you need space, sure. I can back off." Her expression softened, eyes flicking over Lila's face with concern. "Just… be careful, okay?"

Lila nodded, swallowing hard. "I promise, I'll explain soon. I just… can't right now."

Maya pursed her lips, exhaling. "Fine," she said, patting Lila's arm briefly. "Go handle the line. It's picking up again." Her tone was clipped, but there was an under-current of compassion. Lila felt a tiny weight lift from her chest. Maya wasn't fully shutting her out.

She moved to the register, busying herself with fresh orders. A mother with a toddler asked about non-dairy milk, an older couple complained about the radio volume, and a cluster of young professionals demanded an assort-ment of iced drinks. Lila scrambled to keep up, anxiety swirling in her gut like a coiled serpent. She dreaded another slip of magic. Luckily, she only stumbled over small details, like forgetting a syrup pump or mixing up receipt totals.

Eventually, the café music switched from perky pop to a staticky oldies tune. Lila's nerves loosened slightly as the lunch rush began to wane. She was about to breathe easier when she pivoted to clean the wand and scalded her entire forearm on the burst of steam. A tone of frustration bubbled up as she jerked away from the espresso machine.

"Dammit," she spat, wincing at the throbbing in her skin. She shut the steam nozzle, ignoring the customer who looked up in alarm. Maya hurried over, dropping a half-filled coffee cup to check on her.

"What happened?" Maya asked, concern overshadowing their lingering tension.

"Steam burn," Lila gritted out, her voice shaking. "I wasn't paying attention."

Maya quickly guided her to the sink, running cool water over the reddening patch on Lila's arm. The shock of relief made Lila's eyes sting. She swallowed the tears that threatened to fall, determined not to break down in front of a half-dozen people sipping espresso at the nearest tables.

She felt another stab of guilt when she realized Caleb had stood up from his seat, expression sharp as he prepared to intervene. She saw him hesitate, glancing to ensure Maya was handling it. Then he retreated, gaze unreadable. Lila raised her eyes to meet his, anger and gratitude churning together. Her life was wrecked enough without a magical mentor jumping in at every accident.

Still, another part of her wanted to yield to him, let him fix everything. Her conflicting impulses rattled around in her chest.

"It's going to be okay," Maya murmured, dabbing at Lila's arm with a paper towel once the water had cooled the burn. "There's an aloe kit in the back."

Lila nodded. Her voice wobbled when she whispered her thanks. She recognized how she had let fear and secrets poison her mood, but she could not find the words to set it all right. Not yet. Maya retrieved a small tube of cream, gently smoothing it over the reddened skin. The caring gesture was the final straw in destroying Lila's defenses. Her eyes stung fiercely. She forced herself to swallow back the tears, plastering on a stiff smile.

Caleb's presence weighed on her from across the room. She felt his stare even though she refused to meet his eyes again. She wanted to be anywhere else, yet duty and guilt kept her anchored behind the counter. With a last pat on Lila's arm, Maya stepped away, returning to the siphoned tasks of restocking cups and wiping spills.

Time dragged slowly through the rest of the afternoon. Customers trickled in and out, but each new face seemed overshadowed by Lila's swirling dread. She kept repeating the same cycle of polite greeting, forced smile, coffee prep, and anxious glances around the room. Occasionally, she caught a glimpse of Caleb finishing his drink. His expression changed from casual interest to watchful concern as the minutes stretched on. She guessed he debated whether to speak with her in private or give her space.

In the end, he gathered his coat and left without a

word. Lila's heart clenched when he disappeared out the door. A strange emptiness replaced the tension that had crackled between them. She told herself she was relieved. He was making her life complicated, so maybe it was best he went away. But the pang in her chest proved that not even she believed that rationalization.

The clock hit late afternoon, and Maya started the usual cleanup, wiping down stray coffee rings from tables and reassembling the pastry display with fresh items for evening customers. Lila blew out a shaky breath and continued working the register, though she barely made eye contact with anyone. She made it a point to keep busy with a stack of plastic lids, lining them up meticulously. She had scalded her arm more severely than she cared to admit, and the throbbing pain made everything feel more real—like her body was punishing her for this half-life of secrets.

Once the final trickle of customers left, the shop emptied enough that Lila could gaze at the darkening street outside. The late-day light tinted everything in a warmer hue, clashing with her grim mood. A few passing cars cast flashing streaks on the windows. She pressed a cool cloth to her burn and closed her eyes, recalling how the day had unraveled. She had nearly lost her temper with Maya, felt a mix of yearning and resentment toward Caleb, and discovered references to watchers that charged her with the urgent need to call her grandmother.

She found her phone in her apron pocket, turning the screen over in her palm. She would definitely call Evelyn tonight. Her grandmother's voice might offer a calm anchor, or at least a direction. Lila's own pulse thundered with anxiety, but that single decision gave her a sliver of hope: she was not completely at the mercy of the illusions and conspiracies swirling around her. She still had choices, even if they were as small as picking up the phone and whispering, "Help me," into the line.

When she looked back at the empty café, she noticed Maya watching from across the counter, a mop in her hands. The entire day had taken a toll on them both. Maya started to speak, hesitated, then offered a tired half-smile. Lila did the same. She wanted to believe that once she understood the truth, she could fix the distance growing between them.

For now, she had to survive the rest of this shift without another magical mishap or meltdown. The scald on her arm pulsed fiercely as if insisting she misstep again, but she braced herself, determined to keep it together for a couple more hours. Everything about her life felt like a dam about to crack, letting illusions and raw power— forces she barely understood—spill out. Her breath trembled. She could not imagine showing up tomorrow if she did not get answers.

Maya resumed mopping, and Lila set the cool cloth aside. She took another customer's order, trying to steel her mind. This charade could not last forever. The weight of secrecy was too heavy. Sooner or later, she would let it slip. Whether that moment came tonight on the phone with her grandmother or in some future confrontation, she had no idea. She only knew she was tired of being afraid.

She handed off the final latte of the day, her nerves raw from the simple act of smiling. She leaned against the counter and rubbed the ache in her forearm. The day had worn her down until only one certainty remained: everything was off-balance, and she was not sure she could hide it much longer.

NINE

Lila stared at her phone for a good five minutes before she realized she was trembling. The apartment around her felt warped, the air strangely thick after the turbulent week she had survived. A lamp flickered from across the room, casting occasional glints on half-empty coffee cups and rumpled clothes. Though it was well past midnight, she could not fathom sleeping until she made the phone call she had promised herself she would make.

Her thumb hovered over her grandmother's contact. She closed her eyes. Her throat tightened on the first ring, then the second, and by the third, she almost hung up. Evelyn Matthews answered on the fourth with a measured, "Lila?" as though she had been expecting the call all along.

The familiarity in Evelyn's voice made Lila's chest squeeze. Her mouth went dry. "Grandma, hi. I... needed to talk to you." She tried to keep her tone firm, but the words emerged like a shaky exhalation.

For a moment, only a soft static crackled between them. Then Evelyn spoke in a quiet tone that felt like an embrace. "You have questions about it, do you not?"

Lila swallowed hard. Hearing her grandmother's calm acceptance of something that had rattled her for days almost broke the composure she clung to. "I—did something happen before? Something with our family that explains why I'm... making lights flicker or coffee machines short out?"

There was a resigned sigh from Evelyn. Even across the phone line, Lila imagined her grandmother's expression: thoughtful, mildly regretful. "I was waiting for a call like this. Your parents never wanted you to know. They believed you would live better without... the burden of our family gift."

"Gift? Grandma, that gift is threatening to upend my life. I've been trying to handle it for days." Lila realized she was pacing. Her feet kept catching on a stray sneaker beside the sofa, but she could not force herself to sit down.

"You are a Matthews," Evelyn said, voice deepening into something that made goosebumps prickle along Lila's arms. "Our blood has a knack for certain elemental spells. It can skip generations, but it never truly goes away. When you first began having these... surges, I guessed it was only a matter of time before you discovered the Council." She spoke the word so easily that Lila's stomach flipped. "I once worked with them quite closely before I stepped away. It seems times have changed, though, and they would have found you eventually."

Lila's heart hammered. Her entire body tense, she sank onto the edge of her loveseat. A thousand questions roared at once, none of them forming clearly enough to speak. Grandmother Evelyn was rarely so direct, and the casual way she referenced the Council.

"You... you knew about them?" She tried not to raise her voice, but frustration seeped through. "I'm hearing it from you like it's common knowledge. Watching lights spark off my fingertips has definitely not felt normal."

Evelyn's tone softened. "I'm sorry, child. We have always kept those secrets guarded. Your father—my son—wanted no part of it. He rejected the idea that any future child might inherit the Matthews line. He believed burying our lore would protect you. Perhaps he was right for a little while, but magic cannot be suppressed forever."

Lila drew her knees up. Her heart still pounded, but her grandmother's steadiness offered a small comfort, a reminder that she was not imagining all of this. "So, I'm not hallucinating. You're confirming magic is real, and the Council is a bunch of other witches and warlocks who watch new people like me?"

Evelyn exhaled slowly. "They do more than watch, dear. They keep the peace, or so they claim, and ensure illusions or stray spells remain hidden from mortals. Their structure is complicated, and not everyone in the magical community adores them. But if your power has truly awakened, they will seek you out for training. They will demand your cooperation to preserve their secrecy."

A harsh laugh escaped Lila's lips, startling her in the silence of her living room. "That's already happening. One of their people, Caleb Blackwood... He's been... tutoring me, I guess," she muttered, marveling that the word tutor felt so feeble for the warping illusions and surges she had faced.

"Ah, the Blackwoods," Evelyn murmured, recognition laced in her tone. "Their family has served as guardians for centuries. So, you found yourself quite a mentor. Lila, do you trust him?"

She paused, memories of Caleb's intense gaze and quiet concern flickering in her mind. She thought of the night he came to check on her after the Council detected yet another spike in her aura, and the conversations they had shared in her cramped apartment. The memory sent a wave of warmth mingled with apprehension through her core. "I think so," she whispered, letting her honesty slip out. "He saved me from making a scene in the café once or twice. He seems... protective. I've been mad at him, too, because this is all so confusing, but he's never pushed me to do anything except learn control."

Evelyn's tone resonated with unspoken understanding. "Then you should let him help. Running from it will only cause more chaos."

Lila twisted the phone cord between her fingers, finally realizing she was not using a cordless device but her older landline she kept around for emergencies. She swallowed through a knot forming in her throat. "I'm worried my friend Maya will get caught up in this. And I can't just blindfold myself, can I?" She let out a shaky breath. "My entire life is unraveling."

"Little by little," Evelyn said, "you will adjust. It is frightening, but also an inheritance of sorts—one I once thought might never pass down to you. Now, I suspect it manifested stronger than we anticipated."

"Stronger," Lila echoed. The word sent a rush of conflicted pride through her. "Grandma, the Council is arranging some sort of meeting soon. Caleb said they want to see me in a more formal setting. I was resisting it, but I don't think I can anymore." She closed her eyes tight, exhaling again. This conversation felt bigger than anything she had experienced before.

"It is likely a standard summons," Evelyn said. Her voice offered a measured calm. "If you choose to go, do not hide your nerves. Ask pointed questions. Demand to be treated fairly. The Council can be stiff, but they respect conviction. And if you need me, call. I might not live in the city, but I can catch a train if necessary."

"Thanks," Lila whispered, blinking away tears she had not realized were gathering. "I appreciate that. I'm just... reeling. I guess I wanted to hear you say it's not all in my head."

"It is real, dear," Evelyn replied gently. "It has always been real."

They fell silent for a moment, the hush heavy with acceptance. Lila felt a tangle of relief and terror coiling in her stomach. Eventually, she remembered to breathe out. "I miss you," she said softly.

"And I you," answered her grandmother. "We will

speak again soon. For now, rest. Fear will not vanish overnight, but you have help now—even if it comes from a place you never expected."

Lila nodded, forgetting for a beat that Evelyn could not see her. "Thank you, Grandma," she breathed. Then she ended the call, the dial tone droning for a listless moment before she finally set the phone down.

Her mind buzzed, replaying Evelyn's steady assurances, the shock of hearing "gift" spoken aloud, and the sudden knowledge that her father had once refused all of this. The living room lamp flickered again, but no spark leapt from her fingertips this time. She pressed her palms against her cheeks, struggling to quell her racing heart.

When she finally moved, she scooped her other phone from the coffee table and scrolled until Caleb's name appeared. A wave of doubt pricked her. She had given him a piece of her trust. Did she dare contact him so soon? After all, mention of a formal Council meeting had put her on edge for days. But her grandmother's words repeated in her head: Do not hide your nerves. Seek fairness. She inhaled.

She sent him a brief text: "I need to talk. Is it okay if I call?"

His reply arrived minutes later: "Yes, I'm here."

Steeling herself, she dialed. This time, her fingers steadied. Caleb answered on the second ring, his voice low with a gentle edge. "Lila?"

"Yeah," she said, not sure where to begin. "I... I just spoke with my grandmother. She knew about this. She even spoke about you—your family. Apparently, your surname is well known in magical circles."

He released a quiet exhale. "My family has a reputation," he admitted. "They have served with the Council for generations. Some see that as honorable. Others see it as meddling. But I gather you called me for something else?"

"Right," she answered, picking at a stray thread on the couch cushion. "I've decided I can't avoid the Council. I want to meet them. Officially. Even if it terrifies me." Her words emerged in a rush, a confession of acceptance.

Caleb stayed silent for a beat, as if gauging her conviction. "Then I will arrange it. They suggested a neutral spot for novices sometimes: a courtyard in Greenwich Village that is partially warded but not too intimidating. Will that help?"

Her heart thudded at the idea of stepping blindly into a Council domain. "Anything less claustrophobic than some hidden basement is good," she managed, summoning a shaky laugh. "I don't want to be cornered. Not again."

"I understand," he said gently. "We can go in the next couple of days if you like. They will want to see your aura, ensure you can control it in a safe environment. You'll be asked questions, but I will be there."

She let out a breath. "Okay." Another flicker of relief warmed her chest, surprising her. Part of her still fought a frantic urge to flee the city, to erase everything that had happened. Yet another part brimmed with an odd excitement. Even if it meant stepping into the lion's den, this was her best chance to grasp the truth of her power.

"Are you all right?" Caleb asked softly. "You sound—tired."

Exhaustion swamped her senses the moment he named it. "I'm beyond tired. I barely slept last night. But I want to do this. I need to do it."

He murmured a quiet sound of agreement. "Try to rest. Keep your phone by your bed. I will text you the details when the Council confirms the schedule."

"Yeah. Okay." She paused. "Caleb?"

"Yes?"

Her heart skipped a beat at the warmth in his tone. "Thank you. I mean, for giving me space until I was ready to make this call. You could have pushed me. You didn't."

She could hear the faint noise of him shifting, perhaps leaning against a chair or window as he responded. "I never wanted to force you into anything. This is your choice. We can face them together."

His words sent a soft ache through her ribs, an unexpected comfort. "Goodnight," she whispered.

"Goodnight," he replied before the line disconnected.

Lila dropped her phone onto the cushion and rubbed her face with both hands. Somehow, her grandmother's revelations and the knowledge that Caleb stood ready to back her gave her a steadiness she had lacked all week. She rose on shaky legs, moving to her small kitchen table and collecting the scattered papers she had left behind—a few half-hearted notes about magic she had scribbled days ago, a short list of spells gleaned from an online search. They all seemed childish now compared to what she had just learned on the phone.

She walked into the bathroom, flicking on the overhead light that buzzed once, then steadied. Taking in her reflection, she noticed the faint circles under her eyes. A short laugh bubbled up at how firmly the day's events had hammered her: some magical novice she was, stumbling through illusions, scalding her arm on espresso wands, and lying awake at night. She thought of her grandmother's unwavering calm. That presence, and the promise of real guidance, emboldened her. She pictured the coffee machine at The Daily Grind and how easily everything could unravel if she lost control again. Maybe after she met the Council, she would finally learn enough to keep her power in check.

She dragged herself out of the bathroom and back to the living room, scanning the small space. She had never felt so aware of how worn her possessions looked: the faded throw blanket on her futon, the sagging bookshelf loaded with coffee-themed magazines and second-hand novels. This was her life—modest, cluttered, but hers. Now she would invite an entire hidden world in or maybe accept its invitation. Either way, she saw no path backward.

Without turning on the bedroom light, she sank onto her bed and curled up. Her phone screen glowed faintly on the bedside table, the last text from Caleb still visible. Each breath slowed. She clutched the pillow under her head, eyelids feeling like lead. The swirl of tension in her stomach refused to vanish entirely, but beneath it ran a hum of anticipation. She had made her decision—no more half-measures or frantic avoidance.

She closed her eyes. A memory of Caleb's watchful gaze slid into her mind, reminding her of those hushed moments in her apartment, and more recently, the gentle timbre in his voice on the phone. Then she imagined the Council: unfamiliar faces wearing formal expressions, prepared to question her. It should have terrified her outright. Strange that part of her welcomed the confrontation.

A flutter of longing for certainty flickered in her chest. She wondered if her grandmother used to stand at a crossroads like this, adrenaline buzzing because there was no safe path except forward.

Exhaustion finally gripped hold, the last conscious thought etched in bold relief: life would never be the same. She clung to that quiet promise in the last moments before sleep took her, a promise that beneath every fear, something far greater waited to be discovered.

CHAPTER

TEN

Lila woke with her nerves already on edge. She lay in bed, blinking at the early-morning gray filtering through her curtain, every trace of sleep smothered by a knot of dread that twisted in her belly. She had swapped shifts with Maya for this, and she still felt guilty about the flimsy excuse she used: an urgent "appointment" that had forced her out of the café's schedule. Yesterday, Maya's raised eyebrows suggested she wasn't fooled, but a half hearted joke had been enough to earn reluctant acceptance. Guilt throbbed at the idea of deceiving her friend, but Lila reminded herself the secrecy wasn't something she chose casually. The Council needed her to keep magic hidden.

She got ready in record time, leaving her apartment with shoes that squeaked against damp pavement. Her breath formed faint clouds in the chill air. As she walked, her mind churned with fresh worries: would she botch whatever test the Council planned? Would they scold her for not mastering her budding powers quickly enough? She hated how every question burrowed under her skin, building an itch of anxiety she couldn't scratch.

Her phone buzzed while she navigated winding streets in Greenwich Village. The screen glowed with a text from Maya: "Hope your weird appointment goes okay." Lila swallowed hard, guilt surging again. With shaky fingers, she forced a short reply: "Thanks. Will let you know." She refused to add any more details, afraid she might spill the entire truth if she kept typing.

Glancing up from her phone, she scanned the block. Brownstones rose on either side, their brick façades coated in early-morning humidity. A few quiet pedestrians strolled past, none paying her any mind. The address Caleb had given her matched a short archway draped with ivy, flanked by an old wrought-iron fence. The metal gate squealed softly when she pressed it open.

Stepping through, she found a narrow courtyard scattered with potted plants, though most of the leaves looked half-wilted in the weak sunlight. At first glance, it appeared more neglected than hidden. Then she noticed the shimmer—like a faint ripple on the air. She slowed, heart pounding, and spotted Caleb standing near an arched doorway of weathered stone. He wore a tailored coat and carried an air of composure that made her wonder if he ever felt the same jolt of fear that twisted her insides. She still didn't know how he stayed so unruffled.

His eyes flicked up the moment she approached. "You're early," he said softly, barely above a murmur. He scanned the courtyard. "That's good. Fewer distractions."

"I was too nervous to wait around," she admitted. She clutched her messenger bag, counting the seconds until he offered some reassurance. When the silence lingered, she released a breath and tried to keep her tone steady. "What exactly is going to happen in there?"

He seemed to weigh how much to tell her. "Formal introductions," he said at last, his voice calm. "Marcus Steele wants to ensure you fully understand the Council's expectations—and the resources they can offer you." He studied her face, reading the tension in her posture. "Just remember you're not alone, Lila."

She tried to swallow, her throat dry. A faint flutter of warmth filled her chest at his words, though she loathed how off-balance she felt around him. "Right. Not alone."

Caleb lifted a rune-etched token from his coat pocket. It looked small enough to fit on a key ring, carved with a swirling pattern that glowed deep violet in the morning light. He murmured something under his breath—words that felt both melodic and foreign—and the ripple around the doorway shimmered. A gentle breeze brushed Lila's cheeks as if the courtyard exhaled. Then the air parted. Brick turned to shimmering stone, and what appeared to be a solid wall dissolved into a tall entryway. It opened onto an opulent hall with polished floors and high ceilings decorated with etched columns.

Lila couldn't hide the gasp that escaped her. The sudden change tore through her breath. She forced her feet forward. As soon as she stepped across the threshold, an electric tingle danced along her skin, like stepping through a thin veil of static. Her magic flickered in response, making her fingertips warm. She curled them into fists. No showy bursts of power. Not here.

The hallway beyond blurred with motion as robed men and women hurried about. Some carried rolled parchments, others clutched leather-bound books. They all moved with clear purpose, and she noticed how a few paused to glance at her before returning to whatever urgent task awaited them. Anxiety twisted in her gut, the sensation that each pair of eyes measured her as some sort of curiosity.

Caleb guided her deeper inside, one hand lightly resting at her elbow. She tensed at the contact but didn't pull away. His warmth steadied her, though she felt a quiet embarrassment at how much she seemed to lean on his presence. Ahead, a man stood by the marble steps, tall and austere. His hands were folded behind his back, and lines of concentration pinched his forehead. She recognized him from Caleb's description: Marcus Steele. Senior figure in the Council, infamous for his unyielding adherence to rules.

Marcus inclined his head in greeting. "Ms. Matthews," he said by way of welcome. His voice was firm, no nonsense. He gestured for her to ascend the steps. "This way."

Lila inhaled slowly and followed his lead. They passed through a foyer grander than any place she had seen in her normal life: floors of white-and-gray veined marble, chandeliers flickering with an otherworldly glow, tall windows that overlooked an inner courtyard enclosed by illusions.

Marcus paused at the entrance to a secondary hall.

Two Council members in charcoal robes stepped aside, allowing them through. Lila's breath caught when she saw the scale of the new space: the ceiling soared overhead, carved with symbols she couldn't decipher. Arcane energy hummed along the domed walls, making the hair at the back of her neck rise. A cluster of watchers—maybe a dozen individuals, each wearing a different style of robe —milled near the far side, exchanging quiet words.

"This is the preliminary receiving area for novices," Marcus explained briskly. "We evaluate your readiness here before formal initiation. The test ensures you understand the responsibility that comes with your magic." He spoke as though this was a standard procedure, but his gaze flicked across her face, sharp and probing.

She dampened her lips, heart hammering. "And if I'm... not ready?"

He lifted a brow. "Then you'll become a potential danger. Untrained magic has consequences. You must decide if you are prepared to leave behind illusions of life as it was and embrace what you truly are. This path isn't optional for someone with awakened power." He glanced at Caleb, then at Lila. "Your friend here has explained we cannot allow novices to roam unchecked."

A spark of indignation rippled through her. She wasn't a child who needed to be monitored, but she bit her tongue. Fighting the Council right now would only make matters worse. "I understand," she said, voice quiet.

"Good," Marcus replied. "Then, shall we?"

He nodded to a door at the far end, flanked by tall torches flickering with a cold silver flame. Lila felt Caleb step closer, brushing her shoulder as they started forward. Her stomach churned with fresh nerves, but she took the lead anyway, determined not to appear timid.

They walked through an arched doorway into a large foyer that radiated power in every polished surface. The air smelled faintly of incense, a hint of spice that reminded her of the old apothecary shops she had wandered past in Europe but never dared enter. Marcus, still in front, spoke to a robed attendant who jotted notes on a floating parchment. The attendant raised his head, eyes flicking past Lila's face, though he made no comment. He motioned for them to continue onward.

As they crossed the foyer, Lila's gaze roamed the ornate columns adorned with swirling patterns. She thought she saw shapes writhing in the stone—subtle illusions woven into the architecture. It made the walls seem alive, breathing magic from centuries of tradition. More than once, she felt a flicker of fear that something would leap off the stone, but each shape remained part of the carved ornamentation.

Caleb leaned in. "You're doing fine," he murmured, so softly she almost missed it.

She appreciated the reassurance, though her cheeks warmed at the realization that her tension must be obvious. She managed a nod, too rattled to speak.

The corridor bent left, then opened onto another expansive space. This one was quieter, with fewer robed figures. Marcus led them to a dais at the center, where an intricate mosaic underfoot depicted a starburst with swirling runes. Lila hesitated at the edge, noticing how the mosaic glowed faintly around her shoes. Something about it felt alive, as if the emblem recognized her presence.

Marcus turned toward her, setting his shoulders. "You must pass an initiation test," he said, voice echoing. "We call it a proof of control and awareness. Typically, novices demonstrate fundamental spells to show they can avoid harming themselves or others."

Lila's breath caught. Memories of her earliest mishaps raced through her mind: the day she shocked customers at the café, the near-accidents with illusions crackling at her fingertips. Fear curled in her gut. "What if... I haven't practiced anything advanced yet?" she asked.

His expression remained impassive. "We do not expect perfection. We do expect you to demonstrate enough discipline to be safe. The Council invests resources in novices who show promise and caution."

Caleb placed a hand lightly on her arm. "We've covered the core basics," he offered, glancing at Marcus. "She can manage a stable conjuration."

Marcus inclined his head. "Very well." He gestured around. "We have wards here that will contain any mishaps."

The marble under Lila's feet felt suddenly cold. She forced herself to breathe. "All right," she said, voice wavering. Her eyes darted to Caleb. His calm nod gave her the tiniest surge of confidence.

Before she could step forward, Marcus lifted a hand. "A moment. First, you must understand: until you prove you can handle your magic responsibly, your past life stands on precarious ground. We cannot allow novices to cling to illusions of normalcy. This power will reshape you. If you hope to continue your daily existence, you must accept the Council's rules."

His words were clipped, but Lila heard an undercurrent of finality. Her pulse thundered in her ears. Hadn't she already felt that shift? Working at the café had grown fraught with tension. Maya could barely look at her without suspicion. Every day, she juggled fear of exposing magic to unwitting customers. And she had no illusions that life would ever be simple again. But hearing Marcus articulate it so bluntly made her stomach drop.

She nodded. "I understand," she repeated, though a hollow ache spread in her chest.

Marcus studied her a moment longer. Then he placed his hands behind his back and walked further along the dais, beckoning her to follow. Caleb stayed close at her side. Their footsteps echoed in the vast, vaulted silence.

Various robed onlookers had begun to drift closer, curiosity painted across their faces. Lila noticed a few younger faces among them, novices or newer members perhaps. One woman with short, dark hair and a badge pinned near her collar surveyed them calmly, as though evaluating. Several others whispered among themselves, exchanging glances that made Lila's neck prickle with self-consciousness. She gripped the strap of her messenger bag, wishing she had left it behind. She almost felt like an intruder in a sacred hall.

Marcus stopped at a set of tall double doors flanked by two watchers in emerald robes. The watchers bowed their heads in respect to him, then turned those intense stares on Lila. She tried to exhale any lingering panic, feeling it coil in her lungs.

"There is no returning to what you once were, Ms. Matthews," Marcus said, voice echoing off carved stone. "In time, your powers will anchor themselves in every aspect of your life. We must be certain you do not pose a threat—either from negligence or from misguided ambition. You stand on a threshold. Today's test will show whether you can walk forward without harming yourself or others."

Her throat felt tight, but she managed a small nod. "I... I give you my word I don't want to hurt anyone," she said, voice trembling with sincerity.

Marcus raised an eyebrow. "Intent is important, but alone it is not enough. Discipline shapes magic. We will ensure you have the discipline before we permit you to continue unmonitored in this city." He signaled the watchers to open the doors.

Caleb slid closer, lowering his voice so only she could hear. "Keep calm, focus on your breath. You can do this." He gave a tiny smile. "I've got your back."

A wave of warmth rippled through her, though embarrassment crawled under her skin at how quickly she looked to him for support. Despite the swirl of tension, she felt grateful—relieved, even—that he cared enough to stand by her.

The watchers pushed open the doors. A soft glow spilled out, illuminating a corridor with walls inlaid with mosaic tiles that formed shifting patterns when she tried to focus. Green and gold whorls. She sensed a subtle magic thrumming from the corridor itself, a sign that illusions or wards reinforced every inch. Marcus gestured for her to enter.

Her mind spun. She took a shaky step. Her pulse pounded, and every nerve stood on edge. This was the reality of belonging to the Council's world: she was expected to prove her worth so that the city, and humans like Maya, would remain safe from any magical fallout. She hated how final it all sounded, but she also knew there was no alternative. She had felt the raw sparks of her magic threaten to spin out of control before. If some hidden technique could help her rein it in, perhaps it would be worth everything she was giving up.

Marcus cast a final, solemn glance over his shoulder. "Leave behind any illusions you still cling to about a normal life. Magic steps into every corner of your existence. You must be ready for that."

His words settled, heavy as a millstone, on her heart. The watchers stood flanking the passage, their postures rigid. Lila swallowed. She could almost hear her heartbeat echo in her ears. Caleb's presence at her side offered one comforting anchor as she set foot onto the mosaic floor. The patterns beneath her swirled in gentle movement. Had they always swirled, or was that the effect of her own magic stirring?

She realized with stark clarity that nothing would ever be the same. No more illusions of day-to-day normalcy. No more casual coffee shifts without scanning for flickers of power in the corners. She inhaled once, counting to three, and moved forward.

Each reverberating step carried her deeper into the building's magical core, where the test—and her future—waited. She felt her chest tighten at the monumental shift, fear coiling around her spine. Yet she pressed on, acutely aware she could not run from what she had become...and even more aware that part of her didn't want to.

CHAPTER
ELEVEN

Lila felt the severity of the place the moment she stepped inside the circular chamber. Columns of polished stone reached for a lofty ceiling etched with constellations she did not recognize. There were more than a dozen Council members positioned around the circumference in silent expectation. The curl of incense drifted from braziers stationed along the curved walls, and the faint smell of sandalwood made her stomach twist with nerves. She tried to calm her breath, but her pulse thudded in her ears, a pulsing reminder that she was standing at the threshold of something immense.

She sensed Caleb just behind her left shoulder. Even in quiet stillness, his presence felt solid. When she risked a glance back, he dipped his head in a subtle nod. She remembered how, not long ago, he had spoken of this vow ceremony. She had guessed it might entail a formal oath, perhaps an agreement to keep the magical world hidden. She had not realized, until now, that it would involve this measurable aura of judgment pressing in on her from every angle.

At the center of the room stood an ancient table of dark wood, scuffed and scarred with centuries of use. Its edges were carved in flowing lines reminiscent of intricate runes, and a single battered tome rested on its surface. The Book of Oaths, Marcus had called it. In the torchlight, its leather cover gleamed with an otherworldly sheen, the archaic script etched into the surface seeming to glow with diluted silver. Lila swallowed hard.

Marcus Steele, tall and imposing in his formal Council robes, held a quill that glowed with golden ink in one steady hand. His stern features had a certain gravity that shifted the air around him. He fixed Lila with a quiet stare. For one tense heartbeat, it felt as if the entire chamber—columns, braziers, watchers—held its breath.

"Lila Matthews," he said, his voice resonating in the stillness. "This stands as the test of loyalty I mentioned. The Council must ensure each novice who steps into our world does so with both knowledge and humility. You have received instruction, you have glimpsed the scope of your powers, and you have chosen to remain here. Now, you will solidify that choice."

Her throat went dry. She dug her fingernails into her palms for composure and took a step closer to the table. Her pulse thrummed. Caleb's warmth steadied her from behind, as though urging her forward. She told herself she could handle whatever vow they asked of her, although a prickly fear still reminded her she was stepping even further from the normal life she used to know.

Marcus set the tip of the quill against the old book's open page. "The vow you take today demands secrecy, discipline, and your unwavering loyalty to the Council and its purpose: to guard the boundary between magic and mortal life. Do you understand?"

Her heart hammered so loudly she was sure the watchers heard. "Yes," she managed, her voice emerging in a low rasp. She felt too many eyes on her, each pair weighed and measured her worth. Caleb had warned her that novices sometimes balk when they taste the magnitude of this oath. She refused to flinch.

Marcus gestured to the luminous quill. The faint light illuminated curves of golden ink swirling in the air. "Take it," he instructed. "The vow is not lengthy, but it is binding. Speak the words in full, then sign your name. This is how you join us as a pledged Guardian."

She reached out, careful not to let her hand tremble. The quill pulsed with a strangely warm current that crawled through her fingertips, a reminder of magic's undeniable reality. For a moment, she feared she would drop it. A sharp tingle spiked along her palm, and she sucked in a breath. Marcus did not comment, only waited, expression unchanging.

Lila glanced at Caleb's reflection in the polished surface of the table. He gave the smallest nod of reassurance. She exhaled, swallowed again, and focused on the Book of Oaths. The pages had a worn texture, as if scribed over and over by countless novices before her. Faint runes glowed at the corners of each parchment sheet, while the center remained blank except for the golden swirl indicating where she should sign. She tried to keep her breathing steady as her gaze flicked to the vow, which was penned in graceful script.

Her eyes skimmed the text. The vow demanded secrecy, discipline, respect for mortal lives, and a pledge to uphold the magical realm's stability. She recognized certain lines Caleb had paraphrased for her, but seeing them here felt heavier. There was no turning back from this. Closing her eyes briefly, she raised the quill, the golden glow brightening at her touch, and began to speak the words aloud:

"I, Lila Matthews, do solemnly vow to serve and protect the balance between mortal and magical realms. I pledge to guard the secrets of our community and uphold the tenets of discipline in every spell I cast. I bind myself to act with integrity, neither through personal ambition nor malice, but guided by the principles of harmony and respect. I swear to strengthen, not to break, the fragile veil that shields magic from those unaware. In the presence of these witnesses, I offer my loyalty to the Council of Magical Guardians, embracing the path of study, restraint, and unity. May this oath guide my hand and heart, from this day until release is granted or my life's breath ends."

Her words echoed in the chamber. Heat flared along her cheeks, and for a moment, an undercurrent of magical energy pulsed in the floors beneath her feet. She could not tell if that wave of power came from the watchers, the Book of Oaths, or her own heightened aura.

She felt each moment stretch like a plucked string, tension reverberating in the stillness. Marcus's face remained impassive, yet a certain satisfaction flickered in his eyes. He inclined his head. "Now, sign."

Lila dipped the glowing quill's tip against the page, her name forming in luminous script. The letters shimmered white-hot, trailing a golden flare behind each stroke. As she finished the last letter, a surge of energy rushed through her chest, causing her to gasp. She almost yanked her hand away, overwhelmed by the sudden jolt.

Caleb moved closer, his presence a steady pressure at her back. She felt him lift a hand, as though ready to catch her if she wavered. She gritted her teeth and forced herself to remain still. This vow was not a gentle handshake. It was a binding tether that sank into her magic. She felt it coil around her ribcage, warm as a living thing.

Marcus's voice lowered. "These terms ensure confidentiality and ethical use of your gifts, Ms. Matthews. This vow is not meant to subjugate you, but to safeguard the mortal world and our own. If you keep true to this oath, you may preserve the life you value. The Council never intended to strip novices of their daily lives, only to protect them from the dangers of unrestrained magic."

She heard him, but it was difficult to focus on anything beyond the heavy tension winding itself around her heart. The golden ink on the page pulsed once, then sank inside the parchment as though consumed. The page faded to a more ordinary shade, leaving her signature glinting faintly at the center. Courage hammered inside her as she watched magic swirl like fine dust. She shivered.

Marcus reached out to rest his fingertips on the edge of

the open tome. "Your vow is recorded." He turned his head toward the semicircle of watchers. Robed men and women inclined their heads in solemn acknowledgment. Some of them wore unreadable expressions; others had a ghost of a smile on their lips. Faint sparks flickered in the air, reminiscent of a subdued applause. Lila wondered if her own wrists were shaking too much to notice anything else.

She glanced over her shoulder at Caleb, uncertain if she should step back or remain at the table. He gave a small, encouraging nod. There was pride in his eyes, that calm confidence that rarely wavered. The steady hum in her veins calmed, just a fraction. Having him at her side reminded her she was not alone in this strange new world.

Marcus lifted his hands to command the watchers' full attention. His cloak swept behind him in an authoritative arc. "Lila Matthews has committed to uphold and respect the magical limits set forth by the Guardians. From this moment, she stands as a novice under our guidance, bound by the discipline of spell craft and the charge to keep illusions away from mortal eyes. We honor her willingness to protect what must remain hidden."

A faint surge of approval rippled through the circle. It was not a thunderous cheer but rather a collective acknowledgment, as if each Council member contributed a share of magic or silent respect to show acceptance. Lila felt the hush wash over her, the weight of an organization hundreds of years old leaning forward, seeing her as part of it now.

As Marcus's gaze returned to her, his voice softened. "Congratulations, Ms. Matthews. Your journey has only begun." Yet his tone carried a hint of warmth, like a teacher who was pleased with a student's promise. He stepped closer and set the quill aside. "Are you all right?"

She inclined her head in a quick nod, clearing her throat. "I'm... still wrapping my head around the sensation, but yes. I'm all right." She could not describe the invisible coil around her chest, but it was there, a reminder that she had promised something massive and binding. Despite the tingle of lingering magic, she managed to hold herself upright.

Marcus's stern lips twitched as though he nearly smiled. "Good."

Caleb slipped nearer. His arm brushed hers. She felt his quiet concern. "You did well."

She exhaled a shaky breath, tension rattling in her ribcage. "Thanks. I definitely... felt something. Or everything, really." Her attempt at humor came out faint, but a few watchers in the circle allowed themselves a small chuckle. The tension softened, if only slightly.

Marcus returned to the center. With a measured air, he placed one palm flat on the open page of the Book of Oaths. Lila watched the subtle swirl of runes bloom around his hand, verifying that her signature had been accepted. Then he cleared his throat and addressed the room. "We stand witness to this new pledge. May the Guardians keep us united in purpose and guide our novices to wield power with discipline and wisdom."

She suddenly noticed the dryness in her mouth. A wave of relief tinged with apprehension coursed through her limbs. She felt more eyes upon her, some curious, others guarded. They must be sizing her up, wondering if her power, rumored to be unusual, would truly serve the Council now. She forced herself not to look away.

Caleb bent in slightly, murmuring for her ears only. "Breathe, Lila. You have passed the hardest part."

She nodded. It did not feel as though the hardest part was over, yet the immediate formality had concluded, so she took his advice and inhaled. "Could have fooled me," she whispered, voice trembling with exhausted adrenaline.

Behind them, Marcus raised a hand, drawing attention once more. "Everyone, you may offer your greetings. However, keep in mind that Ms. Matthews is still adapting. We expect full decorum." His words carried a hint of protective sternness.

In response, a few watchers stepped forward to speak quietly with her, each in turn offering measured welcomes. Their greetings blurred together: solemn praise, whispered remarks about remembering how disorienting this day could be. Some asked if she needed anything, but most kept a polite distance. Their curiosity lingered beneath their official courtesy.

After an older woman in a charcoal robe murmured her support and retreated, the circle eased back to give Lila space. She turned and found Caleb's gaze steady on her. Her lips parted, searching for what to say. She was grateful for his calm presence, and a part of her wanted to fling her arms around him just to anchor herself. But the watchers were all around, and she doubted that public displays of relief would go over well.

Instead, he offered her a slight smile, one that crinkled the corners of his eyes. "I admire your composure," he said softly. "Many novices stumble right afterward."

She let out a quiet laugh. "I feel like I could still stumble, any second." The coil around her chest had lessened but remained a heavy, pulsing warmth, like a chain linking her to the Council's magic. She was part of them now, which brought a sense of relief and dread in equal measure.

"That's expected," he admitted. "Come. Let's move aside. It can be overwhelming."

She started to follow him toward the arc of watchers who stood near the far columns. Before she could take a second step, Marcus's voice rang out with firm clarity: "Now hear me, members of the Council. Lila Matthews is officially pledged to uphold and respect the magical limits set forth by the Guardians."

His words resonated throughout the chamber, echoing against the high ceiling. A light shimmer of magical energy flitted above the watchers' heads like static sparks. The burnished brazier flames flickered in silent acknowledgment. Then, at last, applause sounded. It was not the rowdy excitement of mundane celebrations. It was subdued, reverent, laced with the shimmering hush that magic could command. Lila pressed her lips together, heart fluttering in her chest. This applause felt like the final chord of a symphony she had never known she was part of.

She could sense eyes searching her face, wondering about her reaction. Her stomach knotted. The vow had anchored her to responsibilities she could not escape. She recalled how just weeks ago, she had tried to cling to her mundane existence behind the café counter. Now she stood at the epicenter of a secret world, bound by a vow that might as well have been braided into her soul.

The impact of that final chord lingered. Caleb touched her elbow gently, guiding her a step away from the center. Her name hung in the air, repeated in soft conversations among watchers. There was no going back.

In that moment, she realized that while the Council considered this a triumphant moment, it also marked the end of everything she thought she knew. A thick tension welled in her throat, because she still felt like the same barista who spilled coffee and worried over rent. But the coil of magical responsibility said otherwise. It was as though a door had closed between her old life and whatever came next.

She stood quietly by Caleb's side, absorbing the applause that drifted through the chamber. The Book of Oaths lay open on the table under the glow of magical torches, her name shining on the page. A warm weight settled on her shoulders, half pride, half reluctance. Under the swirl of voices and flickering torchlight, she wondered if she could ever lift that weight again.

Marcus inclined his head to them, concluding his announcement. The final word left Lila teetering between relief and trepidation. She closed her eyes, letting her breath catch. This was not just a pledge to keep secrets. This was a division in her life's timeline. Her role as a simple coffee-slinger had ended the instant her pen left that page. She sensed Caleb's gaze, and she turned to meet it, finding both understanding and a quiet flicker of admiration.

A chorus of murmured acceptance filled the chamber. The energy of the watchers pressed in for an instant and then began to disperse. Lila reached behind her to press a palm over her chest, where the new magic bond still buzzed. She felt calmer knowing Caleb stood so close.

Marcus's voice carried one last solemn note. "Lila Matthews is now officially pledged to uphold and respect the magical limits set forth by the Guardians."

At that pronouncement, the chamber seemed to brighten, as if the wards themselves gathered in celebration. A soft wave of applause followed, that signaled the ceremony's end. Lila drew a deep breath, heart pounding.

She realized, with bone-deep certainty, that a new door had slammed shut on her old life.

CHAPTER

TWELVE

Lila stood near the end of a marble-floored corridor, still trying to process the whirlwind orientation she had just survived. The Council had wasted no time. Mere hours after formally welcoming her as a novice, they had swept her through a swift overview of safety protocols, conjuration guidelines, and, most unsettling of all, the catalogue of past disasters wrought by untrained witches. Her head throbbed with new terms and the chastising gazes of several stern-faced elders. She understood the undertone of their warnings: magic could be glorious, but it could also destroy cities if wielded carelessly.

Now she waited for Caleb, her mentor, in front of an ornate door. The door opened, and he emerged, wearing a calm, composed expression. Although he was taller than most in the corridor, he had a way of moving that carried no wasted air, no obvious arrogance. His dark coat shifted around him with the subtle grace of a man perfectly used to illusions—even if the corridors themselves were not illusions. A faint swirl of energy lingered in his wake, reminding her that everything about him was steeped in magic.

"You ready?" he asked in a steady voice.

She tried to keep her chin up. "I think so. Could use a coffee, though."

He met her eyes with a flicker of amusement. "We can get you coffee later. For now, we'll focus on your training, starting with basic control."

Lila's stomach did a nervous flip. She wasn't sure what basic control entailed, especially after the orientation's talk of novices accidentally summoning illusions or toppling entire structures with a stray burst of power. Still, she nodded and followed him.

They walked together down a narrower passage lined with glowing sconces. The lights cast amber halos across the stone walls, making the place feel more like an underground crypt than a modern training facility. Lila tried not to stare at the swirling runes carved in the floor. They moved under the sconces' illumination, twisting into patterns she couldn't decipher. She swallowed hard, deciding not to ask too many questions about them right now.

Caleb spoke softly as they approached a sealed iron door. "These runes help contain stray magic. The Council learned that novices who experiment without fail-safes can cause chain reactions. We'd rather keep you—and the rest of the city—safe."

She raised a skeptical brow. "This is all for me? Seems... a little overkill."

"Given what you can do, it's the opposite of overkill," he answered.

She bristled, but there was no accusation in his tone. Instead, it held a mix of caution and respect. She tried to brush aside the anxious flutter in her stomach. She had told herself she wanted to learn. Now that she was actually here, in a corridor that led to a practice chamber full of wards, she felt strangely exposed.

Caleb placed a hand on the iron door, murmuring a phrase that Lila couldn't quite catch. She recognized the gentle, lilting quality of his voice as a magical incantation. At once, a faint ripple spread across the metal surface, then the door clicked open. Warm air rushed out, carrying a subtle, unfamiliar spice that prickled the back of her throat. He held the door for her. She squared her shoulders and stepped inside.

Rows of elaborate sigils ran across the smooth floor, shimmering in and out of view like lazy fireflies. They ringed a wide oval area at the room's center, where lines converged in an intricate pattern. Several glowing crystals perched at the edges, flickering in time with the swirling runes. The ceiling was a polished dome that reflected everything in a softly distorted way, and overhead she could see faint reflections of both her and Caleb, side by side, dwarfed by the chamber's space.

She let out a low whistle. "This feels like stepping into a giant spell circle. Is it always this... fancy?"

Caleb's mouth curved into a small smile. "Utility can be elegant, too. Try not to worry about how it looks. We'll focus on function."

"Sure. Function," she muttered. She folded her arms across her chest, attempting a sardonic stance, though her heart thumped at double speed. "What first? You test me to see if I can blow up a wall?"

"I'd rather we steer you clear of blowing up anything," he said, leading her to the center. "Start by grounding yourself. You can replicate the surge you felt at the café, but in a controlled manner this time."

"That surge nearly short-circuited my entire coffee machine," she murmured, remembering the jolt of green sparks flaring over the metal. She summoned a flicker of courage. "Alright. Just show me where to stand."

Caleb pointed to the center of the pattern. Lila stepped into it, noticing how the runes brightened under her feet. "Focus on your breathing," he said, positioning himself a few paces away. "Magic tends to respond to intention. In the beginning, novices let emotion rule their spells. We want to shift that balance."

She inhaled slowly, exhaled even more slowly. His voice was somehow soothing, though she refused to admit that openly. Her gaze skimmed the lines etched around her shoes. "Okay. Breathe. Then... what?"

"Visualize the energy in your body, the same warmth you felt when it first surged. Let it gather in your finger-tips. Start small, as if you only want to produce a spark. When you feel the pressure build, guide it outward along a single path."

He demonstrated, holding his hand inches above the runes. A tiny pulse of blue light flickered around his fingers before vanishing like a gentle sigh. Lila studied the motion. It hadn't seemed forced—just a tranquil wave of power.

"I can try," she said quietly.

She shut her eyes and inhaled. She sensed the hum in her chest, fluttering with each heartbeat. This time, she coaxed it instead of clamping down. Her arms felt both heavy and electrified. She pictured her close call with the café's milk frother. The memory of neon sparks danced in her mind.

A crackle buzzed around her palms. She opened her eyes in time to see faint greenish light flicker over her skin. The air tingled with raw potential, and a grin tugged at her lips. She felt a rush of excitement.

But the energy flared faster than she expected, responding to the sudden spike in her adrenaline. Without warning, a burst of emerald sparks snapped out from her hands, warping into a wave that rattled the chamber's protective walls. A high-pitched ring shot through the air, and she gasped in alarm as the nearest crystal flickered wildly.

"Watch out," Caleb called. He moved in closer, steps surefooted against the trembling floor. "Don't panic. Breathe."

"Trying," she hissed, voice cracking. She felt an icy jolt of fear at how easily the power had leapt out. Her arms vibrated as though something wanted to surge forth again.

He came up behind her, not quite touching but standing close enough that she felt the calm aura of his presence. "Slow exhales," he instructed. His voice was firm but gentle. "Let your magic settle, or it will flare again. Acknowledge it, but don't let it drive you."

Lila clenched her fists, doing her best to press the roiling energy back under a layer of steady breathing. "I can't believe how strong it got so quickly," she muttered.

"That's exactly why we have this chamber...and these wards," he said. A faint sheen of magic radiated from him, cool and steady, as if he was channeling a signal to her. "Try again but be prepared for the surge."

She steadied her stance, letting the tension slip from her shoulders. Beneath the adrenaline, she recalled the small thrill she'd felt a moment ago, right before the magic roared out of control. She wanted that again, minus the near-disaster. Closing her eyes, she took three long, slow breaths. On the third exhale, she extended her right hand. Hot tingles traveled through her wrist. This time, she guided them, focusing on letting a gentle stream flow rather than a sudden blast.

A thin arc of green light danced from her palm, forming a sparkling ribbon in midair. It glimmered above the runes, fluttering like a tiny banner, then fizzled away in a soft pop. The room fell silent, the crystals around them flickering more sedately. She opened her eyes, not entirely sure she had succeeded until she heard Caleb's soft intake of breath.

"That was good," he said, stepping around to face her with an approving nod. "Not too strong, not too weak."

She allowed herself a small smile. Her pulse thumped wildly, but the sense of control was exhilarating. "I...I did it," she murmured.

"You did. And you can do more," he said, "but let's keep a careful pace."

Her cheeks felt warm, from both effort and the sudden realization that Caleb was far closer than before. She noticed the subtle lines at the corners of his bright eyes, the slight tilt of his mouth that suggested relief. She wondered if he worried she might send another shockwave hurling across the chamber and accidentally flatten him. Or if he was simply proud.

"Give it one more try," he instructed. "Focus on the same feeling. Steady. You're aiming for a spark, not a fire."

She let herself breathe in a measured way again, coaxing the magic up from her core. Each inhalation fueled that green glow, which crawled along her arms in small pulses. She extended her left hand this time, carefully mindful of the shimmering patterns under her feet. A second swirl of green light flickered into being, swirling elegantly before fading. This attempt felt steadier, less frantic.

A pinprick of giddy excitement stabbed at her chest. She wanted to cheer. She settled for a nod, turning to see if Caleb was equally impressed.

He wore the faintest smile. "Good. That's enough conjuration for the moment. Before we try something more advanced, let's make sure you truly understand how to rein it in."

She arched an eyebrow. "I'd hate to see my next meltdown if I don't." Her attempt at sarcasm sounded a bit shaky, but the confidence blooming inside her was real. That second conjuration had felt... right.

"We learn by doing, but we survive by controlling," Caleb said quietly. "You'll find a rhythm. I'll help you."

The sincerity in his expression made her heart pound. Before she could overthink the sudden tension, he reached out, resting a light hand on her shoulder. His warmth was immediate, radiating through the thin layers of her shirt. It was not just physical heat. She sensed the hum of his magic guiding hers, as if he extended a calm thread into the swirling chaos inside her. A strand of embarrassment flared in her mind—this was her teacher, not a potential lover—but she couldn't ignore the shiver of awareness that traveled her spine.

"Relax," Caleb said. "Steady your breath."

She closed her eyes again, letting his presence steady her. With each inhale, she felt the sparks receding, like waves that finally decided not to crash so loudly. His hand lingered a moment at her shoulder, then drifted away. She almost regretted the loss of contact.

The next hour passed in a blur as they tested smaller spells, practicing mindful control. The few times she slipped, conjuring an erratic spark or letting her power spike, he was there to remind her gently that her breathing was the key. They circled the chamber's perimeter, checking each ward line. Caleb pointed out how the swirling runes absorbed excess magic, glowing brighter whenever Lila's energy wobbled. She apologized every time she let something crash against the wards, but he never scolded—only guided.

By the time they finished, she was drenched in sweat, her hair stuck to the back of her neck, and her arms felt like she'd run a marathon with them. Her nerves tingled from the repeated effort. Standing at the center of the runic design once more, she placed her hands on her thighs, leaning forward to catch her breath.

"That's enough for today," Caleb said, voice carrying that calm authority. "You did well. There's a lot of raw power, but you're already learning to center it."

She let out a breathless laugh. "I'm wiped out. But I... I didn't realize how exhilarating it would feel to actually control magic."

He watched her with a careful, almost protective look. "The thrill can be addicting. That's one reason the Council believes in firm training. Raw magic can twist a person's judgment if they treat it like a new rush of adrenaline."

She nodding, feeling oddly proud that she understood. Her entire body buzzed with a mixture of exhaustion and excitement. The swirling runes along the floor dimmed, as if sensing that she had finally quieted down. She could hardly believe this was only the beginning of her magical education. That spark—both inside her and in the air around them—seemed eager for more.

She unzipped the light jacket she wore, wiping sweat from her forehead with a shaky hand. "I guess I'm done punching invisible walls for the day."

He gave a soft laugh, then moved a step closer, his gaze kind. "We'll handle the rest tomorrow. Right now, you need a warm shower and something to eat."

Her cheeks heated again. Standing so near to him reminded her of the moment he had gently guided her shoulder, matching the rhythm of her breathing. She felt compelled to say something witty, or maybe something honest about how grateful she was for his patience. Instead, she only managed a small, awkward smile. The thick silence that followed thrummed with a tension she wasn't entirely ready to name, but she sensed it curling in her belly like a secret.

She cleared her throat, but before she could form words, he took a small step backward, restoring a more formal distance between them. "Do you need help finding your way out of the corridors?"

"I'll manage," she said, trying to sound casual.

He nodded. "I'll lock down the wards. You can head back to the main hall."

"All right. Thank you, Caleb," she added quietly. "You've been... patient with me. That means a lot."

He gave her one last smile that stirred something in her chest. "It's part of my responsibilities as a mentor. And," he paused, "you're worth the patience."

Her stomach flipped again. She couldn't hold his gaze or she might burst into flames right there. Mustering a final nod, she stepped away from him and angled toward the door. The runes underfoot glimmered as if bidding her farewell. Outside the door, the cooler air of the corridor brushed across her flushed cheeks, and she exhaled a breath she hadn't realized she was holding.

She wiped the back of her hand across her forehead, half-lost in a swirl of churning thoughts. She was one session in and already felt the tug of fascination—both for the magic and, embarrassingly, for the man teaching her. The combination made her head spin. She wasn't sure what to do with all that energy, except notice how her pulse pounded whenever she remembered the feather-light press of his hand on her shoulder.

By the time she reached the end of the corridor, her legs ached, and her shirt clung to her skin. She realized she was grinning, though her nerves hadn't fully subsided. The Council's safety protocols had proven their worth, but the real shock was how quickly she had found a spark of satisfaction in channeling her magic. Maybe she really could learn to harness it.

As she lingered in the passage for a moment, pressing a palm against her still-thudding heart, she tasted that familiar electric thrill once more. Magic was potent, heady, and likely more dangerous than she imagined. But the exhilaration reminded her of stepping onto a stage— she felt seen and alive in a way she never had before.

Her gaze drifted back to the practice chamber door, where she could picture Caleb quietly resetting wards, planning next steps, and calmly preparing for the next challenge. Exhaustion jabbed at her, but deeper than that lay a breathless awareness of how her mentor's steady presence made her feel almost brave.

Pressing her lips into a determined line, she turned away, heading for the main hall. She already wanted the next session, even if her muscles groaned in protest. As she walked, she hardly noticed the angular shadows dancing along the corridor walls. Thoughts of conjurations and illusions mixed with the faint memory of Caleb's soft approval. If this was only the first lesson, she wasn't sure how her heart would handle the weight of all the ones to come.

Sweaty, exhausted, and thrilled beyond reason, Lila felt half-terrified by the power she had touched—and by the strange new attachment budding inside her. Yet she couldn't deny the flutter in her chest when she thought about Caleb or the rush of conjuring bright green sparks on command. It was equal parts intimidating and intoxicating. As she placed one foot in front of the other, she realized she was already impatient for more, not just of the magic, but of him. A soft warmth bloomed behind her ribs at the thought, and with that gentle ache of awareness, she knew the boundary between student and teacher was already blurring in ways neither of them had anticipated.

THIRTEEN

Lila arrived at The Daily Grind before sunrise, hoping to smooth the tension coiling inside her with a quiet hour of preparation. Instead, she found herself wrestling with jammed filters and a sour mood that refused to fade. The weight of her new vow felt like a brand searing her chest—she couldn't decide if it actually burned or if the sensation was merely in her head. Either way, her shoulders remained rigid.

Maya, who normally breezed into work with a cheerful hum, scowled at Lila as she collected coffee cups and began setting them in neat rows. "You look like you haven't slept in days," she said, voice low enough that customers couldn't hear. "But it's more than that, isn't it?" Her dark eyes flicked to a faint bruise visible near Lila's elbow. "You better spill soon. I'm worried."

Lila swallowed, hating how quickly her patience frayed. "It's nothing," she mumbled, focusing on rearranging the pastry display. "Just a lot going on."

Maya scoffed, crossing her arms over her aproned chest. "When have you ever kept secrets from me? Don't say it's 'nothing' if you're wincing every time you bump into a counter." Frustration laced her voice, though there was no mistaking the worry beneath.

Their quiet confrontation dissolved the moment a line of bleary-eyed regulars trudged in for lattes. Lila forced a thin-lipped smile, ignoring the unnerving rush in her bloodstream that reminded her of the vow she had taken. Early morning hustle usually comforted her, but she sensed an invisible tether clinging to her soul. The knowledge that she was now bound to a world most people would never comprehend twisted all her usual rhythms into knots.

She cranked the steam wand to prepare a cappuccino, only for the hiss to rattle her nerves. She glanced at her arm and spotted a yellowish bruise peeking out from under her rolled-up sleeve. When had that one happened? She remembered stumbling during a practice session, a wave of raw energy that nearly sent her tumbling over training mats. Now the memory made her chest tighten in embarrassment.

"Watch your back, Lila," Maya urged softly as she stepped around to pass a stack of cups. "If you need help..." She let the words dangle, an offer unspoken but understood.

At the front counter, a disgruntled customer tapped his foot. "Miss? Is my mocha ready yet?"

"Almost," Lila said through clenched teeth. The milk had overshot its froth. She cursed under her breath as she maneuvered the nozzle. Over the noise of steaming milk and half-shouted orders, a headache throbbed behind her eyes.

A sudden surge of frustration made her yank the pitcher too quickly. Hot milk splattered across the counter and dribbled over her wrist. She hissed in pain. Another curse slipped free, earning a startled look from the customer. Maya leapt to help clean up, but Lila refused to let her. Grimly, she dabbed at the spill. Inside, she felt a burning desire to conjure something—anything—to ease the tension. But here, where mundane eyes watched, that was impossible. Walls might have ears, but coffee shops had a full audience.

"Lila, you're jumpy," Maya said in a hushed tone, tossing a wet rag into the sink. "And you're snapping at everyone."

"I'm fine," Lila snapped. When the words left her mouth, she realized how unconvincing she sounded. She didn't mean to sound so harsh, especially with Maya. This job was meant to be her safe place. The normalcy felt more fragile than ever now.

For the next hour, she forced herself to remain calm, though the tension in her neck never subsided. Her small attempts to chat with customers sounded hollow even to her own ears. She apologized automatically whenever she flubbed an order. Through it all, she felt Maya's gaze, equal parts concern and frustration.

By mid-morning, the café had a steady hum of patrons. The sound of the espresso machine and the soft murmur of conversation merged into a frantic blur that normally wouldn't faze her. She lined up fresh pastries, hoping the heat radiating from the display case might soothe her. It didn't.

Then she heard a quiet, familiar voice:

"A black coffee, please."

Her heart gave a traitorous jolt. She didn't need to look to know who had arrived. Still, she glanced up, and there he was. Caleb stood at the far end of the counter in a dark coat, his posture composed and his expression calm. Only his eyes betrayed the same weary tension she felt. He offered her the smallest smile, as if sharing a secret.

She swallowed. "Truly black again today?" she asked in a low voice, trying and failing to keep the edge out of her tone.

He nodded. Under the café lights, his dark hair looked tousled, and the faint line between his brows betrayed concern. She wanted to ask if he was here because he sensed her unraveling or simply because he was fulfilling his usual routine. But she couldn't do that in front of everyone.

"Got it." She turned, shaking off the flutter in her stomach as she filled a paper cup with fresh coffee. Her hand trembled. She pressed the lid down carefully, reminding herself not to burn him. Or me, she thought bitterly. When she handed it over, their fingers grazed. A tremor passed through her that had nothing to do with the scalding liquid.

"Thanks," he murmured. Beneath the polite acknowledgment, she caught a subtle question in his tone: Are you okay?

She gave a curt nod, then muttered something about finishing an order. He headed to a corner table near the front window, settling into a seat with a vantage point that offered a discreet view of the entire space. She noticed how he tilted his phone, passing his hand over it in a gesture she recognized. It was the same warding trick he had demonstrated once before. The air around him seemed to ripple for half an instant, ensuring no one else would overhear if he spoke quietly.

Moments later, Maya elbowed Lila in the side. "Isn't he that weird friend of yours? The one who shows up at odd times?" Her tone carried a suspicion that made Lila's guilt spike.

"He's...helping me with something," Lila said, fumbling for words. She grabbed the wet rag again and wiped an imaginary spill off the counter. "It's complicated."

Maya snorted. "Anything that might explain why you keep running off at weird hours?"

Lila's chest tightened. She forced a stiff smile. "Don't worry about it." When she finally risked meeting Maya's gaze, she saw hurt flicker there before the other woman turned away to hand a latte to a customer.

By the time the rush died down, Lila sneaked out from behind the counter and made her way to Caleb's table as unobtrusively as she could. She kept her distance until she reached the edge of his invisible ward—a slight tingle along her skin. Carefully, she sank into the chair across from him, exhaling shakily.

He regarded her, voice barely above a whisper. "You look tired."

She raked a hand through her hair. "No kidding," she said bitterly. "I need to pretend I'm normal, but I feel like I'm one slip away from the entire café noticing I've... changed."

Caleb's eyes flicked toward Maya, who was wiping tables near the opposite side of the shop. "You've done nothing wrong by wanting to keep your life intact," he said. "But you can't let the tension eat you alive. If you need space—"

"I don't know what I need," she cut in, then immediately winced. She lowered her voice. "I'm sorry. I just...I hate keeping secrets from everyone. Especially her."

"I understand." He reached out as if to place his hand over hers, then paused. Instead, he set his fingertips lightly on the table. The undercurrent of warmth between them pulsed nonetheless. "It's part of the arrangement," he reminded her gently. "For now, at least."

She nodded. The vow, the secrecy, the new training— every piece weighed on her. A reluctant laugh escaped her. "I guess you saw me burn my hand again. Not exactly my best day."

Caleb's mouth curved in a tiny smile. "The wards at your place. They're holding?"

She bobbed her head. "Yeah. I still feel...tethered, though. Like I can't breathe."

His eyes softened. "You'll adapt as you practice. It gets easier."

She opened her mouth to ask something else, but the phone in his coat pocket lit up with a soft glow. He glanced at it, grimacing. A spike of alarm went through Lila. He usually set his phone wards to block everything except Council-level emergencies. If that was buzzing, it couldn't be good.

Caleb pressed his finger to the screen and frowned. "We have to go. Now." He took one last sip, then stood. "They need us for a briefing...urgent."

Lila's pulse kicked up. She had hoped for a quieter morning—time to talk or even breathe before the next wave of demands. But it seemed the Council had other plans. Of course they do, she thought with a jolt of frustration. She rose, wiping uselessly at a stray drip of coffee on her apron.

From behind the counter, Maya caught the movement and shot Lila a sharp look. "Where are you going?" she called out, ignoring the few customers still lingering. The tension between them thickened.

"I need a break," Lila lied, hating herself for it. "I'll be back as soon as I can."

Maya's eyes narrowed. She glanced from Lila to Caleb, now standing near the door. "Is this going to be like last time? You vanish for hours and come back with bruises no one can explain?"

"Maya," Lila whispered, stepping closer. She wanted to hug her friend and apologize for all the secrecy, but a tightness in her throat prevented it. "I promise I'll explain when I can."

Maya didn't look reassured. "Fine," she said, crossing her arms. "Go handle...whatever it is you do. But you owe me a real conversation."

Lila swallowed hard. "I know." Trying to quell the guilt roiling in her stomach, she joined Caleb at the door. Part of her wanted to turn back, but the silent urgency in his expression propelled her forward. The Council's summons. Her vow. The secret brand of belonging to a magical world that the rest of the city knew nothing about. All of it demanded her presence.

They hurried outside, stepping past customers who barely looked up from their phones. The autumn air felt crisp against Lila's flushed cheeks. She hugged herself, glancing sideways at Caleb as they navigated the sidewalk. He typed a quick message on his phone, presumably updating the sender that they were en route.

"Any idea what's going on?" she asked, voice tight.

He shook his head. "Emergency briefing is all I know. The phone alert indicated something bigger than routine updates." The corners of his mouth drew taut. "We should find a private spot to open a gate or get a quick ride. Time matters."

She nodded, though apprehension fluttered madly in her chest. "I'll text Maya in a bit," she said, mostly to herself. "Try to calm her down. I hate leaving her like that."

"What you're doing is for everyone's benefit, including

hers," Caleb said firmly. "She won't understand now, but hopefully someday."

They walked briskly, weaving around pedestrians. Lila caught her reflection in a window: a pale-faced woman in a rumpled café uniform, eyes shadowed with fatigue she couldn't fully hide. Selecting this path hadn't been simple. Each day, she felt the friction of juggling two lives. And now, with the Council beckoning, she couldn't even finish her shift without more crises landing on her doorstep.

At the corner, they paused for traffic. Caleb looked at her with a piercing concern that made her stomach flip. She noticed the fine line on his brow, deeper than usual. Something in that gesture told her this wasn't just a routine briefing. A tension clung to him, too, like a storm cloud waiting to break. Whatever had triggered the Council's call, it wasn't minor. Her chest tightened at the thought of stepping blindly into another layer of secrets and threats.

"How bad do you think it is?" she dared to ask.

"Worse than we'd like," he murmured, gaze scanning the busy street. "I can't say more until we're there, but...be prepared."

Wordlessly, she nodded, her pulse drumming in her ears. A sense of foreboding coiled in her belly. Maya's guarded expression still haunted her, but there was no turning back now.

They crossed the street. As they rounded a corner, Lila noticed Caleb's posture tense, as if he expected illusions or watchers to appear at any second. The smaller details of normal city life—taxi horns, distant chatter, birds fluttering above a street vendor's cart—felt surreal. She was no longer part of simple Manhattan routines, not entirely. Even though she still held a barista's paycheck, her real obligations lay elsewhere.

She thought of Maya's anxious stare one more time, a pang of shame gripping her. Keeping secrets frayed every friendship, but how could she explain that her new pledge meant involvement in a realm so hidden and dangerous? The vow forbade straightforward answers. The best she could do was survive the next crisis and pray she didn't alienate her friend completely.

When they reached a quiet alley between two towering buildings, Caleb tapered his pace, phone still in hand. "We'll vanish from here. You won't be late if you can manage to come back later, but that depends on the Council's timeline."

Lila offered a resigned shrug. "I'll deal with the fallout."

He focused on a subtle swirl of magic in the air, presumably a small ward to cloak whatever he planned next. As he lifted a hand, she stepped closer, noticing the tightness in his jaw and the faint lines of worry etched across his features. That deeper concern sat lodged in his eyes, fueling a fresh wave of unease.

He reached out, faint energy humming between his fingers, and she placed her palm gently over his. Even in the chill of the alley, his warmth comforted her. She managed a flicker of a smile, although anxiety churned in her gut.

"I guess we've got no time to waste," she murmured.

He nodded, voice subdued. "No time at all."

She clung to that brief flicker of closeness, then released a breath she hadn't realized she was holding. Storm clouds drifted overhead, turning the sky as gray as the swirling thoughts in her mind. She noticed how his brow furrowed deeper now, like an open warning that things were about to escalate yet again.

FOURTEEN

Lila stood in front of a tall, carved door that led into a cramped Council briefing room. Heat radiated from her cheeks despite the faint chill drifting through the stone corridors. She had passed these Council halls only a few times since her induction, but tonight, tension permeated the very air. The flickering orbs suspended from the vaulted ceiling made the space feel even smaller. The orbs glowed a soft silver, pulsing in and out as if reacting to the unease rippling across every person gathered.

She swallowed hard and adjusted the collar of her jacket. She could still catch faint traces of coffee clinging to the fabric from her deflated morning at The Daily Grind. Her throat felt dry, and her pulse throbbed with anxious energy she could not quite contain. Stepping carefully over the threshold, she followed Caleb Blackwood into the room.

Caleb paused to usher her in, his coat shifting against his lean frame. He gave her a short, reassuring nod before guiding her toward an open spot along the curved wall. She sensed the concern vibrating off him, though he tried to appear calm. The others in the room included mentors and novices—exactly five novices stood huddled in small clusters, exchanging uneasy looks. She did not know them well. A woman in a sleek black coat fiddled with the tassels on her sleeve, while a narrow-faced man clutched a small warding stone. They, like Lila, wore expressions caught between curiosity and fear.

Marcus Steele presided at the front of the space. His posture was as rigid as the tall staff at his side, his gray hair trimmed close to the scalp. Though Lila barely knew him, she recognized the weight of authority whenever he spoke. Several other guardians stood at his flank, arms folded or pressed behind their backs. A hush seeped over the gathering as Marcus's gaze roamed across them.

"We have called you all here for one reason," Marcus announced. His voice carried along the walls with a deliberate ring. "The Council faces a dire threat that cannot be understated. There has been a theft."

The orbs overhead flickered, and Lila's stomach twisted. She did not blink, aching to catch every detail. Theft felt like a broad word, but the grim set of every guardian's mouth told her this was not routine. Caleb inhaled, and she caught the subtle tension in his jaw. He had alluded earlier to a crisis but gave no specifics, likely to keep her from panicking.

Marcus's glare swept the novices. "The missing object is called the Nexus Prism." He paused to let the name settle. "This relic is legendary for its ability to amplify magic to catastrophic levels. If misused, it can peel open the very barrier protecting mortals from what we do. It can reshape illusions into reality itself."

A chill snaked through Lila's core, forcing her to clamp her arms tight around her middle. She felt as if an invisible hand was gripping her lungs. She had only begun to learn how to craft modest sparks of magic safely. The idea of a relic that could take that power and expand it beyond control made her skin crawl. She glanced sideways at Caleb.

He lifted his chin and spoke. "The wards around the Prism's last known storage site were destroyed." His voice was low, brimming with subdued anger. "Someone... powerful... tore through them with little effort."

A ripple of unease moved through the novices, and Lila swallowed the knot in her throat. She noticed how Caleb did not specify names. He likely knew more than he was letting on. She could sense the deeper layer of worry behind his blue eyes. Almost unconsciously, he shifted his stance closer to her, as if prepared to put himself between her and any threat in the room.

Marcus tightened his grip on his staff. "We have reason to suspect that the thief aims to harness the Prism's ability to distort or amplify illusions. That means novices are now in danger. An untrained mind stands little chance against illusions sexpanded by the Prism's power."

He turned his attention pointedly toward the five novices. Lila's heart hammered, her gaze darting between the stoic guardians and the wide-eyed novices beside her. She recognized a tall boy near the other side of the room—

he had joined the Council's newest ranks only a few weeks before she did. His face had gone pale. A second novice, a curly-haired woman wearing thick-rimmed glasses, shifted uncomfortably and tightened her fingers around a wooden focus in her hand.

One of the mentors cleared his throat. "Is there any possibility the thief wants to sell the Prism on the black market?" he asked, but his voice trembled.

Marcus's mouth pressed into a thin line. "We cannot dismiss that. Yet we see signs pointing toward a more insidious plan. People have no reason to seek the Prism unless they intend to exploit its illusions or rip open the boundary between worlds. The relic itself is too volatile to trade casually, and those who handle it risk being consumed by it."

A heavy silence pressed on Lila's ears. She dared a small question, forcing her voice not to crack: "What... happens if illusions bleed into everyday life?" She thought of her coffee shop, of unsuspecting customers who might see glowing runes or shapeshifting wards. She remembered how close she had come to inadvertently exposing magic when her power first flickered across a milk frother. The idea of that phenomenon multiplied a thousand times by the Prism made her stomach churn.

One of the guardians, a severe-looking woman on Marcus's left, answered curtly. "Then we risk mortals discovering us en masse. We risk panic on a citywide scale. The Council has worked for centuries to prevent that."

Her words were clipped. Lila felt a flash of defensiveness but remained quiet. She was no stranger to mistakes

—her entire induction had been riddled with near-disasters—and shame still burned at the memory of scalding milk exploding from the café's espresso machine that morning. The difference was that she had done those things by accident. Whoever stole the Prism seemed bent on sowing chaos for personal gain.

Marcus exhaled sharply, then resumed. "The Council urges every one of you to maintain a strict code of silence. Discussions of the Prism, even among yourselves, must be handled with absolute discretion. Failure to stay quiet could give the rogue warlock—if that indeed is who we face—exactly what he wants."

Heat prickled across Lila's neck as she detected unspoken tension behind Marcus's authoritative words. A rogue warlock powerful enough to destroy wards in shambles. Caleb had mentioned the severity of illusions and the possibility that a cunning mind lurked behind them. Lila recalled how rigid Caleb's posture became whenever illusions came up. She had once or twice asked him about dangerous warlocks in the city, but he had sidestepped her every time.

She stammered under her breath, "Are we absolutely sure it's a... warlock? Couldn't it be a group?" She was not sure why she asked that question. Perhaps she needed to convince herself that one individual being that strong was impossible.

No one rushed to correct her, which only heightened the pit in her stomach. Caleb gave her a warning glance, a subtle shake of his head. She swallowed more uneasy questions. Her mind spun with the dread of confronting someone so formidable that entire wards had fallen.

Marcus frowned. "At this time, the Council has not confirmed the identity of the thief. We believe a single orchestrator stands behind the break-in. Whoever it was, they knew exactly how to bypass our normal defenses."

Lila slipped her hand into the pocket of her coat, finding nothing there to soothe her rising anxiety. She had never felt so small. She recalled the first time she revealed magical sparks in front of Maya—how everyone wrote it off as faulty wiring. Now she stood in a room where the entire magical community faced exposure if illusions escalated.

A rustle broke among the novices as one, a stocky young man in a green scarf, lifted his head and asked, "Why not galvanize the Council's best guardians? Why tell novices like us?"

Marcus exchanged a look with several elders. Finally, the tall man with short-cropped hair, standing near Marcus, cleared his throat. "You have a right to know the threat that might target you. The Council wards around new initiates can only protect you so far. If the thief decides to test illusions on novices, we need you to be prepared. Pay attention to your mentors' instructions and practice control."

Prepared, Lila thought, unable to suppress a hollow laugh inside her head. She had struggled to keep a single conjuration from exploding the training chamber walls. How was she supposed to fend off illusions super-charged by this Prism? She felt the faint vibration of regret in her fingertips. If she had realized how deeply she was stepping into danger, would she still have signed that oath?

She looked at Caleb again. He kept his arms folded, eyes narrowed with a fierce concentration. She wanted to demand answers from him. Why did he seem a hair's breadth away from storming out of here? Who could be strong enough to shatter the Council's wards? He clenched his jaw, and she sensed a storm of guilty knowledge swirling behind his calm facade.

Marcus's voice cut through her racing thoughts. "We will continue investigating. Until further notice, do not walk anywhere alone unless you have a stable ward or a capable mentor at your side. Illusions might prey on an unsteady mind. The best defense is vigilance."

A short gasp worked past Lila's lips. She tried to mask it by brushing a lock of hair behind her ear. The same prickling dread that overcame her days ago at the café, when she realized how rapidly her life was changing, now barrelled back with full force. This time, an entire city might be at stake.

She forced a question out, even though it came in a shaking whisper. "What... can novices specifically do if illusions start appearing around us?"

A handful of guardians exchanged looks. The severe-looking woman from earlier stepped forward, greenish runes glinting at her wrist. "First, you attempt to ground yourself. Basic self-control. Use a focusing object—a ring, a crystal, anything you have practiced with. If illusions intensify, call your mentor or a Council contact as soon as possible. You are not alone, though you may feel that way if illusions start shaking your sense of reality."

Caleb's voice emerged, quieter than before: "Lila." He said her name in a level tone as though reminding her that they would handle it together. Despite the flurry of tension behind his eyes, he tried to project steady reassurance.

She inhaled through her nose, willing herself to keep it together. "Right," she managed, though her heartbeat pounded so loudly she wondered if everyone in the room heard it.

Marcus lifted a hand, calling for final silence. "One more thing. We suspect the thief—the warlock or group—may attempt to recruit or pressure novices who show promising magic. Raw power is valuable. They might dangle illusions, advanced techniques, or the empty promise of independence. Do not be deceived."

At that warning, a faint murmur swept the novices gathered. Lila clenched and unclenched her fists. The notion that novices like her could be treated as pawns made her stomach churn. She could picture it now: illusions used to coerce them into betraying the Council's secrets or distrusting their mentors. She wanted to believe she would never fall for such temptation, yet her anxiety prickled. She was barely learning how to cast a steady spark. If illusions overwhelmed her, how would she even know what was real?

Satisfied that his words had sunk in, Marcus turned to the crowd. "You are dismissed. Your mentors will receive further briefings. Trust your assigned guardian or come to me if you see anything suspicious. For now, remain vigilant and discreet."

In one fluid motion, he lowered his staff and stepped aside. The orbs overhead dimmed, flickering from silver to a softer glow, signaling the close of the meeting. Lila stayed rooted, uncertain if her legs could carry her out the door. The novices began shuffling to the exit, while the guardians huddled among themselves for hushed discussions. A few voices rose in stern whispers: references to old archives, or unconfirmed sightings of illusions near obscure corners in the city. She felt Caleb's presence beside her, steady even if charged with tension.

FIFTEEN

Lila's first clear thought that morning was that it had to be illegal for the sky to look so gray and cold. She could barely feel her nose, let alone rally her spirits as she trudged after Caleb across the warped wooden boards of an abandoned pier on the Hudson River. A brisk wind cut through her jacket and stung her ears. Darkness still clung to the horizon, hinting that dawn was close but not yet merciful enough to bring any warmth.

She glared at the choppy water lapping against the pier, cursing herself for agreeing to meet him this early. She wanted coffee. She wanted sleep. The swirl of fatigue pressed against her mind, a reminder of how late she had stayed up pouring over magical notes. Instead, here she was, ankles throbbing in the chill, waiting for instructions that might involve dodging an incoming wave or conjuring a shield while half-frozen.

Caleb stood at the end of the pier, dark coat pulled tight around his body. His hair looked slightly damp, or maybe it only appeared that way. He turned at the sound of her footsteps, his intense eyes reflecting just enough concern to keep her from screaming about the hour. She hugged her arms around her torso and tried not to shiver.

"Tell me again why we thought training at dawn was a good idea," Lila said, her teeth chattering. She blew a shaky breath into her cupped palms. The wind flicked her hair into her eyes, and she batted it away with a disgruntled huff.

He leaned against one of the rotting pier pilings. "We need isolation. This quiet stretch of the Hudson is perfect for working with water-based energy." He gestured at the open expanse. The water slapped against the posts, producing a low, rhythmic roar. "It is also less likely that we'll find prying eyes."

Lila scowled. "I'm appreciating the dryness of prying eyes. At least they'd come with a heated building. My entire body is numb."

He offered an apologetic half-smile. "We'll warm up with some movement. Are you ready?"

She wanted to say no, but the time for hesitation had passed. After everything she had endured—sleepless nights, illusions haunting her thoughts, the Council's wary instructions—she recognized that progress never arrived comfortably. But she could still mutter complaints. That was her right.

"I guess I'm ready," she managed. Then she huffed when another breeze made her stumble. "As ready as a half-frozen barista can be, anyway."

He stepped closer, executing a neat circular gesture

with his hand. The air at his fingertips turned faintly iridescent, shimmering like sunlight on rippling water. Lila leaned in, curiosity nudging aside her discomfort. He guided the energy outward, and in the soft gloom, she saw the shimmering illusion expand into a translucent shield shaped like an oval mirror. Strands of pale blue light flickered across its surface, almost giving the shield a glassy texture.

Caleb pressed a gentle palm against the illusion's center to demonstrate how it rippled in response to touch. "This is a water-style ward," he explained. "Illusory by nature, but it has substance if you channel enough focus. The idea is to draw on the fluidity of the environment. Here on the pier, it might be easier to tap into the motion of the waves."

Lila nodded, eyes on the shield. She reached out a tentative fingertip. The surface felt cool, almost pliant, before it curled away like a rolling tide. Fascination replaced some of her grumpiness, if only for a moment.

Caleb let the illusion fade, stepping back so that the breeze tugged at the edges of his coat again. "Your turn," he said. "We want to practice forging a shield and maintaining it under pressure. If illusions escalate in the city, you might need to defend yourself quickly. The Nexus Prism is still missing, so we have no idea how powerful illusions could become if an enemy tries to strike when your guard is down."

Mentioning the stolen Prism sent a flicker of anxiety through her chest. She swallowed, rolling her shoulders in an attempt to dispel the tension. "You're sure it's wise to use water wards when I haven't exactly mastered fire or earth or... anything?"

He arched an eyebrow. "Confidence, Lila. You have ability, and we've already seen how your elemental inclinations can adapt when you concentrate. Water might be tricky, but the city is on an island surrounded by water. Better to fail here, in relative safety, than out in a real attack."

That logic made sense, frustrating though it was. Lila stepped along the pier, searching for a stable spot not lacquered with algae. As she lifted her hands, a small swirl of her own energy trembled in her palms. She struggled to keep her teeth from chattering and forced her mind to connect with the movement of the waves below.

One breath in. The brisk air stung her lungs. She pictured the water's steady rhythm. Another breath out. The swirl of magic in her grasp brightened, forming slender threads of aqua light. She felt a moment of excitement. She was doing it. This was real progress.

"Focus. Keep your stance rooted," Caleb reminded. He moved behind her, not quite touching but close enough that she could feel his presence.

Lila crafted a rough shield shape, smaller than Caleb's demonstration but enough to create a barrier the size of a large serving tray. She bit her lip, determined to hold it steady.

"Nicely done," he said in a calm tone. "Now let it expand a bit more."

She tried to push energy outward, but a rush of impatient frustration clamped down on her concentration. The wind rattled the pier, and cold water sprayed her ankles, seeping into her shoes. With a gasp, she lost her grip on the shield, dropping it in a flicker of watery sparks that splashed on the boards.

"Ugh," she muttered, stepping back to avoid the trickle streaming across her toes. She was shivering now, her socks soaked. "This is miserable."

Before she could steady herself for another attempt, Caleb stepped to her side and touched her elbow lightly. "Again," he said.

Her jaw tightened. She exhaled, ignoring the scalding ache of her toes. Turning her focus inward, she visualized the wave patterns in the river—small, repetitive pulses. Tuning out the biting wind, she let her magic align with that gentle push-and-pull. A faint swirl of liquid light formed in her hands, and she willed it to grow into a barrier that could withstand more than a faint gust.

The shield shimmered into being, a pale turquoise disc arcing before her. This time it appeared steadier, broad enough to cover her from shoulder to waist if an illusion attacked. She managed three slow breaths, mind whirling from the strain. Then she spotted movement at the corner of her vision. One of the rotted boards near her foot cracked, making her flinch. That sudden jolt of adrenaline destabilized her control.

Her shield, along with her carefully hoarded energy, flared out in a chaotic burst. The leftover magic pressed forward like a rogue gust of wind. Caleb, caught in the wave, stumbled. Lila yelped and tried to rein it in, but the force reversed direction, nearly slamming into her own chest. She panicked and spun aside, slipping on the slick wooden planks. Her arms flailed until she toppled over with a splash, soaking her knees and elbows in freezing water that pooled on the edge of the pier.

Caleb lunged across the platform, sliding on one knee just as the final wave of conjured force rattled the boards again. He reached for her, pulling her upright before the next surge drenched her completely. His coat, too, ended up soaking along one sleeve, and water dripped from the hem onto his scuffed boots.

She shivered, her heart pounding. "Shoot, I'm sorry," she managed, pressing a hand to her forehead. Cold droplets trickled down her collar, and her cheeks burned with embarrassment.

Instead of scolding her, he let out a low, husky laugh, his breath visible in the raw morning air. She blinked at him in confusion, expecting a stern reminder about discipline. He only gave her a warm, almost teasing look.

"You are more than capable of generating power," he said softly, helping her gain her footing. "We need to refine how you control the final release." His gloved hand lingered on her elbow, steadying her as she fought to stand without slipping again.

A surge of heat rose to her face. She didn't know if it came from his nearness or from embarrassment at nearly blasting him off the pier. The tension in her body unclenched just enough that she caught herself smiling, albeit shakily. Her hair hung around her face in damp clumps, and her waterlogged shoes squished beneath her weight.

"So I basically fail spectacularly, but you laugh?" she asked, half-amused, half-sulking.

He tilted his head. "You succeeded in generating a real shield. That is progress. The chaos afterward, well... it is part of learning." He sounded genuine, not mocking. "And you are allowed to get frustrated, but not to the point of giving up."

She realized how close they stood, the tips of their boots nearly touching. Between them, the faint pulse of magic hovered where their wards collided, as though their combined energies recognized each other. For an instant, neither spoke, and the cold receded behind something undeniably warmer.

The sky behind the city skyline began to lighten at that moment. A hint of pink and gold spread across the clouds, casting a pale glow over the water. It drew their attention, and Lila's breath caught when she looked back at Caleb. In that early dawn luminescence, his eyes seemed gentler than usual. She felt her heart flutter, confused by the intensity.

He, too, seemed caught in the silence. She thought he might say something about the training, or maybe scold her for nearly soaking them both. Instead, they shared a soft glance. Her pulse thrummed in her ears. She found her gaze sliding to his mouth, though no words passed her lips. A subtle warmth filled her chest, the kind of warmth she rarely felt under these dire circumstances.

After a delicate beat, he cleared his throat and separated them with a slight shift of weight, though the motion felt reluctant. "We should keep going," he said, not quite looking at her. "We still have to practice under greater pressure."

"Right," she answered, trying to grasp the swirl of sensations that had ignited in her. She pushed the thoughts aside. Training first. Emotions... later. "Let me try again without going for a swim."

He nodded. That momentary softness didn't vanish, but it tucked itself behind his usual composure. She inhaled and summoned a new surge of energy, eyes narrowed at the water's glint. Despite the renewed chill in her legs, she felt steadier, as if the unexpected closeness they'd just shared fed a small spark of confidence deep in her gut.

They continued for another hour, cycling through illusions that Caleb conjured to test her. One manifested as a swirling pattern of misty shapes diving from above. Another turned the far side of the pier into a rolling mirage of sea foam that rushed at Lila's shield, scattering droplets around her. Whenever she faltered, Caleb offered calm corrections. Whenever he conjured illusions meant to startle her, she tried to anchor herself in the rhythm of the tides. She slipped up multiple times—once even blasting a chunk of planking loose, forcing her to stumble backward just to keep from tumbling into the river again.

By the time morning fully bloomed in a hazy wash of flat sunlight, the pier looked even more battered than before. Lila's socks were thoroughly soaked, and her aching muscles screamed for rest. Yet she felt more accomplished than she had since the last time she managed a simple charm without setting off unintended consequences. Each time she summoned a watery shield, it held a little longer under Caleb's illusions. Each time she nearly lost control, it took less effort to recover. Though the mistakes left her laughing weakly with frustration, she could sense the progress.

Finally, she dropped her hands with a sigh. "If I keep this up, I'll have no feeling in my toes ever again."

Caleb surveyed the dreary pier, then gave her a nod. "We have done enough for one morning. You need dry clothes, and I suspect you need something hot to drink."

She let out an exhausted scoff, pushing soggy bangs away from her forehead. "A triple shot latte wouldn't be out of place."

He signaled for her to follow as he walked back toward the rickety steps that led to a sloping path along the river. They left the shimmer of illusions behind, though watery droplets still clung to their coats. The early light spread across the water in gentle streaks, painting the surface with ripples of orange. Lila felt her limbs protesting with each movement, but a small surge of satisfaction kept her upright.

Despite the complaining she had done earlier, she couldn't hide a tiny sense of pride. She had nearly blasted him off the pier, yes, but she had managed real spells under harsh conditions, a testament to how far she had come in her training. Caleb's rare laugh echoed in her mind, and she found herself smiling at the memory, no matter how her cheeks heated at the thought.

They trudged side by side until the pier gave way to a cracked sidewalk, and then they continued along a scraggly row of trees. The wind carried an occasional hint of garbage from the city's underbelly, but Lila's heart remained buoyed by that trace of victory. Her exhaustion warred with an undercurrent of excitement she couldn't completely suppress.

She gave Caleb a sidelong glance. "Thanks for not chewing me out every time I messed up."

He shrugged, adjusting the collar of his coat. "Encouragement often yields better results. You learn from your mistakes if you have space to correct them. I believe in your potential."

Her chest warmed again. She thought of the Council's concerns and the cryptic warnings about illusions. That weight hadn't vanished, but at least she didn't feel quite so alone facing it. She nodded, deciding that she wouldn't dwell on stingy Council elders or the threat looming in dark corners, at least not this second.

They crossed a quiet street before heading into a residential neighborhood that soon connected to a narrow back passage Lila recognized. Her boots squelched with each step, an absurdly loud reminder of her bruised toes, but she kept pace until her arms began to tremble. Finally, as they turned a corner, they paused under the overhang of a shuttered store. The city had begun waking up, horns bleating in the distance, early joggers glancing warily at the pair dressed in wet clothes. Lila felt adrenaline separating from her bloodstream, leaving behind a pleasant weariness.

Caleb studied her face. "Shall I walk you to your place?"

She shook her head, though she appreciated the offer. "I'll be fine. Besides, I can't imagine you need an audience while you freeze to death in that coat. Get some rest, too."

He allowed a faint smile, almost affectionate in the delicate morning light. "In that case, I will see you soon. We can review your progress later tonight if you want to practice more illusions."

She nodded, chewing the inside of her cheek. "I'll text you," she said softly. "Thanks again."

He inclined his head in a polite farewell, then folded another ward around himself, likely to keep his already soaked sleeve from breaking into a chill. She turned, ignoring the way her pulse jumped when she caught him looking after her. As she continued toward her apartment blocks away, she let herself savor that small flicker of warmth behind her ribs. The wind threatened to disperse it, but she locked it away, determined to hold on.

As she walked toward home, the fierce training had granted Lila a small but tangible kernel of confidence. She felt stronger than she had hours ago, as if the icy morning had forged a sharper sense of her own capability. Even so, a low hum of unease settled beneath her relief, reminding her that the theft of the Nexus Prism was no random heist. Standing on the threshold of her apartment, she sensed that something larger lurked just out of sight. Their morning session on the pier had offered a glimpse of what she could accomplish, but it also exposed the raw truth: they were circling the edge of a much bigger underworld, and every day brought them closer to a confrontation few people outside the Council could possibly understand.

CHAPTER

SIXTEEN

Lila's shoes squelched with every step as she reached her apartment building's dimly lit lobby. Water pooled around her ankles, the result of dodging half-frozen puddles all the way from the Hudson pier.

She stepped onto the old tile floor, noticing a faint shudder in the overhead light. Flickering fluorescent bulbs cast jittering shadows down the corridor, amplifying every scuff of her footsteps. The landlord had promised to repair the lighting weeks ago, but Lila no longer took such mundane assurances to heart. She ran her tongue across dry lips, forcing her shoulders to relax. At least once she got inside, she could strip out of these wet socks and try to forget that the entire city might be on the brink of a magical crisis.

Her apartment door stood at the far end, painted a dull beige that looked gray in the weak light. She paused before it, aware that she was still keyed up with leftover adrenaline from the water-based training. Slowly, she forced a breath through her teeth and tensed her fingers around the keys. The wards Caleb had insisted they set—minor protective spells to keep strangers from slipping inside—should lend her some comfort. Yet a strange sensation made the tiny hairs on her neck prickle. She swallowed, disliking how the air here felt stagnant, almost heavy.

Fishing a second key from her keyring—the one tied to a subtle locking ward—she slipped it into the deadbolt. The lock clicked, but her wards didn't deliver the familiar gentle tingle against her fingertips. Instead, she felt only a faint shiver that told her the wards were present but frail. Confusion knotted her forehead. Had the wards weakened from disuse or from some oversight?

With a soft grunt, she turned the key the rest of the way and stepped inside. A single overhead light buzzed to life, illuminating her cramped living room. The meager warmth of the place managed to chase away the chill, but it did nothing to quell the uneasy feeling creeping up her spine.

She took one step over the threshold, then froze. A slip of paper lay on the floor, just inside her door, as if someone had pushed it under the seal. The edges curled slightly, as though it had been crammed hastily. Her heart gave a jump. Nobody else should have had access to her apartment. The wards, flimsy as they might be, were intended to repel uninvited visitors. Yet here, plain as day, was a note that did not belong.

Careful, Lila closed the door behind her. She bent to

pick it up, eyebrows drawing tight as she read the message:

Beware who you trust. The Prism changes everything.

The words were scrawled in a hurried, spiky script. The note's corners looked smudged with what might have been city grime or residue from a dirty glove. Her heart kicked hard against her rib cage, each thump a warning that she was in deeper than she'd realized. She flipped the note over, hoping to find a clue to its sender, but the back held only a faint residue of chalky dust.

She raised her gaze, scanning the small entry area for more signs of intrusion. At first, nothing seemed amiss. Her coat rack leaned precariously, same as always; her corner shelf still held the fussy little succulent she tried not to kill. Then she looked down near the door. A faint scuff of footprints in the dusty corner near her doormat drew her attention. She sidestepped to get a better look. The prints looked like smooth skid marks, as if someone had dragged their shoe or pivoted abruptly.

"How...?" she whispered. She had assumed that the wards Caleb and the Council had helped her set would keep interlopers from crossing the threshold. Clearly they didn't work on whoever left this note.

Her pulse hammered, an involuntary recognition that someone powerful—or at least cunning—had bypassed her protective spells. She carefully toed off her soaked shoes, then peeled away her socks, leaving them in a soggy heap near the baseboard. A wave of panic seized her. She hated that her mind leapt immediately to Sebastian's illusions or a traitor from within the Council. The guardians had stressed the possibility of infiltration more than once. Their repeated reminders to keep her head down rang in her head, fueling her worst fears.

Hastily, she flicked on another light and stumbled toward the couch. The entire apartment felt colder than usual, as though the presence of that note had leeched the warmth from the air. She settled onto a frayed cushion, heart beating so loud she swore it would rattle her chest. With shaking fingers, she fished her phone out of her bag. In the bright screen glare, she saw her reflection—pale cheeks, eyes wide with worry, damp hair plastered to her forehead.

Her first thought was to call Maya, simply to hear the comfort of a friendly voice. But Maya had no idea how deep this rabbit hole went, and Lila couldn't risk piling more danger on her best friend. Caleb, however, was the one person who would come without question, the one person who understood exactly how precarious all of this was.

She pressed his number, dread coiling in her stomach as each ring sounded in her ear. Every passing second felt like stepping deeper into a vortex of unknown threats.

"Lila?" He answered on the third ring, voice hushed. Static flickered for an instant, then cleared.

She licked her dry lips. "C-Caleb." She drew a shaky breath, fighting to keep her voice steady. "I—someone left me a note under my door. It's about the Prism... They somehow got through the wards." The words tumbled out in a frantic rush.

A beat of silence, then his tone sharpened. "You're sure the wards were still in place before you left this morning?"

"They were," she whispered, pressing a hand to her forehead. "I checked.

Caleb said. "Are you safe? Is anyone else there?"

"I'm alone, but I'm not sure I feel safe. The note says 'Beware who you trust.'" She glanced down and smoothed the paper flat on her lap. "It mentions the Prism. And the handwriting... it's so shaky, like the person was in a hurry."

Caleb's voice grew firmer. "I'll be right there. Stay inside. Keep your phone nearby."

He hung up, leaving the apartment quiet except for the low hum of the refrigerator. Lila sagged against the couch. The text shimmered in her vision, the note's meaning echoing behind her closed eyelids. She tried not to give in to hysteria, but the suggestion that someone had specifically targeted her stoked a creeping paranoia. The Council's words came back to her: illusions, infiltration, the stolen Nexus Prism. It felt like a boulder pressing on her chest.

Minutes later, a light knock on her door made her jump. She practically flew from the couch to the peephole. Caleb's familiar profile was framed by the weak hallway light. She unlatched the door quickly, relief flooding her muscles.

He slipped inside, shutting the door behind him with deliberate care. She noted the tension in his posture—the rigid line of his back, one hand flexing at his side. He wore a dark coat over what looked like a hastily thrown-on shirt. The trace of nighttime stubble on his jaw gave him a ruffled edge she couldn't help noticing, even in her distress.

"Did you see any sign of forced entry?" he asked immediately.

She hesitated, gesturing vaguely at the faint footprints. "Not forcing, exactly. But there's that scuff, right there. Someone definitely stood in that corner." The anxious quaver in her voice made her cringe. "They got past the wards without setting off an alarm."

Caleb crouched by the footprints and pressed two fingers to the floor. He concentrated, likely scanning for magical residue, but after a moment he shook his head, brow pinched. "They masked their aura. I can't detect left-over magic. Whoever did this was thorough." He rose and turned to her, gaze dark with worry. "Let me see the note."

Silently, she handed it over. He read the words, tension deepening across his features. For a second, fear flickered behind his eyes. She caught it before he quickly schooled his expression. That flicker made her gut twist. If Caleb was frightened, that wasn't a good sign.

He set the note down on her coffee table with deliberate care. "The Council will investigate. They'll dispatch watchers to sweep the building for illusions." His voice sounded calm, but she had known him long enough to sense the undertone of concern. "For now, promise me you won't answer your door unless you confirm who it is. If you see or sense anything out of place, call me right away."

She folded her arms against her chest, nodding too

vigorously. "It just feels...like a warning. Or a threat. Or both."

"People who want the Prism do more than issue warnings," he murmured, glancing around the room. "But it's possible they think you know something about it."

"That's what scares me," she admitted. "I'm a novice, Caleb. I only know fragments from the Council briefings. It's not like I have valuable intel."

His jaw tightened. "The best lies often hinge on partial truths. They may believe you have a direct link to the rumored power in your family line." He hesitated, then crossed the small space to where she stood, lowering his voice. "For someone skilled enough to slip wards, intimidation works best if they think you're alone and vulnerable."

She swallowed hard. "I hate that they could come and go and we'd never know." Sliding a glance at the note, she recalled the angled letters. "It's like they're taunting me. They said 'Beware who you trust.' That's not exactly subtle."

Together, they settled on the couch, the small overhead lamp casting a meager glow. She pulled a blanket over her damp legs, hugging it to her body in an effort to chase away the chill. She noticed Caleb scoot closer, close enough that she heard the soft rustle of his coat as his shoulder brushed hers.

"You realize," he said after a moment, "this might be connected to infiltration within the Council. If it's a traitor, they could be stirring fear to keep you on edge. They know novices are prime targets for illusions."

Her stomach knotted like a twisted dishrag. "So even the guardians I'm supposed to trust could be compromised?"

His sigh felt heavy in the hush of the apartment. "I'm not sure how deep the corruption goes. But we've seen sabotage before. The wards in the city have been tampered with more times than I can count."

A wave of frustration sparked in her chest. "If the people supposedly protecting us are also the ones who might be feeding Sebastian or any other rogue warlocks information, then where does that leave me? Or the others?"

For a long beat, Caleb said nothing. He simply let the question hang in the stale air. Then he carefully placed a hand on her forearm, giving a reassuring squeeze. "We keep alert. We lean on those we know won't turn on us. You can trust me," he added quietly, as though he realized how hollow the Council's guarantees must feel right now.

She met his gaze, and for a fleeting moment, she found comfort in those intense eyes. The tension between them hummed, a mixture of fear and closeness that neither had asked for but both felt compelled to acknowledge. Her pulse leaped, uncooperative in the face of danger. She let her gaze slip lower, noticing the way his fingers lingered on her arm.

"Caleb..." Her voice emerged softer than she intended. "Thank you for coming so quickly."

He offered a small, rueful smile. "You're my responsibility. And you're more than that." Warmth flashed across his expression, just enough for her to see the conflict within him. "I can't let anything happen to you."

The admission stirred something deep in her chest. She shifted under the blanket, heart pounding louder than before. She wasn't certain if it was the panic from the note, the weight of illusions gnawing at her trust in the Council, or the quiet promise in his words. Perhaps it was all three threads woven into one potent swirl. The moment crackled with unspoken possibilities, and she knew they both felt it.

But she was too rattled to focus on the deeper desire tugging at her mind. She tore her gaze away, fiddling with a loose thread on the blanket. "I'm just... I'm scared that if we can't even keep one small apartment warded, we won't stand a chance against illusions across the entire city." Her voice faltered. "It's all unraveling, isn't it?"

Caleb's hand slid from her forearm to grasp her trembling fingers. "We're working to reinforce the city's wards. I spoke with Marcus earlier—he's gathering a team to trace any tampering. More watchers will be assigned to novices.

"You're still damp from our session. Why don't you take a hot shower and change into some warm clothes. I'll be here when you finish."

"Yes, thank you. I am chilled to the bone," she said as she went to her closet and pulled out a sweater and a pair of jeans. "I'll be quick," she said as she hurried into the bathroom. Ten minutes later she felt so much better when she exited the bathroom and rejoined Caleb on the couch.

A clock on the wall ticked away the seconds. Outside,

the city might have been full of horns and distant chatter, but inside her apartment, the quiet felt oppressive. At length, they spoke about the possibility that a rogue guardian had singled her out. Caleb speculated about ways illusions could bypass wards—perhaps by layering a false identity or forging a signature. Lila occasionally chimed in with scathing remarks about how powerless she felt in this situation.

At some point, she realized Caleb was sitting so close that their thighs brushed. A pang of longing sparked in her chest, sudden and urgent. She tried to chase it away, reminding herself how unsteady she felt, how the day's events had left her raw. The swirl of conflicting emotions made her heart ache.

He seemed to sense the shift. The back of his hand grazed her knee, a fleeting contact that left a spark of warmth in its wake. She met his gaze again, and her breath caught. She saw the same desire flicker in his eyes, an echo of what she felt. Yet the tension of the day—the ominous note, the infiltration fears—hung in the air like a barrier neither dared press through.

She pressed her lips into a thin line, summoning a shaky smile. "I'm sorry," she whispered. "My mind is all over the place. This is the last thing I needed to find today."

He brushed a strand of damp hair behind her ear, his fingertips ghosting across her cheek. "Don't apologize. You had a right to call me."

A faint flutter stirred in her stomach. Closing her eyes, she forced a steady breath. These feelings—this closeness

—would have to wait. She was too tense, and the awareness of looming dangers made every nerve in her body scream for caution. As if sensing her conflict, Caleb withdrew slightly, though he kept a supportive hand on hers.

Several more minutes passed in low conversation, strategizing small ways to improve her wards or set up a discreet alarm charm. He insisted he would leave behind a protective token near her door, a subtle layering of illusions that might deter any further intrusions. She nodded, feeling a grateful jolt that at least she wasn't entirely defenseless.

Eventually, though, exhaustion crashed over her, dulling the edges of worry until her eyelids threatened to shut. Caleb noticed. His thumb brushed across her knuckles, and he rose from the couch with slow, careful movements. "You need rest," he said gently. "I'll stay if you want, but if you think you'll sleep better alone—"

Her throat constricted. She badly wanted him to stay, to anchor her in this swirling uncertainty, but she couldn't ask that of him. Too many raw emotions roiled inside her. She managed a nod that would serve as acceptance of his departure. "Thanks," she murmured, voice thick with fatigue. "I'll be all right. I'll...call if something happens."

He gazed down at her, a storm of unspoken words behind his eyes, then leaned over to press a careful, lingering touch to her shoulder. It wasn't quite a hug, certainly not a kiss, but that half-embrace gave her a small spark of comfort in the dim lamplight.

"I'm a phone call away," he murmured, his breath a soft brush against her hair. "No matter the hour."

She offered a tired smile in return, every muscle heavy with worry and residual adrenaline. He left quietly, footsteps fading down the hallway until she heard the gentle click of the outer door. Only then did she let out a long, trembling breath. The note lay on her coffee table, an accusation of how precarious her life had become.

She flipped off the main lamp and walked slowly to her bedroom, a dull ache forming behind her eyes. The apartment no longer felt like the haven she once cherished. Over in the corner, the wards Caleb had promised to reinforce flickered faintly, but she couldn't shake the suspicion that a more cunning presence could bypass them again.

She wondered who would stoop to leaving such a message under her door. She wondered how soon another threat might manifest. And worst of all, she wondered if the Council's security—her security—had already slipped beyond recovery.

Eventually, her eyes drifted shut, though sleep brought only uneasy half-dreams of swirling illusions tapping on her windows. The single shining relief in that moment was the memory of Caleb's hand enveloping hers, a fleeting promise that she wasn't alone in this unsettling fight.

CHAPTER

SEVENTEEN

Lila's eyes were gritty from sleeping too long, she realized it must have been at least ten hours since Caleb had left. She got up and stretched and looked out the window that glowed with the faintest tint of purple, hinting at an imminent dawn that arrived all too early. Her heart thudded in her chest, matching the tremor in her fingers.

She quietly made a decision: she would call her grandmother. Evelyn Matthews had always seemed to possess a reservoir of secrets—old family lore disguised as bedtime stories. Growing up, Lila had dismissed the tales as pure invention. Now, after all she had witnessed, she suspected those stories held answers that no one else could give.

Turning on her laptop, she propped it atop a couple of old cookbooks so the camera faced her properly. Her hair was a tangle of exhaustion-induced waves, and purple shadows bruised the skin beneath her eyes. Dawn light through the window turned her reflection ghostly. She took a moment to blot her face with a towel, inhaled, and hit the button to initiate a video call.

Anxious seconds passed, the ringing drawing out like a string. It felt odd to call at such an hour, but Evelyn was an early riser—or so Lila recalled from childhood visits. Just when Lila feared her grandmother might still be asleep, the screen flickered. Then Evelyn's familiar face appeared, framed by loose, silvery auburn hair.

"Lila?" Evelyn's voice was soft and a little breathless. "Is everything all right, dear? It's so early."

Relief swelled in Lila's chest, so swift it made her eyes sting. She cleared her throat, trying to steady her voice. "Gran, I—sorry to wake you. I was afraid you'd be busy later."

Evelyn tilted her head. Concern deepened the faint wrinkles at the corners of her eyes. "Never apologize for needing me. You look so pale. Have you been sleeping at all?"

"I finally collapsed for the past ten hours." Lila twisted one hand into the hem of her oversized shirt, unsure how to even begin explaining the chaos that her life had become. She forced a shaky smile. "Gran, I need your help. Something...you always hinted that our family had a special history." She swallowed, remembering the swirl of illusions she had seen and the talk of stolen relics. "I need to know about the magic—and about these relics you used to talk about when I was little."

Evelyn's expression shifted from gentle worry to a more guarded, knowing look. Lila recognized it as the way her grandmother always looked when confronted with truths she had kept close for years. Something about that gaze made Lila's pulse race. The older woman exhaled softly, then gave a small nod, as if deciding there was no turning back from this conversation.

"All right," Evelyn said quietly. "Ask me what you need to know."

"Gran," Lila began, voice unsteady, "people have mentioned...a Nexus Prism and illusions that might tear open a barrier between normal life and magic. I keep hearing how my family—our bloodline—has ties to artifacts that can bridge realms. Is that true?"

Evelyn hesitated. Her lips pressed into a worried line, then she spoke with a quiet gravity. "Yes. The Matthews line has long been connected to relics that can cross the threshold between worlds. The Prism is only one of them, though it is perhaps the most dangerous if used for ill."

Lila's heart pounded, each beat thudding against her ribs. She sank into a chair, hugging one knee against her chest. "So it's real. And we might be right in the middle of a crisis involving it."

She glanced warily at her front door, half expecting shadowy footsteps to approach. The apartment felt colder than before. Dull light from the rising sun illuminated motes of dust dancing in the air. Every inch of her body ached with tension, but she refused to let herself close the laptop or walk away. She needed answers, no matter how terrifying.

Evelyn's eyes flicked downward for a moment. "I withheld many details because your father insisted you be kept from magic. He forbade me from teaching you anything when you were still a baby. He never told me exactly why, but he was adamant that I not pass along the traditions. Perhaps he believed he was protecting you." She sighed. "Magical ability often skips a generation, Lila. In our family, it seems it has chosen you."

Lila's breath caught. She had never probed her father, Thomas, about magic. He was practical, almost rigid about normalcy. She vaguely recalled overhearing arguments between him and Evelyn, but never the context. Now the pieces fell into place, painting a picture of secret tension in their household.

"So that's why I never saw you do spells while growing up," Lila said numbly. "Even though you told stories about illusions, wards, and...other realms. You were always hinting. You said they were fairy tales."

"I did what I could without breaking his trust," Evelyn replied, sadness in her eyes. "I am sorry. Perhaps I should have rebelled more. But when your own son pleads with you to keep his child away from magic, it weighs heavily. I knew better than to scoff at his feelings. He was frightened."

Lila's gaze roamed her cramped kitchen, taking in the chipped counters and the pile of mismatched plates. Thin lines of warded magic ran along the ceiling from corner to corner, placed there only days ago. She wondered if hundreds of small decisions over the years had guided her to this moment—an apartment in Manhattan, a job at a café, and an explosive awakening of power she never sought.

She had so many questions, her head felt ready to

burst. "Gran, do you know anything about...well, about an amulet? Caleb mentioned there might be an artifact that can neutralize dark magic. People keep talking about illusions escalating. If the Prism is in the wrong hands, is there something out there that can stop it?"

Evelyn's focus sharpened. For a flicker of a moment, her gaze darted toward something off-camera, as though she was recalling a detail kept in years of memory. Then she returned to the conversation, her face carefully controlled. "There are indeed references in our lineage to an amulet that can buffer or even cancel certain kinds of corrupt magic. The writings about it are old, scattered across family journals and letters. Some believed it was only myth, though I always suspected otherwise." She paused. "Your great-aunt mentioned it once. She called it a key that connects to ancient wards."

Hope fluttered in Lila's chest, emotions tangling with her dread. The possibility of a solution—anything to keep illusions from spiraling out of control—felt like a lifeline. She leaned forward, ignoring the ache in her stiff shoulders. "Gran, do you know if the amulet exists, or where it might be?"

Evelyn grimaced. "I wish I had a neat answer, but the truth is our records are incomplete. I have little more than scraps describing its design and rumored purpose. Over time, pieces of our heritage were lost or destroyed. This is a heavy secret to share, and I can't be certain it will help. But if the Prism is truly stirring again, you need every advantage."

Lila swallowed. "I'll take any scrap of advantage I can

find." Something in her tone wavered, and she pulled free the knot in her hair, letting the loose waves tumble around her face. Faint pink rays from outside were cresting the window ledge. She swallowed convulsively and admitted to a deeper fear. "I keep thinking...what if I'm too late? What if illusions are too strong? I had...there was a warning note someone left under my door, and the wards on my apartment weren't enough to keep whoever delivered it from crossing the threshold."

Across the video feed, Evelyn's eyes darkened with quiet concern. "Oh, sweetheart, that is very serious, and quite scary." She sighed softly. "I never wanted you to shoulder such threats. But our bloodline has always been tied to magical relics, especially those bridging realms. It isn't fair, yet it is part of who we are. You have to trust your instincts. Remember that power doesn't define you; how you wield it does."

Lila felt a stir of warmth in her chest. Her grandmother's words soothed some of the raw edges in her mind. She brushed her fingertips over a faint bruise on her arm left by an earlier mishap letting that small ache remind her why she was fighting so hard to grasp the truth.

Unbeknownst to her, a faint hum resonated near the wards that Caleb had placed around the apartment door. If she had listened closely, she might have heard a gentle shift of magical current, but the low hum of her fridge and the soft static on the laptop's speakers masked it. Focused on her grandmother's face, she gave no thought to the possibility that someone else might be listening.

Evelyn exhaled again and spoke gently. "As for your

parents, I know you might feel compelled to tell them, but please refrain, at least for now. Your father was firm in his stance against magic in your life. He might react badly, and we don't want to add that turmoil while illusions pose such a threat. Let me speak to him if it becomes unavoidable. He is my son; he might listen to reason... eventually."

A pang of sadness cut through Lila. She despised keeping secrets from family, yet it felt like the only choice. Thomas Matthews had always been distant about the past. This new truth about him—how he feared the same magic Lila now struggled to control—unnerved her.

She nodded slowly. "All right. I'll wait. I won't mention any of this to Dad the next time they call."

Her grandmother offered a small, reassuring smile. "Thank you, dear. I truly believe it is for the best, at least until we know more." Then Evelyn's gaze softened further. "In the meantime, I will look through old letters in my possession. Perhaps I can find a firm lead on that amulet. Because if illusions are truly spiraling out of control, an artifact that neutralizes dark magic might be helpful."

Lila's stomach twisted at the seriousness in Evelyn's voice. She recalled the fear in the eyes of certain Council members when the Prism was mentioned. If something as potent as that relic was on the loose, they needed every ounce of help. The memory of reading that ominous note in her apartment sank like a stone in her chest. But at least Evelyn believed a solution might exist.

As they spoke, the room brightened bit by bit. Sunlight climbed the wall behind the kitchen counter. Shadows crept toward the small fridge plastered with pinned receipts and coffee-themed stickers. The entire apartment felt caught between night's secrecy and the day's promise of clarity. Lila could almost imagine this half-light as a metaphor: half in the dark, half in the uncharted brightness of truth.

"I'll keep your confidence," Lila said in a hushed tone, whether to calm herself or reassure her grandmother, she wasn't sure. "Thank you, Gran. I...didn't know where else to turn."

Evelyn blinked, her gaze warm as she set her jaw in quiet resolve. "You can always turn to me. I should have been more open sooner, but I didn't want to expose you to dangers you weren't equipped to handle. Even now, I wish none of this weighed on your shoulders. But if we do nothing, the city and countless people could be at risk. Your father believed denial would keep you safe. I understand why he thought so, but that time has passed."

Lila's throat tightened. The city. The unsuspecting millions swirling through Manhattan's streets, so wrapped up in their normal lives that illusions and wards would seem straight out of a myth if they even knew. She pictured her friend Maya's worried face, and the confusion in Caleb's eyes as illusions grew bolder by the day. Her mind buzzed with the weight of so many lives. And she was only just discovering her own place in a world of hidden magic.

"Is it terrible that I'm...relieved to hear you confirm it's real?" she asked. "I felt like I was losing my mind. At least now I know it comes from our family history, not some random fluke."

"Relief is not terrible," Evelyn said gently. "Magic is part of you. Accepting that is the first step. You will learn to direct it, to let it strengthen you instead of frightening you."

Lila closed her eyes briefly, letting that encouragement splinter the thick dread that clung to her chest. A fragile feeling of hope flickered inside her like a match in the dark. Yes, illusions prowled the city, and a stolen Prism threatened unimaginable chaos. But there might also be a hidden heirloom, her birthright, capable of changing the outcome.

She nodded, words sticking in her throat. "I—I'm sorry for calling so early," she whispered without meeting the camera directly.

"Never apologize to me for that," Evelyn said, a spark of affection brightening her voice. "This is important. And if things worsen, I will come to the city. I suspect my presence might be needed soon." Her tone carried a hint of regret, as though this entire scenario was an inevitability she had prepared for in silence.

CHAPTER

EIGHTEEN

Lila felt each step reverberate beneath her feet as she crossed the threshold into the Council's grand entry hall. The entire chamber shone with pale marble pillars and polished floors, reflecting every flicker of enchanted torchlight. Several robed figures wore expressions of severe concentration, barely glancing at her arrival as they hurried in and out of a side corridor. Their hushed whispers reminded her of a hospital at midnight, tense and buzzing with the promise of bad news.

She moved forward, heart picking up speed, her arm brushing Caleb's sleeve. He kept pace with her, quiet yet alert. His presence offered a fraction of comfort, though his jaw was set in a way that could have indicated worry or focus. She noticed a faint line of tension at his temple and realized he was just as unsettled as she was.

When they reached the circular chamber where key Council members gathered, Lila straightened her shoulders. At a glance, she counted over a dozen witches and warlocks arranged in a semicircle around a broad mahogany table. Marcus Steele stood at the center, back rigid, with a single sheet of parchment balanced before him.

Marcus beckoned them in without preamble. "Lila Matthews," he said in a measured tone. "We appreciate your prompt arrival."

She nodded, though the dryness in her mouth made speech difficult. Caleb's reassuring tilt of the head helped her claim a breath. They stepped onto the smooth marble floor within the circle of elders, each Council member regarding Lila as if she were an exhibit under glass.

"We have several matters to address," Marcus continued. His voice echoed in the high-ceilinged space, making it feel even more cavernous. "Your training progress, as well as certain... irregularities that have come to light."

Lila's stomach clenched. She knew exactly which "irregularities" he meant. Her mind leapt to the note someone slipped under her door, the footprints that bypassed her wards, the phone call with her grandmother at dawn. She pressed her palms together, fighting the impulse to snap at them in frustration.

One female elder with iron-gray hair coughed delicately. "You are a novice, Miss Matthews, yet you have had multiple magical incidents of note, correct? Not only an accidental spark at your workplace but also these more recent... ringings of your aura." She bent her gaze to the parchment in front of her. "Our watchers have sensed them more than once. Are you lacking discipline in your training, or is there another reason these flares continue?"

Before Lila could answer, another Council member—a tall man wearing glasses—cut in. "Is she even stable enough to proceed with advanced instruction? We already know illusions can disrupt novices. If she is prone to these spikes, we may be placing more than her own safety at risk."

Heat rushed to Lila's cheeks. She struggled to find her voice, torn between defending herself and acknowledging that her magic had been uneasy all week. Caleb moved half a step closer, still silent, but she sensed him gathering words to speak on her behalf.

Marcus tapped the parchment. "Well, Miss Matthews? Speak for yourself. We need to determine your readiness."

Lila dragged in a breath. "My training is progressing," she said, maintaining eye contact with Marcus. "I practice daily with illusions and wards. Caleb has tested me extensively under controlled conditions. The... irregularities you mention were unintentional, but I'm learning to control them."

Caleb nodded. His tone was measured when he finally spoke. "While Lila's power has spiked at inconvenient times, her control is improving. She has shown quick adaptability with wards and a strong sense of elemental grounding. I believe advanced training is the next logical step."

An older warlock draped in crimson robes gave a derisive snort. "That remains to be seen. We have also received troubling news of an unknown individual bypassing Miss Matthews's warding spells." He folded his arms across his chest. "An ominous note was left in her dwelling, referencing the Prism, if I understand what I've been hearing. Miss Matthews, can you explain how it is possible that your wards were so easily breached?"

"Because someone skilled enough wanted inside," she said quietly. "We set up minor wards, but—" She forced herself not to glance at Caleb. She refused to throw him under any scrutiny if she could help it. "I am new to these spells, yes, but the wards were functional. Whoever came in did it without triggering a single alarm. That suggests infiltration beyond ordinary magic."

A murmur passed through several elders. She sensed the undercurrent of blame centering on Caleb again. As though accusing him of not training her properly, or suspecting he had left some backdoor open. Lila stiffened at the notion. She wanted to bark that none of this was Caleb's fault, that the city was crawling with illusions thanks to the Prism's theft, but she bit her tongue.

Marcus's stare tightened. "Given that you already faced intimidation from an unknown source, do you believe you can continue your training without jeopardizing Council security?"

"I can," Lila insisted, voice breaking slightly. She cleared her throat. "I would prefer not to give them the satisfaction of frightening me away. My powers won't suddenly vanish if I hide in my apartment."

An elder from the edge of the group, a woman wearing silver runic bracelets, leaned forward. "We are deciding whether you will remain a novice with limited responsibilities, or whether we accelerate your instruction. If we deem you too great a liability, there are other options." Her tone made Lila's skin crawl, as if being locked away for her own good was a possibility they might consider.

She swallowed, wishing her pulse would slow down. "I want to learn. If the Prism is as dangerous as you say, I want to do my part. Hiding or forcing me into some corner will not help us face illusions across the city."

Marcus lifted a hand. "Very well. On that point, at least, we appear to have consensus that an untrained witch is more risk than an educated one. Therefore, the Council sanctions advanced training for Lila Matthews—supervised closely by her assigned mentor."

Caleb's shoulders relaxed minutely, and Lila felt him exhale. Yet the tension at the edges of the chamber didn't lighten. Several watchers traded skeptical looks, as if uncertain whether she was truly a solution or just another problem.

The female elder with the iron-gray hair spoke again, her voice clipped. "But do not mistake this sanction for unbridled freedom. One miscalculation with illusions or wards could compromise us all." Her words dripped with cool disapproval.

"Understood," Lila said, jaw clenched. On one hand, relief that they were not locking her out of training. On the other, she hated this feeling of dancing on the edge of a sword, where one slip might ruin everything.

Marcus inclined his head, satisfied for now, then he cleared his throat. "There is another matter. We have learned that you recently communicated with someone outside our typical novice guidelines, yes?" He paused for dramatic effect. "Your grandmother, Evelyn Matthews."

Lila froze. She had predicted that question might come up, but the blood drained from her cheeks all the same. She could practically feel the eyes of every Council member upon her. At the periphery of her vision, she caught Caleb turning slightly, as if uncertain whether to meet her gaze.

Marcus continued. "We know she is well-versed in older magic. We also know you spoke with her at length. Did you glean any new information pertinent to our efforts in retrieving the Nexus Prism?"

Her heart hammered. She remembered the video call at dawn, her grandmother's quiet admission of their bloodline's connection to certain relics, and that subtle hint about an amulet. She had not revealed the amulet's existence to the Council. She doubted Evelyn wanted that detail freely shared. Worse yet, Lila had not anticipated that Caleb might mention it so soon. She shot him a sidelong look, frustration coiling in her stomach.

"She is my grandmother," Lila said slowly, each word measured. "We spoke about the family's background, yes. She... answered some questions about the legacy of illusions and relics, but she wasn't able to confirm anything concrete about the Prism's current location."

Marcus stepped closer, his boots tapping loudly against the marble. "So, you claim." His eyes flicked toward Caleb. "Did you, by chance, fail to mention how thorough or frequent these calls might have been, Mr. Blackwood?"

Caleb's jaw tensed. He finally met Lila's eyes, and she read the regret there. She realized he had likely reported her contact with Evelyn because the Council demanded it, not necessarily because he wanted to betray her confidence. Yet the revelation stung all the same. Her pulse thrummed with anger. She had shared those personal details with him thinking he would keep her grandmother out of the Council's crosshairs, at least for a while.

Lila tried to steady her voice. "Yes, I have contacted her. I am not concealing that. She is family. I would appreciate the courtesy of deciding how much I share about my personal calls." Her protest sounded downright sullen in the echoing chamber.

A stern older warlock on the left side gave a pointed cough. "We do not question your right to speak with family, Miss Matthews, but Council novices must remain fully transparent about any outside magical influences. You understand the stakes here, do you not?"

She swallowed against the surge of resentment. "I do understand. If my grandmother had something that helps with illusions or the Prism, I would share it for the good of the city. I have not withheld crucial knowledge. Her insights are simply... broad references to our lineage."

Marcus studied her with a cool, assessing gaze. "See that you maintain that cooperation. Your grandmother's knowledge of older wards may be vital. We do not want her—nor anyone else—to compromise official channels."

Lila clenched her fists at her sides, nails biting into her palms. She despised how they implied she might sabotage them if she withheld secrets. As though she could be tricked or swayed. A heavy silence settled, broken only by the faint flicker of the mage-lights overhead.

Marcus exhaled, then folded his arms. "The Council thus officially endorses your advanced training. Caleb Blackwood, you will intensify Miss Matthews's regimen—more illusions, more practice controlling surges. We cannot afford a novice with unpredictable magic in the city right now. If she is to be an asset, she must be prepared to face illusions head-on."

A wave of conflicting emotions coursed through Lila: relief that she was not sidelined, frustration at their condescension, and a seething anger that they had dragged her grandmother into official suspicion. She felt singled out, each elder's stare making her want to crawl out of her own skin.

One by one, the Council members gathered their parchments or notes. Some gave polite nods toward Lila, but she noticed the way they whispered among themselves—not quite trusting her. She wanted to stand firm, to insist her lineage did not make her a danger. The sense of being tested in every breath made her chest tighten.

Before she could release that tension, Marcus fixed his gaze on her once more. "We will expect regular reports of your progress, Miss Matthews. Any deviation, any unexpected surge, you are to notify us immediately."

She inclined her head, unable to keep the spark of resentment from creeping into her eyes. "Fine." The single word balanced between acceptance and challenge.

"Dismissed," Marcus said curtly.

Lila forced herself to turn on her heel, wishing her pulse would settle. She had barely taken two steps toward the ornate double doors when the elder in crimson robes called out, "Caleb, remain here for a moment. We have additional questions about your methodology."

Lila paused, glancing over her shoulder. Caleb met her gaze, his expression weighted by concern, but he nodded once, signaling she should go. The unmistakable tension in his posture told her he did not relish staying behind. A swirl of uneasy guilt flashed in her chest as she realized how precarious his position was. He was defending her daily in front of these intimidating elders.

Still, she felt a pang of betrayal that he had reported her private call with Evelyn. Maybe it was not betrayal—maybe it was duty—but the sting left a bitter taste in her mouth. She pressed her lips together, flicking her gaze down. The Council had forced him to share. The pang lingered, though, and she let that frustration simmer unspoken.

She slipped out the double doors into the corridor outside. Steam from the bright sconces along the walls created small halos of light, leaving pockets of shadow between them. Her breathing was too quick, echoing in her ears. She forced herself to take one steadying inhale, then paused. She looked back just in time to see Caleb, still near the half-circle of elders, throw her a final lingering glance. Beneath the seriousness in his eyes, she spotted genuine concern.

CHAPTER

NINETEEN

Lila paused atop the smooth marble steps just outside the Council's main briefing chamber, her pulse skipping in uneasy rhythm. The gleaming corridors around her echoed with low voices and shuffling footsteps, all charged with an anxious tension that made the very air feel denser.

Marcus Steele, severe and unreadable as ever, emerged from one of the side rooms and beckoned softly to Caleb. A slight scuff of boots on polished marble told Lila that Caleb was approaching from her left. She glanced over her shoulder and saw him step forward, shoulders tense beneath a fitted black coat. He inclined his head in a brief acknowledgment of Marcus, though the faint pinch between his brows betrayed his concern. Lila felt the tug of curiosity in her chest. Marcus had not summoned her name, which meant she was not officially included in this conversation, but she had a feeling that it concerned her all the same.

Curiosity prickled along the back of her neck. She needed to hear what was happening, but the Council was known to guard sensitive information with illusions and wards. If they decided to seal the corridor, she would have no right to intrude. Yet the entire hallway felt too wide for secrecy, and the fact that Marcus was not leading Caleb into a private chamber told her this might be less about hush-hush conspiracies and more about an urgent update that had to be shared now.

Lila hovered a respectful distance away. Her gaze settled on Marcus's face, noting the sharp lines of tension at his temple. She had come to recognize that look. It spoke of important intelligence, something that changed stakes for everyone in the Council's orbit. She edged closer and concentrated until she could hear the low cadence of his voice.

"We found a warding cloth," Marcus said, not bothering with a typical greeting. "It was recovered from a break-in at our Midtown outpost."

Caleb's eyes narrowed. "What kind of break-in?"

"A forced entry," Marcus answered in a clipped tone. "Minor relics were taken, though the thieves did not breach the deeper wards. The cloth bears a crest, one our watchers identified as belonging to the Shell family."

Beside a tall marble pillar, Lila tensed at the unfamiliar name. Her curiosity flared again, and she dared to shift one step closer. She saw Caleb's reaction clearly: his lips parted in shock, and for an instant, a haunted look darkened his gaze. He almost dropped the small leather-bound notebook in his hand.

"Sebastian," Caleb said quietly, as though speaking the name caused him physical pain.

Marcus nodded. "I suspect he is the one behind it. We do not have absolute proof he led the raid himself, but it is enough to confirm our suspicions. The same warlock the Council has feared might be tied to the Prism's theft. It is indeed Sebastian Shell."

Painted orbs of mage-light floating near the ceiling cast shifting patches of brightness over Caleb's face. He looked as though someone had yanked the ground from beneath him. Lila's heart pounded as she witnessed the depth of upset passing through his features. She tried recalling all the times Caleb had mentioned a past friendship with a man named Sebastian who had been like a brother to him but they had parted badly. He had always spoken in vague terms about "a lost friend."

Marcus cleared his throat before continuing. "We located the cloth near the largest vault door at the outpost. The wards were faulty, almost like they had been tampered with from within, but we are not certain. A few relics, mostly lesser items, are gone. However, the infiltration alone is worrying enough." He paused, then softened his voice. "The elder watchers now think Sebastian Shell is truly at the center of these illusions. This ties him to the Prism's disappearance, but also to the smaller sabotage plaguing our outposts."

Caleb closed his eyes, expression grim. "He was never a small-time threat. If he set his mind to it, he could infiltrate nearly any ward. He always had a talent for illusions and manipulation. I just... did not expect him to go this far."

At that last phrase, Lila's chest tightened. She recalled how hesitant Caleb had been to discuss the person responsible for the Nexus Prism theft. He had seemed both frustrated and guilty, a potent mixture that hinted at personal involvement. Now she realized that the missing puzzle piece was Sebastian Shell, someone who had once been a brother-in-arms to Caleb. A cold swirl of dread rippled through her, knowing that if illusions were indeed intensifying in the city, they might have the cunning mind of Sebastian behind them.

Marcus exhaled and placed a hand on Caleb's arm, an unusually gentle gesture for the stoic leader. His voice dropped to a near murmur. "I know you blame yourself for not intercepting him sooner. I know he was your friend. The Council has its share of regrets, too. But that is in the past. This threat is bigger than guilt."

Caleb looked up, and his voice grew tight with emotion. "I should have seen it, Marcus. Years ago, I noticed how fixated Sebastian was on illusions that crossed ethical lines, but I chalked it up to his ambition. I wanted to believe he would never turn against the Council in such a brutal fashion. By the time I realized, it was too late."

For a moment, nobody spoke. The corridor beyond them felt still, as though the normal hustle of witches and warlocks had yielded out of respect for the conversation. Somewhere down the hall, an acolyte cleared his throat and moved away, sensing that he should give a wide berth to the discussion.

Slowly, Lila inhaled and let the air fill her lungs. Her heart thundered. If Sebastian was behind the illusions in the city, then the infiltration at her apartment—the ominous note, the footprints bypassing wards—could be only the tip of a much deeper network of manipulations. She thought she had begun to grasp the danger. Yet there was a sense of finality creeping in as she realized how personally Caleb felt this betrayal.

Marcus placed his hand on Caleb's shoulder again in a show of camaraderie. "This is not about blame. It is about stopping him. Given this new evidence, I want you to intensify your vigilance. Keep your eyes open on all lines of communication and check for illusions wherever they might worm through. We cannot afford another infiltration, especially not by someone with Sebastian's talent in misdirection."

Caleb swallowed hard and nodded. "Understood."

Marcus hitched in a slow breath, his gaze sliding from Caleb to the gorgeous but forbidding corridor around them. "Ensure that novice Matthews maintains her training at a faster pace, too. She has demonstrated strong magical potential, and we need every advantage if Sebastian tries to target her. We suspect he might. The Matthews heritage is valuable, and if rumors of a missing relic or amulet in her family line hold any truth, then it is all the more reason to keep her prepared."

Lila found her cheeks heating. A swirl of emotion emerged: relief that the Council saw her as an asset, nervousness at the mention of her family's relic, and a pinch of embarrassment that they spoke about her in a public hall. Some days, she felt as though the entire Council watched her every move. She managed to step forward, clearing her throat just enough so they would notice her. With an awkward half-wave, she approached.

Marcus turned, seeming unsurprised by her presence. The corners of his mouth dipped in a solemn frown. "Miss Matthews. You heard enough?"

"Just enough," Lila answered, letting her gaze flick to Caleb. She saw the sorrow etched in his eyes, and her pulse gave a sympathetic stutter. "Is it true, then? The infiltration in Midtown is connected to the same warlock who stole the Prism?"

Marcus confirmed it with a single nod. "Everything points to Sebastian Shell."

Lila parted her lips, uncertain what to say. She glanced at Caleb, who seemed to be struggling to compose his thoughts. She stepped closer to him, heart pounding with concern. "I'm sorry," she whispered, hoping the sincerity of her words could break through the shield of guilt radiating from him.

He gave her a tense smile. "Thank you. We always feared the thief might be Sebastian, but seeing tangible proof dredges up old regrets." His voice roughened. "We trained together. He was brilliant, charismatic, always pushing boundaries. It never occurred to me that those boundaries would crumble into a betrayal like this."

She hesitated, wanting to do something to ease the burden in his eyes. Instead, she extended her hand and rested it lightly on his forearm. It was a simple touch, but he seemed to draw steadiness from it. A faint, fleeting warmth flared where her fingers connected with his coat sleeve.

Marcus took notice of the gesture. His intense stare flicked between them, but he did not comment on it. Instead, he gave a measured nod. "I will leave the teaching to you, Caleb, at least for the immediate future. Miss Matthews, I advise you to keep your wards strong and your senses sharper. If Sebastian begins targeting novices with known potential, he may attempt illusions that break your guard."

"Understood." She tried not to shiver at the possibility. The thought of illusions so refined they could slip past her newly learned wards made her stomach twist.

Clearing his throat, Marcus turned his focus back to Caleb. "Continue intensifying her training. Push beyond the basics if you must. Once you finish that, I want you to conduct an additional inspection of the wards around our smaller outposts, especially the one near East 43rd. That site is not as secure as Midtown or the main Council facility, and I fear Sebastian could strike again."

TWENTY

Lila hugged her thin jacket tighter as she followed Caleb down the damp steps leading into the old subway tunnel. A stale draft greeted them, carrying the smell of rust, mildew, and something she could only describe as restless shadows. Each footfall echoed farther than it should have, as though the passage were inhaling their presence. She tried not to think about the rats or roaches that might nest here. Instead, she focused on the wards Caleb was quietly raising, his voice low and sure as he spoke a few quiet phrases that slipped like threads of magic through the air.

He moved with practiced ease along the tunnel's entrance, pressing his palm lightly to various chunks of broken concrete and chipped tile. Wherever his fingertips met the wall, a gentle glimmer of silver flared, then faded as if consumed by the darkness. Lila watched, her heart pounding fast. She marveled at how deceptive his calm manner could be. Despite the tense circumstances, he always seemed to contain everything in a single measured breath.

When he stepped back, he gave a small nod. "That should keep anyone outside from noticing stray sparks," he murmured in his usual even tone. "We can train without drawing curious mortals."

She inhaled, trying to quell the rising nerves in her chest. She'd had juggled her entire week—swapping shifts at the café, telling half-truths to Maya about a "class commitment after hours"—just to make time for this. Her next shift hovered in the back of her mind, reminding her that she needed to be up early tomorrow and present some semblance of normal. But right now, normal was a distant concept, lost in the abandoned tunnel.

"I can't say I love the ambiance," she said, forcing a wry grin. "It's like we stepped into a black-and-white horror flick."

Caleb's mouth curved in a half-smile. "It isn't pretty, but it's secluded enough. Besides, the flickering lights overhead will help you practice focusing under less-than-ideal conditions."

She glanced upward where battered fluorescent bulbs dangled from metal cords. They sputtered in rhythmic bursts, casting uncertain shadows across the dripping walls. The entire place felt like the set of a ghost story. She reminded herself that she was here for a reason. The few illusions she had managed over the last few days still felt dangerously raw, and the importance of controlling them was paramount. She would do whatever it took.

"All right," she said, shutting her eyes for a brief moment. "Let's do this."

He guided her a dozen steps deeper. The ambient gloom expanded, broken only by the occasional flicker of a stubborn bulb overhead. She tried to ignore the slight tremor in her fingertips. Magic simmered under her skin, eager and impatient.

"You're going to create a barrier," Caleb explained. "This time, I want you to regulate it with your breathing rather than relying on the immediate surge you feel."

She gave a tight nod. "A real barrier or an illusion?"

"An actual ward shield. The illusions come later. First, we strengthen your stamina so you don't get drained halfway through a real fight." His firm tone lacked condescension. If anything, she sensed pride woven into his instruction. But it also carried the faint shadows of worry.

She braced her feet on the slick ground, ignoring the cold that soaked through the thin material of her sneakers. Closing her eyes, she exhaled long and slow. A gentle warmth rose in her core. She'd learned to summon that feeling by visualizing some internal flame. Though she was no expert, she had begun to sense the difference between a frantic rush of magic and a carefully harnessed current.

"Good," Caleb said softly. "Now feel the air around you. Imagine weaving your energy outward until it forms a shell."

Her heart hammered. She released her breath, picturing a transparent dome expanding from her center. Slowly, a wavering film of greenish light shimmered around her. She struggled to maintain its shape, pressing the boundary outward until it was large enough to encircle her body. At first, it flickered along the edges like a candle about to snuff out. She clenched her teeth, pushing more magic into it.

A bead of sweat trickled down her temple. The flicker stabilized, finally rounding into a full protective barrier that enveloped her like a sphere. She hazarded a peek, marveling at the faint lines of luminescent threads woven in the gloom.

"Impressive," Caleb said, stepping carefully around her. "Now hold it steady, even if I do this."

He raised a hand and sent a tiny spark—no bigger than a sparkler flash—directly at her shield. The impact made the barrier quiver. Lila felt a pull in her gut. She inhaled, willing the ward to stand firm. Crackling energy danced along the outside of her dome before dispersing into the moist air.

She allowed herself a small grin. "I did it."

"You did." He nodded once. "Now keep holding and add another layer beneath it. Could you try conjuring an additional ward inside the first one? The second layer should remain separate but reinforcing."

Another push of magic. Her arms trembled, but she managed to form a second, thinner shield that pulsed like a transparent shell just a few inches from the first barrier. The strain doubled. Sweat dripped down her back, and she felt her breath turn ragged. She forced herself to keep going. Caleb's gaze stayed locked on her, measuring every shift in the energy.

When she started to falter, her vision speckled with dancing black spots. She let out a ragged exhale and lowered her arms. The wards collapsed in a flash of green sparks that scattered across the dark tunnel.

"Son of a—" she grumbled, cursing as the magic fizzled. The luminous residue marred the air for a few seconds before fading. She wiped the back of her hand across her forehead. "I almost had it."

"You pushed a bit too hard." Caleb offered his hand. She leaned on his support for a moment, catching her breath. "For stamina, steady perseverance is more important than intensity."

She let his words settle, then nodded. "I'll try again."

They repeated the exercise three or four times, each attempt taxing her more than the last. Lila's shoulders ached and her lungs burned, but she refused to give up. On the final round, she conjured her shield, reinforced it, and even withstood three flicks of Caleb's conjured sparks without total collapse. By the end, her head swam. She released the ward with a sigh, arms trembling as if she had done hours of real physical labor.

Caleb's voice was gentle. "That's enough wards for now." He passed her a metal canteen from his jacket pocket. She drank greedily, the cool water soothing her parched throat. "When you practice alone, remember your breath is the anchor. Don't overreach too soon."

"Right," she rasped. "Breathing. Got it." Another drop of sweat trickled between her shoulder blades.

They moved to the next segment of training. He pivoted, scanning the far end of the tunnel. The flickering fluorescent lights barely reached that far, leaving large swaths in murky darkness. With a calm motion, he raised his right hand and conjured the faint outline of a phantom shape. It appeared a few yards away, wreathed in drifting shadows. Lila's chest constricted at the sight. He'd shown illusions before, but rarely did one set her nerves ablaze so abruptly. This particular phantom shape flickered with dully glowing eyes and elongated, spectral edges that seemed to shimmer between existence and void.

"As you know," Caleb said, his voice echoing faintly in the gloom, "Sebastian excels at illusions. Sometimes they'll appear real enough to attack you. They can vanish when you strike, or they can twist your sense of direction, so you become lost in your own mind."

Something in her stomach clenched. She recalled how easily illusions had rattled her before—she would see them in the corner of her eye, or sense them creeping along walls. She remembered how powerless she had felt. But now she was learning, strengthening. She straightened her spine.

"I'm ready," she said softly, squaring her shoulders. "Show me."

The phantom drifted closer. She caught her breath when it swirled around a broken pillar, momentarily taking the shape of a gaunt figure with outstretched arms. Even though she knew it was Caleb conjuring it, her heartbeat thundered as if facing a genuine threat.

"Try your ward," he instructed. "Stay calm. Don't let your fear feed the illusion."

She opened her palms, calling on that well of magic

once again. Her ward shimmered to life, a protective barrier that surrounded her torso. The phantom lunged with a sluggish, half-gliding motion. She pressed her legs into the ground, focusing on the solidity of her stance. The illusion slammed the outer edge of the ward with a thrum of energy, and for a brief moment, she wavered. She clenched her jaw and exhaled through her nose, keeping the ward intact.

Caleb dispelled the phantom with a flip of his wrist, leaving the tunnel in silence once more. He gave her a level look, then stepped nearer. "How does it feel?"

She felt a swirl of adrenaline in her belly. "Terrifying," she admitted, letting out a shaky laugh. "But at least I'm not screaming or flailing."

"You handled that well."

"Thanks, mentor," she teased lightly, trying to hide how unsteady she still felt inside. "So, illusions can physically interact sometimes?"

He nodded. "If the caster invests enough power, illusions stop being entirely ephemeral and can cause real injury. Sebastian's illusions are known to be lethal under the right circumstances. Especially if someone already feels fear or doubt."

She clenched her fists, absorbing his warning. "He uses that fear to strengthen them?"

"Yes, precisely. You have to remember that illusions feed on your mind as much as they harness external energy."

They ran through six or seven more illusions. Each time, she forced her ward up, steadied it, and tried not to jump when the illusions clawed at the barrier. She lasted longer with each attempt, ignoring the dull ache in her arms. Once, she faltered, and the phantom's arm grazed her shoulder with a cold tingle that shot goosebumps down her entire body. She hissed, throwing out a final burst of magic that scattered the illusion into wisps of curling smoke. Caleb watched, silent but alert, always ready to intervene if things went sideways.

When he finally lowered his hand to signify the end of the exercise, Lila's forearms practically quivered from the extended effort. The entire tunnel swam in and out of focus, and she sagged against a nearby patch of wall. Past experiences had taught her the beginnings of magical fatigue. Still, her pulse raced with satisfaction. She had begun to see real progress—no illusions had completely undone her this time.

Caleb eyed her carefully. He was sweaty too, his dark hair clinging to his forehead. She found herself mesmerized by the faint rise and fall of his chest beneath his fitted jacket. A faint flush of pride lit his features when their eyes met. He looked like he wanted to say something, but paused.

"How are you feeling?" he asked, stepping closer.

She opened her mouth to say she was fine, but the words got stuck. Her heart thumped. The closeness of him, combined with the adrenaline still in her veins, sent a dizzy rush over her. Her gaze lingered on the curve of his mouth.

The air between them felt different tonight—charged, not just from the magic or sweaty exertion but from something deeper that had been quietly building for weeks. She thought about how he had guided her, sometimes with excruciating gentleness that belied his serious demeanor. She remembered the many times he had shielded her from danger and how she had grown to trust him, leaning on him more than she had ever leaned on anyone else.

She swallowed hard and managed, "Exhausted, mostly."

His slight grin said he understood the unspoken layers behind her answer. Without warning, he slipped an arm around her shoulders in a brief, comforting gesture. The contact made her skin tingle. She was still panting, so standing still in his arms felt almost surreal. She caught a whiff of soap and faint cologne, mixed with the tang of sweat. It flustered her more than she cared to admit.

"Excellent work," he said softly. "You've come so far."

His words dripped with warmth. She was about to mumble a shy thanks when she realized how strong his arm felt around her, how the heat of his body made the cold of the tunnel vanish. Her heart pounded in her ears. The rest of the tunnel seemed to fade from her senses. Feeling brave or reckless—maybe both—she rested her hand tentatively on his chest. A burning awareness pulsed between them, unsaid but undeniably growing.

Caleb's breath caught. Their eyes locked, and she saw an echo of her own conflicted longing. For a moment, it felt like they might close the distance. She swayed closer, caught up in the intensity reflected in his gaze. She was suddenly sure they would kiss.

He hesitated, his hand still on her shoulder. Then his

expression twisted in an apologetic mix of regret and self-control. Slowly, he let his arm drop. The moment snapped like a taut string releasing under tension.

"I'm sorry," he said, stepping back, voice low enough to almost vanish under the distant hum of the failing fluo-rescents. "I... We can't. You're my student. My responsi-bility is to train you properly."

TWENTY-ONE

Late-afternoon sunshine glinted through The Daily Grind's glass storefront, strobing across the counter where Lila Matthews fumbled a fresh stack of paper cups. She was tired after several opening shifts in a row, having squeezed in magical training whenever she could, yet she forced a smile at each curious customer who approached the register. Sharp scents of espresso and caramelized sugar coated the air. The place was lively today, though she sensed something uneasy threading through the usual bustle, as though even the mundane customers could sense an undercurrent of tension.

"Lila, table four wants a refill," Maya called, balancing a tray of pastries with one hand. She caught Lila's eye and mouthed, "You good?" with a concerned tilt of her head.

Lila nodded, though she suspected Maya saw right through the forced brightness in her grin. She turned to the espresso machine, fiddling with the steam wand as she measured out ground beans. Her mind drifted against her will, recalling illusions she had barely warded off at home the week before, and the ominous sense that Sebastian's influence was stretching into every corner of the city. Not that she could chat about it with half a dozen impatient patrons in line. She slid a mocha latte across to a harried mother, then turned to greet the next arrival.

The next customer was a stranger who moved with slow, almost measured steps. He appeared to be in his late twenties, with features partially hidden beneath a charcoal-gray fedora. Thick-lensed glasses concealed much of his eyes, but Lila noticed he didn't actually look at her. Instead, he studied the café's scuffed floor, as if searching for something invisible at his feet. His long coat brushed the tile with each step.

"What can I get for you today?" Lila asked, voice steady but polite. The man hesitated, then recited an order that made her eyebrows rise in surprise.

"I'll take a triple-shot cappuccino," he began, quietly. "Use coconut milk. Add two pumps of vanilla, but half-sweet; top it with a spin of cinnamon, then whipped foam, three drizzles of caramel around the inside of the cup, and... a dusting of cocoa on the final layer."

His words fell into an almost rhythmic pattern. Lila blinked, trying to commit the complicated sequence to memory. On any other day, she might have joked about how he was missing the kitchen sink, but something in his deliberate tone made her uneasy. She realized her shoulders had gone stiff. She tapped the order into the register, reading it back to him to verify she had it right. He nodded, still avoiding her gaze as he slid crinkled bills across the counter.

"Sure thing," she murmured, stepping over to the espresso station. Her mind buzzed with speculation. Most complicated orders came with a dash of excitement or at least an explanation about preferences. This guy offered nothing. She tried to shake off her suspicions. It was a coffee shop, after all, and unique requests happened daily. But she picked up a strange tension that set every hair on her neck standing.

She carefully pulled three tight shots of espresso. The hiss of steamed coconut milk filled the air while she measured the vanilla pumps. Beside her, Maya shot her a sympathetic grin. Lila layered the foam and drizzled the caramel in neat little circles, finishing with a fine dusting of cocoa. She placed a sleeve around the to-go cup, checked the label, and turned to deliver it.

The man had retreated to a corner table, where he sat alone, his gaze fixed on the condensation ring left by a previous customer's drink. She approached slowly, her heartbeat thudding in her ears. The café's cheery chatter became muffled, as if her own anxiety tuned out the surrounding noise. She set the drink on the table.

"Triple-shot cappuccino with coconut milk and... the rest," she said, forcing a polite laugh, though it faltered when he finally lifted his head.

"Thank you," he said in a low murmur. His eyes remained obscured by the tinted glasses, even indoors. Before Lila could respond, he fumbled in his coat pocket. A flicker of something small brushed her fingers under the table's edge—an envelope, folded thin as a slip of paper. He pressed it into her hand so discreetly she almost doubted it happened. Then, he took the cup and strode out.

She stood there, shock prickling through her limbs. In a few seconds, the door's bell jangled, and the stranger disappeared onto the busy street. No one else seemed to notice her confusion. Customers continued sipping their lattes, flipping through their phones, or debating what pastries looked best in the glass display. Clutching the thin envelope, she quickly slipped it into the pocket of her apron.

She retreated to a corner behind the display of sweeteners, scanning the café to ensure no one watched. Her hands trembled as she unfolded the note. In slanted handwriting, it read:

Fortune and a better life awaits you with no rules and no one watching your every move. Someone will be in touch soon.

Her pulse jumped. She read the message a second time, her mouth going dry. Something about the phrasing hinted at dark promises—an invitation to break from the Council's structured rules. Maybe an effort to recruit her into a rogue circle of witches who wanted more freedom. Or, more likely, a coded whisper that Sebastian Shell's network had begun to entangle novices in tall tales of liberation. Could it be a trap? Every line bristled with possibility.

"Lila?" Maya sidled up, brow furrowed. "You look pale. Are you okay? Did that guy say something weird?"

Lila forced a smile and stuffed the note back into the apron pocket. "Nothing. He just... left in a hurry," she managed. For a split second, she considered showing Maya, but the memory of Council hush orders squeezed her chest. Maya already knew some of the truth, but the Council still demanded caution in how much they disclosed. She tried to steady her nerves, took a deep breath, and got back to work, though the note's words lodged in her mind.

All day, she remained on autopilot, preparing cappuccinos and croissants without fully tasting or smelling anything. By closing time, her thoughts were an anxious swirl of speculation. Customers trickled out, and Maya locked the door with a final wave. Lila cleaned the machines and wiped down tables, the usual ritual that kept her hands busy, but her heart had not slowed its frenetic pace.

Eventually, she finished the last chore and hurried out into the dusk air. The sky was a wash of purples and oranges fading into the night, and the hum of city traffic droned in her ears as she tucked the note into her jacket pocket. She had texted Caleb earlier, asking him to meet at her apartment. He had responded with a thumbs-up emoji—his subtle nod that he would come as soon as the Council briefing ended.

When Lila pushed into her apartment, she was relieved to find him already there, jacket slung over a chair and an orb-light flickering in the corner to keep illusions at bay. He rose from the couch the moment she closed the door.

"You're definitely unsettled," Caleb said, voice laced with concern. "What happened?"

She tossed her keys onto a side table. "A customer... or someone who was definitely not just a normal customer, came in. Left me this." She fumbled in her jacket pocket and handed him the folded paper.

His eyes narrowed as he read it. She watched fury spark in the set of his jaw, though he kept his voice calm. "'Fortune and a better life awaits you with no rules'... That's a clear reference to Sebastian's recruitment lines. He's stirring up trouble among witches who resent the Council. I've heard rumors that his allies promise novices total freedom from oversight."

Her stomach twisted at the mention of Sebastian. She hated the way that name tightened her chest. "So, you think it's him?"

Caleb exhaled harshly. "It has his stink all over it. Consider the illusions we've seen creeping across the city. He's fanning flames of rebellion, persuading witches—especially new ones—that they can practice however they want, no Council, no wards, no restrictions about mortal secrecy."

A wave of anger rippled through her. She recalled how illusions had nearly cost her sanity that week. The Council wasn't perfect, but life without any protective structure sounded even more dangerous. "Should we go to Marcus? The Council needs to know Sebastian's people are making direct contact with novices."

Caleb clenched the note in his fist and let out a tense growl. "Normally, yes. But right now, rumors are flying everywhere, and we don't have solid proof. A single note could be brushed off as a hoax or a misguided attempt by some rebellious witch, especially if the Council's leadership is already swamped with illusions in half the boroughs."

She nodded, though the tension in her shoulders didn't ease. "It feels like every day, he's pushing deeper into the city's underbelly. There's a reason he's recruiting novices. He probably hopes that the less experienced among us will follow him out of desperation."

Caleb rubbed a hand over his face. He looked exhausted, faint circles under his eyes betraying several sleepless nights. She wondered if guilt also weighed on him—he never quite shook the memories of Sebastian's early illusions. "We'll keep the note. Maybe we can cross-reference the handwriting with something in the Council's infiltration files. Do you remember anything else about that man who delivered it?"

Her mind replayed the scene. "He wore tinted glasses inside, wouldn't meet my eye, and spoke so quietly you could miss it. The coffee order was unbelievably elaborate. Triple-shot, coconut milk, half-sweet vanilla, cinnamon, caramel... everything. Like he wanted me not to notice the real reason he was there." She pressed her lips tight. "I got a weird vibe. I'm almost certain he wasn't a typical mortal."

Caleb's eyes flickered with recognition. "He might be a messenger. Sebastian used to recruit random warlocks or witches adept enough to pass illusions unsuspected. That man could be an underling delivering invitations or threats." He breathed out a choice curse, his brows drawing together.

Lila stepped closer, feeling his frustration like a static charge in the room. "We can quietly alert Marcus. Maybe not a full alarm but at least let him know recruitment is happening. If we wait too long, Sebastian's network could grow bigger. And we have no idea how widespread these illusions are right now."

Caleb's jaw worked as if he weighed the best course of action. "I promise we'll loop in Marcus soon," he said. "But you haven't seen the Council's climate these last couple of days. They're dealing with break-ins at magical supply shops across the city—small robberies that might be linked to Sebastian's illusions. There's a risk that if we flood them with partial intel, they'll dismiss it as rumor. Or they'll overreact and send watchers to clamp down on novices en masse, which might push more witches into Sebastian's arms."

A low ache spread behind Lila's eyes. She felt caught in a labyrinth of illusions she couldn't see, guided by a Council that was too overwhelmed to take decisive steps. "So, what do we do? We can't just ignore it."

Caleb let out a grim sigh. "We don't ignore it. We keep an eye out for anyone else who might hand you a similar note. We watch for illusions in the café or near your apartment. We gather enough evidence to show the Council that this is a real threat, not just rumors in the underground." He glanced at her with a mix of anger and apology. "I'm not happy that the best plan is to wait, either.

But we need actual proof of Sebastian's infiltration. The note alone isn't enough."

She straightened, crossing her arms. "I guess you're right. Everyone's so on edge. We have illusions springing up left and right, magical supply shops being raided, novices feeling abandoned by old Council politics... It's all swirling into chaos."

He folded the note and handed it back to her. "Hold onto that. I'll reach out to a few contacts—guardians I trust who aren't drowning in the Council's red tape. Maybe they've heard stories about novices being lured with promises of 'no rules' or loads of freedom to cast illusions without risk."

For a moment, she said nothing, her mind returning to the memory of the stranger's soft voice. This was no random invitation. They must have known who she was, or at least guessed she was a rising witch. A chill settled over her skin. The city felt more claustrophobic than ever.

Caleb hid a faint shudder as if he sensed the same. "Sebastian is capitalizing on fear," he muttered. "He'll drive wedges between novices and the Council, feeding them pretty lies of power. If these illusions keep ramping up, we'll see novices either panic or jump to his cause."

Lila swallowed hard. She pictured unsuspecting students, wide-eyed at the lure of magic with no oversight. "What about the break-ins you mentioned? Are they related to relics or potions or something else?"

"From what I heard, some local magical shops—like small apothecaries or runic supply places—have reported missing crystals, stolen potions, even partial tomes that vanished from behind locked cases. Whoever's doing it is either unbelievably skilled in illusions or aided by inside knowledge." His voice turned sharper. "We can guess who has that kind of skill."

Her heart pounded. The puzzle pieces formed a grim picture: Sebastian's agents quietly collecting supplies, novices drawn in by the promise of unrestrained magic, illusions weaving fear across the city. The lines between rumor and fact blurred. She could already imagine novices vanishing or betraying Council watchers to join him.

"Then we stay alert," she said, trying to sound braver than she felt. She closed the distance and placed a hand on Caleb's arm, finding a measure of comfort in the warmth of his presence. "We can't let him isolate novices. There's already enough confusion."

He covered her hand with his own. "Agreed. We'll track down every thread we can. But until we have more than a cryptic note to show Marcus, we wait. We gather. Then we strike."

She nodded, though her chest remained tight. Caleb's resolve steeled her for a moment. The city might be caught in illusions, but standing side by side, she felt far less alone.

She stepped away, tucking the folded paper into one of her kitchen drawers. "I'm holding you to that. The moment we see something else suspicious, we talk to Marcus."

"Absolutely," he replied with a final, frustrated exhale. The tension in the small living room thickened, but at least they had each other in this uncertain fight. Settling onto her couch, she tried to will her nerves to calm. She refused to let Sebastian's cryptic invitations break her focus—even if they rattled her more than she cared to admit.

Outside, the evening shadows gathered across the streetlamps, and horns honked in the distance. Somewhere out there, illusions whispered in hidden corners. And that note's promise lingered like poison in her thoughts: a better life, no rules, no watchers. She knew enough by now to recognize the lie. The only question was how many witches would believe it before the Council realized just how tight Sebastian's grip on the underworld had grown.

CHAPTER

TWENTY-TWO

Lila's breath caught in her throat as she lifted her gaze to the towering doors of the Council's assembly hall. Echoing footsteps from passing guards merged with the muffled rumble of conversation inside. She stood on the smooth marble landing with Caleb at her side, the two of them summoned amid a new wave of unrest swirling through the city's magical underbelly. She didn't fully know what she might find beyond those doors, but her heart thudded from a mix of apprehension and the lingering memory of illusions that had rattled the wards in Midtown.

Caleb pressed his palm lightly against her lower back, guiding her forward. She noticed how tense his posture was, despite his outward composure. The Council's messages had sounded urgent, urging them to attend a crisis briefing with no delay. She swallowed and pushed through the doorway, stepping into a tall, circular chamber ringed with long tapestries of constellations—a tangible reminder of how mystical tradition overshadowed modern New York.

The high windows cast beams of daylight across the polished floor, illuminating a semicircle of guardians waiting to deliver their statements. Marcus Steele, standing near the center, beckoned them both closer. He wore an expression that could only be described as grim. The tension crackling off him reminded Lila of a taut wire, ready to snap at the slightest vibration.

"Thank you for coming," Marcus began. His voice carried an edge that no one in the hall could miss.

Lila and Caleb moved to the center of the floor, where other Council guardians stood in hushed clusters. An uneasy quiet followed, each set of eyes raking over Lila's face as if they expected her to produce illusions herself. She kept her chin high, determined not to reveal the knots roiling in her stomach.

One woman with silver-streaked hair and a cloak embroidered with protective runes spoke next. "The illusions are becoming blatant," she said. "We have scattered reports from nearly every borough. Just earlier this morning, a swirl of ghostly shapes danced through Union Square. People assumed it was an eccentric art performance."

Another guardian, a tall man with a clipped beard, added, "Subway wards are being tampered with by unknown hands. Civilians are stepping onto trains and swearing they see entire cars vanish, replaced by flickering images of dancers or bizarre creatures. Most dismiss it as a glitch or some elaborate set of stunts, but we know better.

The illusions are too well-crafted. They show a polished mastery that can't be random." He looked gravely at Lila, though not accusingly.

She nodded, her throat still tight. The images he described reminded her of illusions she had barely fended off in a deserted tunnel weeks ago. Sebastian's cunning had evidently advanced whether or not the Council was prepared.

An older guardian with a hawk-like stare caught Lila's attention next. "Our preliminary sweeps dispelled many illusions before they caused real panic, but this is a pattern, not a coincidence. We suspect Sebastian Shell's involvement, of course. The question is how he's orchestrating it on such a large scale."

Caleb's voice cut in, calm yet resonating with tension. "We've seen illusions at the edges of the Council's wards. He seems to be testing for weaknesses. If we want to contain this, we'll need broader surveillance. We can't rely on random squads to spot illusions after the fact. It's time for a more organized watch."

Marcus leaned forward, arms crossed. "I appreciate your assessment, Caleb. But to deploy watchers in such an extensive way... that would risk too much exposure if we're not careful."

Lila felt a twist of frustration. Mortals who witnessed illusions were already chalking them up as viral stunts or new media experiences. She understood that the Council feared drawing attention to itself, but caution had a cost. "If illusions are ramping up so quickly," she ventured, voice somewhat tremulous, "wouldn't a strong, proactive approach be better than constantly cleaning up? Every-one's on edge."

The guardians were suddenly quiet. Lila felt a prickle of self-consciousness under their scrutiny. She was only recently inducted into the Council's official ranks, yet she kept speaking, spurred by the memory of illusions creeping across the café windows the other day. Fear had already reached her doorstep. Turning a blind eye wouldn't work forever.

Marcus inhaled slowly. "We face another problem as well." He gestured for a younger guardian near the back to step forward. The young man approached, clearing his throat nervously.

He spoke in a subdued voice. "Stray illusions are one thing. But we also have reason to believe someone inside the Council itself might be relaying information to Sebast-ian. Certain infiltration attempts from previous weeks suggest an inside hand. Our wards over crucial records were undone too systematically. That's not random sabotage."

A wave of tension rippled through the assembled guardians. Low murmurs erupted: confusion, anger, denial. Lila's pulse skipped. The Council had hinted at infiltration before, but hearing it stated openly made her stomach plunge. She glanced at Caleb and noticed his jaw tighten. The notion of someone feeding details to Sebas-tian brought old guilt flickering across his features. He'd told her that Sebastian had once been his friend. She suspected doubts plagued him whenever Sebastian's advantage came to light.

"We can't discount the possibility that Sebastian has an informant," the older guardian with the hawk-like stare confirmed grimly. "Reports leaked out suspiciously fast. He always seems two steps ahead whenever squads arrive to dispel illusions."

Marcus scanned the faces of each guardian. "The more we rely on broad Council operations, the more we risk tipping off the traitor—whoever they may be. That is why I hesitate to allocate large-scale resources."

Caleb's frustration was palpable. He bowed his head slightly, then spoke. "We need a middle ground. Sending a few watchers into scattered parts of the city won't suffice. The illusions are too widespread. But if we remain idle, illusions will provoke a bigger crisis, possibly forcing us into a full-scale reveal."

A man in a dark green cloak shifted on his feet, laying out a long, thin scroll. "We do have a handful of discrete squads at the ready. They're well-trained in illusions, prepared to intervene quickly before mortals can identify anything supernatural. That's how we've contained the damage so far—small, localized teams that can vanish at a moment's notice."

Whispers broke out again. Lila searched each guardian's face, trying to gauge how they felt about the risk of an internal traitor. Most eyes remained neutral, but a few glances flitted around, suspicious or guarded. No one wanted to accuse each other openly, but a simmering doubt hovered beneath the formalities.

Marcus exhaled. "We must do more. Yet we must also protect our strategic knowledge so we don't hand Sebastian a blueprint of any citywide defense. The Council has decided that, moving forward, illusions reported by the public will be tagged as potential Sebastian sightings. Only small squads—handpicked by me and a few advisers —will respond."

Lila caught the faint note of finality in that statement. She understood Marcus's logic, but it chafed. The entire city was seeing illusions pop up at street fairs and subway stations, and the Council's official stance was to answer with minimal squads. She clenched her fists at her sides. Whether people recognized illusions as real or not, confusion would spread. She wondered how many close calls it would take before fear turned into panic.

Another guardian, broad-shouldered and older than Marcus, stepped out of the semicircle. He cast Lila a long look. "Your role in this, Lila, is to remain vigilant. We know you've had close brushes with illusions before. Do not underestimate Sebastian's cunning. If he's riling up illusions in public venues, he might also target novices directly, especially those with a unique lineage."

Marcus nodded briskly. "We summoned the two of you here for one main reason: to ensure you remain fully aware of Sebastian's growing confidence. He toys with illusions in broad daylight and still manages to slip out of reach. He is dangerous, and anyone who crosses him unprepared could find themselves in a living nightmare of illusions."

A hush settled over the hall again. Lila felt the press of the Council's combined focus, as if they were a single entity that breathed tension and exhaled instructions.

Standing so near Caleb warmed her from within. She drew strength from his presence, from the gentleness that always underscored his unwavering discipline.

One last guardian raised a hand. She wore a series of crystal beads in her braided hair. "We must address one final matter. Rumors say illusions have surfaced around old wards beneath the subway lines. Some watchers have glimpsed apparitions that vanish the moment you look directly at them. Mortals see it as elaborate mischief, but if it escalates, we won't contain it easily."

After a brief nod from Marcus, she continued. "Let no one here forget that illusions can mislead entire groups in seconds. Sebastian might orchestrate a false lead to lure watchers into traps. And if a traitor within our walls feeds him deployment schedules, who knows how many illusions he can send to sabotage us."

That last statement ignited a fresh wave of anxious mutters. Accusations flitted from one side of the room to the other in hushed tones. Lila's chest constricted, hearing how real it all sounded. The possibility that the Council itself cradled a spy rattled her more than she wanted to admit.

Marcus cleared his throat sharply. "That is enough. We called you today so no illusions of ignorance remain. The threat grows, not recedes. Now, I want every guardian here to reflect on how best to proceed without letting vital information slip into the wrong hands." His gaze seemed to bore through them. "And if you discover anything that might indicate an inside leak, come directly to me. The last thing we need is distrust splintering our ranks."

Lila's shoulders tensed. The Council's structure already felt fragile, each new revelation of illusions or sabotage chipping away at unity. She could almost sense restless energy in the room, a pulsing note of suspicion that might flare into outright accusations at any moment. She hated it. She wished she could remain invisible, but her new place among them made that impossible.

Marcus exhaled slowly. "As for you, Caleb, we respect your request for additional resources. But for now, I'm instructing you to keep your circle small. We can't risk mapping out our entire approach if a traitor is feeding Sebastian data. Do your best to track illusions in key hotspots. Station watchers in subtle patterns. No large sweeps without explicit approval from me."

Caleb inclined his head. "Understood," he replied, though Lila sensed the tension knotting in his voice.

"Good," Marcus said, turning to the rest of the guardians. "You are dismissed until further notice. But remember this: Don't underestimate Sebastian's cunning. He could be behind any street spectacle, any flickering face in a subway reflection." His tone dropped to a near growl. "We must remain watchful."

Lila stood beside Caleb, discreetly trying to quell the swirl of worries rising in her mind. She recalled illusions on the sidewalk, illusions in graffiti-splashed tunnels—each instance had escalated so quickly that she was running out of space to breathe. Now, the Council's ultimatum forced her to accept that it all could get worse if Sebastian's infiltration was deeper than they guessed.

As the crowd thinned, the tension in the chamber still

hovered like a physical presence. Murmuring pairs of guardians peeled away, stepping into side corridors and smaller briefing rooms. The newly delivered warnings weighed heavily on every face Lila saw.

She glanced at the mosaic patterns on the floor, wondering how many centuries of magical negotiations had taken place in this hall, and whether any were as fraught with paranoia as today's. Before she could dwell too long on that thought, Marcus approached. He offered a curt nod, then motioned them away, effectively signaling that her and Caleb's presence in the official meeting was concluded.

Once dismissed, she and Caleb exchanged uneasy glances, their shoulders brushing as they moved across the marble foyer. They passed the tall pillars lining the exit, the hush magnifying the sound of their footsteps. Fragments of whispered conversation still reached them —guardians discussing traitors, illusions, and the unceasing riddle of Sebastian Shell.

The moment they were alone, Caleb pressed a hand to her arm, drawing her gently aside against a column. His breath fell warm on her ear, voice quiet but urgent. "We have to stay alert. Knowledge is our weapon, and vigilance is our shield. We can't let ourselves be lulled by illusions or misled by rumors. We must keep our circle small, just like Marcus suggested, and figure out how to track the illusions without tipping off whoever is leaking secrets."

Lila swallowed the knot of dread lodged in her throat. "He's everywhere," she whispered, recalling fleeting apparitions that might have been Sebastian's doing. "We won't detect every sign, not if he can slip illusions into crowded streets and vanish."

"That's why we can't afford to move blindly," Caleb said. "But we'll figure it out. We always do."

She nodded, feeling the faint pressure of his hand. The idea of illusions stretched across the city, and a possible traitor lurking within Council walls, made her skin prickle. There was no safe place, no single plan that guaranteed success. Still, she clung to the steady warmth in Caleb's gaze. If anything could keep her grounded, it was the trust pulsing between them.

She let out a shaky exhale and stepped away from the pillar. Outside, daylight beckoned, but it felt like the city's bright sun hid a hundred lurking shadows. The Council's words echoed in her mind: do not underestimate Sebastian's cunning. If illusions could appear as harmless stunts, if watchers could be deceived, then the ground beneath their feet was unsteady at best.

Caleb's solemn stare conveyed the same worry. Yet his presence was reassuring enough that Lila found a small spark of resolve. She shook out her hands, hoping to quiet the tremor in her fingers. "We should go," she murmured softly. She refused to let her fears show too plainly, not while suspicion clawed at everyone's nerves.

He inclined his head, expression troubled. In unspoken agreement, they headed past the foyer, near the wide exit doors that led to the hallway beyond. She protected her amulet from curious looks, tucking it fully out of sight. Guardians parted to let them through, and as she walked, Lila felt the weight of stares at her back. Whether out of envy or mistrust, she couldn't say.

Dread coiled tight in her stomach. There was no easy solution, no direct path to cornering Sebastian when illusions could glide through the city's busiest avenues without raising alarm. Yet she refused to surrender. If illusions were the game, then she and Caleb would match wits with the cunning warlock who once called Caleb a friend. Knowledge and vigilance. She repeated those words in her mind, praying they would guide her well.

They reached the corridor leading out of the chamber. The hush cast by thick marble walls followed them, tinted by distant echoes of guardians debating hidden infiltration. Without a word, she felt Caleb's hand brush hers, the brief contact sending a jolt of reassurance through her. Once they were past earshot, he squeezed her arm gently, his voice low in her ear.

He spoke the thought before she could. "We'll handle this together," he murmured.

She met his gaze, heart pounding. "Yes. Together."

With that, she turned from the grand hall, stepping into the corridor's cooler air. Her shoulders were rigid, each step forcing her to ignore the dread crawling up her spine. Whether illusions lurked in broad daylight or secret corners, they remained one misstep away from chaos. But as she recalled Caleb's hand on hers, she found a thin thread of hope. She could do this. Perhaps they all could, if they kept their eyes open.

The hallway ended in a smaller atrium, quieter, empty except for a single candlelit sconce flickering on the far wall. Her pulse thrummed in her ears. She felt the faint brush of Caleb's shoulder against hers, steady and reassuring. The ways in which they found comfort in each other never failed to amaze her, especially when everything else was so uncertain.

He leaned close. "Let's keep watch for illusions around transit hubs first," he said. "Maybe try to identify patterns in Sebastian's appearances. I'll coordinate with a few watchers I know I can trust." He lowered his voice further. "No wide broadcasts that anyone can intercept."

Lila nodded, her throat tight, thinking of half-glimpsed illusions that vanished into crowds. She forced a swallow. They would have to be meticulous and subtle. Perhaps that was the only way forward.

Caleb's hand remained on her arm for a moment longer, his gaze traveling her face. "Knowledge and vigilance," he repeated.

She tried to smile. It came out as a tense quiver at the corners of her lips. "I won't let him corner us," she said.

Neither of them spoke of the traitor or the possibility that illusions might breach even the Council's strongest wards. Yet the unspoken weight of that threat pressed against them both. She steeled herself with a final nod.

Then, raising her chin, she stepped away from the shadows of the atrium, Caleb alongside her, their soft footsteps leading them toward the next hallway. The faint hum of enchantments in the air reminded her that illusions wouldn't vanish on their own. The city needed them awake, alert, and unburdened by fear.

Once dismissed, she and Caleb exchanged uneasy

glances, their shoulders brushing as they walked away from the marble foyer. The moment they were alone, he pressed a hand to her arm, his voice quiet but urgent, reminding Lila that knowledge and vigilance would be their greatest weapons. Lila nodded, swallowing the knot of dread lodged in her throat, fully aware that Sebastian's trap could be anywhere—and that they were expected to navigate it blind.

CHAPTER

TWENTY-THREE

Days later, Lila slid a stack of paper cups along the countertop, fighting off a flutter of anxiety that kept tightening her chest. The Day's Specials board squeaked each time she updated the chalk lettering, and the steady sound of steaming milk nearby only made her nerves prickle. She tried to focus on the mundane tasks at The Daily Grind, hoping routine would smother the more unsettling truths spinning in her thoughts.

The midmorning crowd pressed in. Customers clamored for triple-shot espressos, soy milk lattes, or sweet caramel concoctions. She forced a bright smile as she took each order, mentally chanting that she was fine, that these bruises on her wrists could be explained away. Yet her heart gave a little jolt whenever she moved her arms too quickly, because the ache reminded her of the backfiring shield that had slammed into her forearms days before. She pushed the memory aside, determined not to let it show.

Maya wove through the crowd, deftly passing mugs to waiting patrons. Her short black hair glinted under overhead lights, and the concern in her eyes was obvious every time her gaze drifted to Lila. Maya's frown deepened whenever Lila winced or clutched a frothing pitcher too tight.

When the line finally thinned, Lila reached for a cloth to wipe the espresso machine. Maya sidled up beside her, crossing her arms over her apron. "You're tense," Maya said in a low murmur that barely carried above the machine's whir. "I saw you flinching all morning. Want to tell me what's going on?"

Lila's grip on the cloth tightened. She forced a small laugh that sounded hollow to her own ears. "I'm just sore from these...self-defense classes I've been taking. Maybe I overdid it." She bluffed as casually as she could, not daring to meet Maya's eyes. She managed a shrug, but she felt Maya's steady scrutiny.

"Self-defense classes?" Maya's tone was openly skeptical. "You've got bruises on your wrists, and that looks more serious than a friendly spar." She reached out, but Lila twisted away, pretending to tuck the cloth back onto a shelf. The movement sent a flare of pain up her forearm, and she swallowed a hiss of discomfort.

They were interrupted by a man in a rumpled business suit, tapping the counter for his cooling coffee. Lila ducked around Maya with forced cheeriness, served him, and plastered on her best customer-service smile. The man grumbled about his wait before stepping aside. By the time Lila turned, Maya was still there, arms folded, eyebrows knit together.

"You and I both know something's off," Maya muttered, voice subdued. "You used to tell me everything, Lil. You'd give me all the nitty-gritty details, whether it was landlord drama or weird boyfriends. Lately, you barely say a word about anything."

Lila's pulse thrummed in her ears. She considered blurting out that illusions had been plaguing her nights, that she had accidentally triggered protective wards that went haywire, that she belonged to a covert magical community no one outside the circle was meant to know about. She bit the inside of her cheek and caught herself. The Council's oath demanded secrecy. And beyond the rules, she wanted to keep Maya safe from all this madness.

Lila exhaled slowly. "I'm not trying to hide from you," she said, attempting to sound sincere. "It's just...some weird personal stuff I've got to handle on my own. But I'm okay, really."

Maya studied her, biting her lip. The empathetic frustration in her eyes cut deeper than any angry outburst would have. "All right," she said, though her uncertainty was plain. "But I'm worried. If you need anything, my phone's on until three in the morning. You reach out, you hear me?"

Lila nodded, swallowing guilt. "I hear you."

They left the conversation hanging in painful limbo, returning to their tasks. Maya rang up customers while Lila kept the espresso machine going at the busiest points.

Threads of conversation and bursts of laughter filled the air, yet Lila couldn't shake the sense that Maya was shooting her glances every chance she got, searching for clues Lila refused to share.

As the hours dragged on, Lila tried to distract herself by perfecting latte art: a simple heart, a swirl of foam shaped like a leaf. Whenever she steadied her pitcher, she had to remind herself to keep her shoulders relaxed so her arms wouldn't tremble. She was painfully aware that each movement pressed against the blossoming bruise on her left wrist.

Customers cleared out in late afternoon, and a stillness fell over the café. The neon sign outside flickered repeatedly, innocuously enough for most people to assume faulty wiring, but Lila sensed an undercurrent of magical energy snagged in the city's wards. She gritted her teeth and forced the unsettled feeling away.

Maya approached with fresh pastries, her expression softer. "Toss these in the display, then take a second for yourself," she suggested. "You look like you need to breathe."

Lila accepted the tray with gratitude. "Thanks, Maya."

At closing time, Lila busied herself with cleaning tasks: wiping countertops, stacking cups neatly, and washing stray utensils. Every time she glanced toward the main door, she half-expected to see a sign of trouble or an unexpected magical visitor. I'm getting paranoid, she told herself. But the city felt more precarious than ever, and she couldn't pretend otherwise.

Maya finished loading the dishwasher, then locked the front door. They shut off the big overhead lights so only two lamps and the faint glow from the street illuminated the interior. Lila was about to switch off the display lights too, when the door's old bell jingled. Someone had slipped in at the last second. She spun, startled, until she recognized the tall figure removing a coat.

Caleb. He paused in the doorway with his usual quiet self-assurance. Tonight, he wore a simple black jacket, and a subtle tension lined his posture. Lila's pulse skipped. She lifted a hand, ready to greet him with some semblance of normalcy, but Maya's voice cut in.

"Apologies, we're closed," Maya said with a polite but firm tone, hands braced on her hips.

Lila managed a small smile. "He's fine, Maya. I, uh, told him to drop by before we shut down so he could grab something. I have a pastry for him." She hoped that sounded convincing.

Maya narrowed her gaze and whispered, "Are you two dating?" She gave Lila a look that said we'll talk about this later. "I'll finish wiping tables."

As Maya stepped away, Caleb approached Lila in the faint light. She caught the subtle concern in his intense eyes. Beneath it, a quiet relief at seeing her in one piece. She wanted to fling her arms around him, to unload the stress churning in her head, but Maya's presence kept her pinned in place. Instead, she offered him a soft pastry wrapped in paper.

"Raspberry croissant," she whispered, throat tight. "I didn't get the chance to, um, ask you earlier."

He gave a nod of thanks and gently rested his hand over hers, so briefly she might have imagined it. "We need a moment," he murmured. He flicked his gaze toward Maya. "Is your friend...?"

"She's about three seconds away from dragging the truth out of me," Lila said under her breath. "But I can't just unload everything on her. You know the vow."

His jaw clenched. "I understand."

From across the café, Maya pretended to be busy aligning chairs, but Lila felt her friend's curious stare. The tension in the air crackled. Caleb took a step closer, his voice dropping. "I'll do a ward for privacy." He hesitated. "Quietly."

Lila exhaled, nodding. She set the croissant on the counter, scanning around to ensure Maya was still busy. Caleb slid his hand into his coat pocket, discreetly brushing the runic inscriptions on a small talisman. A faint shimmer fluttered in the air around them, so subtle it might just be a trick of the café lights. The noise from outside dampened, as if someone had turned down the volume on the entire street.

His low voice resonated in the stillness. "Have you sensed any illusions near here today?"

She shook her head. "No, but the sign out front flickered a lot. I'm not sure if it's just old wiring or something else."

He studied her face, eyes lingering on the bruises along her wrists. "You're hurt worse than you let on, aren't you?"

A surge of shame coiled in her stomach. She wanted to

hide her arms behind her back. "I didn't realize that shield was going to recoil so forcefully," she admitted. "It caught me off guard."

Caleb's gaze was steady, more concerned than angry. "I warned you about practicing advanced defense spells alone. At least let me or a Council-approved mentor watch your movements." He paused, expression softening when she looked away. "I'm not scolding you. I just...don't want you hurt."

Her throat tightened. "I know. Thank you."

He reached out, fingertips ghosting over a faint bruise on her forearm. He bent down and gently kissed the bruise on her right wrist. Then he kissed the one on her left. Heat flared in his touch, and it took every shred of willpower not to grab him and kiss him in that moment. That was dangerous, especially with Maya here. Even with the ward, Lila could feel the line between her double lives trembling.

The hum of the ward reminded her there wasn't much time before Maya realized something was off. She cleared her throat and nodded toward the door. "You should probably go soon. Otherwise, Maya might corner us both."

Caleb's features flickered with a hint of wry humor. "All right. But we need to talk more in-depth. Can you come by my place later?"

She hesitated, mind buzzing with obligations, illusions, bruises, and secrecy. "Yes," she whispered. "Text me if you get any new intel first, or if the Council calls us in."

He withdrew the small talisman from his coat pocket, muttered a few soft words to deactivate the muffling ward, and gave her a final, significant look before stepping away. With the ward dropped, the café's normal acoustics returned, bringing back faint street sounds and the hum of refrigeration behind the pastry case.

Maya glanced over, her eyes flicking between Lila and Caleb with open curiosity. Lila pretended to be busy packing leftover pastries. Without another word, Caleb thanked Maya quietly for the croissant and left. Lila struggled not to watch him go.

The door closed behind him, and Maya locked it again. Silence expanded between them, broken only by the subtle clink of stacked mugs. Lila's nerves prickled. She dared not look at Maya, certain her friend's scrutiny would unravel her forced composure.

Eventually, Maya crossed the room, stopping at the corner table they reserved for their post-shift breathers. She gestured for Lila to sit. Dropping onto a chair, Lila kept her apron twisted in her lap. Maya slid into the seat across from her.

"You know," Maya began, voice much gentler than before, "I'm not mad that you have secrets. Everyone's allowed some privacy. I just hate seeing you worn down." She leaned in, scanning Lila's face. "Those bruises look painful. If you're in over your head with that guy, you can trust me."

Lila swallowed back the confession sitting on the tip of her tongue. She wanted to vent about illusions, protective wards, break-ins, and Council briefings. She wanted to tell Maya that the city wobbled under magical pressure no mortal could fully understand. But the vow—and her fear of pulling Maya into dangerous crosshairs—rotted her words. Instead, she picked her phrasing carefully.

"I appreciate it," she said. "I've got...a lot going on right now. Some of it's not mine to share, you know? But I promise I'll tell you if there's something you can really help with."

Maya nodded, though the lines on her forehead didn't ease. "I see the way you two look at each other so I'm not stupid that something's going on. Just take care of yourself, okay? I'm right here, even if you can't say everything."

Lila managed a weak smile. "You're the best."

They sat there a moment longer, the café lights casting long shadows on the worn floor. Outside, sirens wailed in the distance, but it was impossible to know if it was normal city chaos or something more sinister. Lila felt the weight of the day pressing down on her, from the shield backlash to the half-known illusions skittering around the edges of her consciousness. The only real solace was Maya's unwavering friendship. Yet even that comfort felt fragile, tested by secrets Lila couldn't reveal.

Eventually, they both stood. While Maya gathered the final bits of trash, Lila flipped over the CLOSED sign in the window. She tried not to think about the look of cautious affection on Caleb's face moments ago or the thrill of his kisses on her wrists. Instead, she busied herself with mundane tasks: flipping off lights, counting the register.

They said goodnight at the corner. Maya headed home with a backward glance, and Lila forced a wave, pretending there was no trouble that couldn't be solved by a good night's sleep. But inside, she felt the rumble of an approaching storm she dared not name. Steeling herself, she walked away from The Daily Grind, replaying Maya's expression of concern in her mind. If illusions loomed behind every flickering light, then Maya's fierce loyalty might be all that kept Lila tethered to something real.

CHAPTER

TWENTY-FOUR

Lila sat cross-legged on the worn rug in her apartment's cramped living room, arms resting lightly on her knees. She closed her eyes and tried to inhale the stale evening air without flinching. She usually found meditation soothing. Tonight, though, her chest felt tight, as if some invisible weight pressed down on her ribs. No matter how she tried to push it aside, an uneasy sensation clung to her, and she struggled to focus on any sense of calm.

The overhead lamp flickered with a faint click, so subtle that she doubted a normal person would notice anything unusual. Yet she felt the shift as if it were a tremor under the floorboards. She opened one eye and glanced toward the hallway door that led out to the corridor. The small, rectangular space at the door's base remained dark, but the shadows played tricks on her mind. A few times, she swore she saw flickers at the edges of that gap, like stripes of movement where there should

252

have been nothing. She tried to dismiss it as a byproduct of fatigue.

She breathed in again, deeper this time, and forced herself to return to her meditation. The Council had recommended developing steadier concentration, especially after repeated illusions disrupted her daily life. Caleb had insisted that practicing a grounding exercise each evening would improve her control. She could practically hear his voice in her ear, advising her in that quiet, methodical tone. Think of your center. Steady your breathing.

She exhaled. For a moment, she considered lighting the single lavender-scented candle she kept by her bedside. The comforting aroma might settle her nerves. Still, her muscles quivered, and the tiny hairs on her arms stood on end. She felt watched. A wave of frustration passed over her. The city's illusions, and any underhanded tactics used by Sebastian or other rogue casters, had no right to sneak into the only private refuge she had.

She shook off the thought. If Sebastian had truly gained the ability to plant illusions in her apartment, she had bigger problems than a lost sense of privacy. In the silence, the building's old pipes sounded almost like a voice. Lila paused, a chilling twist settling in her gut, hair prickling at the nape of her neck. She willed herself not to bolt upright. She tried to maintain an air of composure, or at least keep her posture neutral enough that any lurking presence wouldn't sense her fear. She counted to three in her head, inhaled, held her breath, and exhaled slowly. Her vision fluttered when she thought she heard the faint scrape of something from the far side of her door.

She could not remain passive anymore. She whispered a few words of a basic protective incantation, letting a thread of greenish energy channel into her fingertips. A sense of warmth glided down her arms, the air around her lifting in a subtle swirl. She extended her hands, shaping that magic into a half-formed circle on the faded rug. This circle was meant to keep illusions at bay and protect her from stray malevolent energies. She had read about the technique in one of guidebooks Caleb had given her.

At first, the circle brightened the shadows. She felt a calm she had been craving for hours, a shift in the atmosphere that reassured her she had the slightest bit of control in a city teeming with illusions. Then, as her breath settled, she noticed a flicker at the edge of the protective boundary. The corner of her living room dimmed, as if the overhead lamp failed to reach that area. Something about that darkness moved.

Her heart thumped. She tried to repeat the incantation, but her voice fell to a whisper. She forced the words out: "Spiritus... revelare..." Her accent cracked at the last syllable. The ring of energy trembled, dimming for an instant. She blinked, and the shadows across one wall elongated. A shape flitted across the plaster. Translucent, shifting, it resembled a warped silhouette of a person.

She swallowed a cry, determined not to let it break her concentration. Her arms shook, and the half-formed green circle snapped too wide. A surge of power left her abruptly, and the lights in her apartment flickered off for half a breath. In the sudden gloom, she saw it clearly: a silhouette with a suggestion of limbs, some bend and curve that formed a mouthlike shape. She could not hear actual words, but a whisper caressed her mind: He already knows you. The voice was ice in her ear, neither masculine nor feminine but eerily in-between.

Her pulse exploded through her body. She leaned forward, pressing her palms to the floor in an effort to hold her protective circle. The air around her crackled, and the shape stretched outward, the corner of her living room distorting as if viewed through a warped lens. She coughed out a strangled sound, fighting the urge to scream. He already knows you.

Panic thundered. Her circle collapsed in on itself, and she half-crawled, half-scooted backward until her shoulders met the edge of the couch. The whisper repeated, each syllable latching onto her racing thoughts. She fumbled for a ward she had memorized. The words refused to come. The stench of static electricity flooded her nostrils, or maybe it was her own fear that made her imagine it.

At that moment, she heard footsteps in the corridor outside her apartment. Heavy, urgent footfalls. Relief and sudden dread mingled in her stomach. If it were Sebastian or a minion, she would be trapped. She braced herself, searching for the pepper spray she usually kept by her door. Her eyes flicked to the coffee table. She had left it there earlier, but it was out of reach now.

The doorknob rattled. She almost sobbed with relief when she sensed the faint hum of a familiar ward. The door jerked open, and Caleb rushed inside, hair disheveled and breath uneven. He took in the sight of her crouched on the floor in a half-failed protective circle, the living room lights spurting in erratic flickers. Without a word, he moved to her side, hand cupping her shoulder. His expression was grim, and the swirl of illusions that had tormented the corner receded at his presence.

"You're all right," he murmured, voice taut. "I was across town when the Council wards detected a dangerous surge from your apartment. I had to come."

"I... something was here," she choked, eyes flicking wildly toward the still-shifting shadows by the wall. "I saw—shadows. Heard a voice. It said—'He already knows you.'"

Caleb's jaw clenched. He shifted to position himself between her and the gloom, as if shielding her with his entire frame. The flicker in his eyes told her he suspected Sebastian was behind this, or some twisted echo of his illusions. Standing tall, he lifted his right palm, muttered a sharp incantation, and cast a shimmering net of protective light across the living room. The shape at the corner hissed and dissolved, leaving only a dim afterimage. Lila felt like she had just staved off a nightmare, yet her heart hammered as though it might burst from her chest.

He took a shaky breath and turned back to her. "I'm sorry," he said in a low, tight voice. "I never should have left you alone tonight. Sebastian is getting too bold, creeping into private spaces. He must have recognized your magical signature. These illusions are personal—designed to terrify."

She swallowed hard. "It worked," she managed to say, voice trembling. "I've never felt... so sure... that something was coming for me right here in my own apartment."

She rose on unsteady legs, and Caleb steadied her with a hand at her elbow. The contact sent a warmth through her limbs, momentarily grounding her. He exhaled, scanning the corners to be certain the illusions were inactive. Then he pulled her gently against him, as if verifying she was real. She noticed the tension in his shoulders, the way his breathing was still ragged from sprinting across the city.

He pressed his forehead to hers, voice quiet. "I hate that we're always waiting for illusions to strike. Seeing you like this—" He trailed off. His heart pounded under her palm, and a faint swirl of energy lingered around him, an echo of the wards that had drawn him here.

They stood like that, letting the moment settle. She felt cocooned by him, secure in this small embrace amid the uproar of illusions beyond the walls. She inhaled the faint scent of his skin, that unplaceable mix of soap and something faintly herbal, maybe leftover traces of a warding ritual he had performed earlier.

Caleb stepped back enough to check the wards again. His eyes flicked to the door. "Let me make sure we're sealed off from any other illusions."

She nodded, though the thought of him letting go unnerved her. He moved with brisk precision, crossing to the threshold and tracing a sign with his ring finger along the frame. Pale lines of runic script glowed for a moment, then vanished into the wood. He did the same along the window. Outside was only the hush of distant street traffic, but Lila could not shake the impression that danger skulked just beyond sight.

He returned to her, eyes scanning her face. "No more illusions should slip in," he murmured. "Not unless Sebastian tries a direct assault. If he does, I'll sense it."

She nodded, swallowing the lump in her throat. "Thank you."

He ran a hand through his rumpled hair, releasing a slow exhale. "I'm sorry I couldn't get here sooner. The second I felt the ward surge, I knew you were in trouble, and my mind raced to the worst possibilities."

She managed a thin, wry smile. "I'm still here, so it wasn't the worst. Just... horrifying."

His eyes flicked to her mouth. They both stepped closer. Caleb put his arms around her and pulled her into a comforting hug. Then he lifted her face upward and kissed her lightly on the cheek.

He brushed his thumb across her cheek. His voice dropped to an intimate hush. "I hate that he touched your mind, even for a second. He should not have that power over you."

"None of us should give him that power," she replied, but her breath hitched. Her awareness caught on the curve of his lips, the tenderness in his gaze as he studied her expression.

Caleb's gaze flicked toward the corner of the room, as if verifying that the shadows had truly receded. Then he looked back at her, determination shining in his eyes. "To hell with letting him scare us in our own homes."

She watched him hesitate, the tension in his posture telling her he was wrestling with a choice. He had always been careful, always a step back. But she saw the spark in his eyes now, the charged awareness that neither illusions nor Council rules could quell. Some invisible barrier broke within him. He let out a shaky sigh. "To hell with it," he said, almost to himself.

Before she could ask what that meant, he pulled her close again. His lips met hers, and the shock of it sent a jolt through her entire frame. She stiffened for a heartbeat, but the warmth of his mouth drained her resistance in an instant. She grasped his arms, fingers curling into the fabric of his coat. A muffled sound escaped her throat. It might have been relief or longing—but it pulled her deeper into that kiss.

He exhaled a soft, needy sigh against her mouth and pressed her closer. The tension that had bound them for weeks burst into a storm of tangled desire. Each time she gasped for air, he brushed mindful kisses along her cheek, her jawline, then returned to her mouth. She felt his fingernails skim the back of her neck, and a delicious shiver rippled across her skin. Fear receded, replaced by a trembling sense of surrender. In that moment, there were no illusions or flickering shadows. Only his body anchoring her to the here and now.

She let her arms slide around his shoulders, marveling at the strength in his hold. The pounding of his heartbeat matched her own galloping pulse. Her mind whirled with relief, fear, yearning. Her fingers drifted into his hair, tugging softly, and his answering groan made her belly flip. Memories of all the times they had stood too close, gazes locked, tension humming like a fault line, flooded back. Every unspoken desire, every near-touch, found its voice now.

He parted from her lips only long enough to press a ragged kiss to the side of her neck, breath hot against her skin. She tilted her head, allowing him closer, her heart hammering so hard she could barely hear anything else, not even the hum of the refrigerator. She let out a soft exhale when he trailed his mouth back to hers, each kiss deeper than the last. She tasted a hint of coffee on him, that faint bitterness she had grown so used to in her café life, but it mixed with something else, something purely Caleb.

They edged toward the couch without conscious thought. She stumbled lightly, knees bumping the cushion, and he wrapped an arm around her waist to keep her upright. The intensity between them rattled her. She welcomed the rush, the sizzling wave that tore through every nerve. The old wards or illusions on the periphery no longer mattered. She pressed against him with a quiet urgency she had never felt so strongly before.

Their kisses grew nearly frantic, full of pent-up frustration and shared relief. Her hands slid beneath the collar of his jacket, feeling the warmth of his neck, the pulse beating there. He breathed her name against her lips, voice so low it sent a pleasant ache through her chest. She responded by tugging him closer, swallowing his next words with her kiss.

He returned it with equal fervor, one hand cupping her

face while the other gripped her hip. The entire apartment seemed to revolve around them, no illusions, no dark corners, only the present moment. Her legs weakened under the torrent of sensations, and she sank onto the couch cushion, bringing him with her. A small part of her mind screamed that they were diving too fast, but the bigger part savored the sensation of his body pressed to hers, all that tension they had carried for so long.

When his lips trailed to the base of her neck, she gasped, her fingers clenching the fabric at his shoulders. Searing warmth coursed through her veins, and she arched against him, every cell in her body awake and alive. He let out a quiet groan, sounding as undone by the moment as she felt.

Just as her breathing threatened to spiral further, she sensed him slow. He lifted his gaze, their eyes locking in the faint lamplight. Both of them were winded, hair tousled, faces flushed. The air buzzed with so much unspoken emotion that it was difficult to form a coherent thought. They hovered there, still intimately close, his forehead grazing hers.

She struggled to read the expression in his eyes. Part raw desire, part tender concern. His chest rose and fell in rapid bursts, and he lightly brushed a thumb across her cheek. She realized her own breath was unsteady, pulse hammering without mercy.

He whispered her name, voice thick with feeling, and she nodded weakly, not sure what she was agreeing to except that she wanted him to stay right here, warmth against warmth. She reached up, grazed her knuckles along his jaw, and he leaned into her hand. A faint hesitation crossed his features, as if he waged a silent war with himself.

His lips parted, and he kissed her again, slower now but still consuming every thought in her head. Her heart glowed with reassurance. She was no longer alone with her fear; a gentle but unstoppable warmth anchored her, chasing away the last remnants of the darkness that had haunted her earlier.

They paused only when she turned her face to catch a breath. He caught her lower lip between his, then released it, his fingers tangling in her hair. Her eyes drifted shut, welcoming another wave of kisses that made her entire body sing. A part of her mind felt dizzy from adrenaline, though it mingled with a trembling relief that he was actually here. Every inch of her body thrummed with awareness.

They slowed again, the whirl of urgency tempered by the simple need to breathe and process the moment. His forehead rested against her temple as they sat tangled on the couch, locked in a closeness that neither had dared before. Lila exhaled shakily, letting her fingers settle on his shoulders.

She opened her eyes, gaze drifting across his features, memorizing the shape of his mouth, the gleam in his eyes that revealed an unguarded longing. He pressed a soft kiss to her temple, then her cheek, promising comfort in every subtle gesture.

Outside in the hallway, the building's pipes clanked again, and a faint hum of city traffic reminded them that the world still turned. But in that moment, sealed in the privacy of her small apartment, neither illusions nor the threat of shadows dared break them apart. He held her as though determined to keep her safe from everything the night might hold.

Her lips parted, seeking his once more. He responded instantly, guiding her deeper into that heady sensation that left them both breathless and flushed. All the tension, the near-misses, and the thrills of magical danger poured into each kiss. Even the flickering lamp could not keep pace with the heat between them. For the first time in days, Lila felt truly alive.

She brushed a strand of hair from his forehead, letting her fingers linger on his temple. He watched her intently, a silent question in his gaze, an invitation to continue or to find a moment's rest. She answered with a half-smile, leaning in to press another deep, lingering kiss to his lips. She felt him exhale into her mouth, relief and hunger mingled in that breath.

Their hearts hammered, and their lips steadily explored each other in the hazy light. Time blurred, each second thick with yearning. At last, Lila pulled back to inhale, chest heaving. She rested her forehead against his, letting out a soft, breathless laugh. The corners of Caleb's mouth twitched in a smile, almost shy, and he brushed his fingertips across her flushed cheek. Though the adrenaline still coursed through their veins, they both recognized the boundary they approached.

For a quiet, tethered moment, neither spoke. They stayed close, hands gently roaming from shoulders to waist, lips occasionally seeking another quick, fervent kiss. The world felt suspended in those shared breaths, haunted illusions banished from the cramped apartment. Lila closed her eyes, letting the warm brush of Caleb's fingers along her face coax the last of her shaken nerves into something softer, safer.

She recognized that everything had changed. She curled her fingers into his shirt, anchoring herself. She could still feel the echoes of fear trembling in her muscles, but that terror no longer ruled her. All she sensed now was his steady presence and the unspoken promise that, whatever illusions or dangers prowled the shadows, he would protect her.

He lowered his head for another deep kiss. She welcomed it fully, letting the tension slip from her body. With their mouths pressed close, her heartbeat thundered, and his pulse thrummed where their chests touched. They stayed locked in that sultry moment, a gentle but insistent current carrying them past every lingering fear, until all that remained was the heat of his lips and the unspoken promise that they would not face the night alone.

CHAPTER
TWENTY-FIVE

The next afternoon, Lila braced her palms against the cool marble tabletop, wishing her heart would stop hammering long enough for her to catch an even breath. The sealed chamber smelled faintly of incense and old vellum, a solemn reminder that she was deep in the Council's domain. All around her, magic-hued orbs floated in the silent air like anxious fireflies, casting shifting shadows onto the faces of the gathered guardians. Each orb flickered with an image: a ward fracturing above a city block, illusions spiraling around unsuspecting neighborhoods, entire corners of Manhattan shifting in and out of shimmering unreality.

She barely recognized half the guardians seated or standing along the chamber's perimeter, but all wore the same grim expression. They watched the orbs with tense shoulders, scribbling notes or passing small runic markers to each other. Marcus Steele stood at the head of the room, unyielding as always, his stern face illuminated by the glimmer of an orb that showed a battered ward near Midtown. He had called this emergency session barely an hour ago, issuing a summons so urgent that Lila and Caleb had dropped everything to hustle through hidden corridors, candlelit in half-shadows, to reach this room.

Caleb Blackwood stood at her side, posture rigid yet collected. Once, he might have tried to calm her in quiet ways—a squeeze of her hand or a subtle nod—but tonight he appeared just as rattled as she felt. She noticed how his dark hair clung to his forehead, a sign of the rushed journey that had brought him here. A faint blue glow pulsed in the ring on his finger, reflecting his growing alarm.

At the center of the chamber, a large hemisphere of shifting light displayed a repeated clip of illusions rampaging through a busy street. The illusions blurred the lines between reality and fantasy, causing distorted shapes to dance along the pavement. More than a few guardians cursed under their breath when they saw pedestrians stumbling, uncertain what was real and what was not. Although spells kept most of these events out of the public eye, some illusions had grown strong enough to break through cautionary wards.

"We have entire blocks facing these phantasms," a female guardian muttered from a seat to the left. She wore a robe fringed with silver thread. "They vanish as quickly as they appear, making it impossible to stage a direct response."

A tall, dour warlock on the opposite side of the table nodded. "My patrol found two wards near City Hall unraveling before our eyes. Three illusions manifested in the span of a minute, each one sending city workers scrambling. Council speak is worthless unless we plug the holes in the wards immediately."

Lila's attention shifted to the main spectacle: a swirling vision of pages going blank in a massive tome. She recognized the distinctive leather cover from a few of the Council's archives: Grimoire of Echoes. This venerable text normally recorded magical events in real time, a living record of the city's arcane happenings. She felt a chill scrape down her spine at the sight of entire paragraphs dissolving into white space. For many guardians, the Grimoire's abrupt silence signaled a deeper threat than illusions alone. It meant knowledge itself might be under attack.

"What is Sebastian doing to the Grimoire?" Lila asked under her breath. She was aware that Marcus, overhearing, cast a glance in her direction. Marcus had little time these days to correct her about protocol—he seemed just as worried as she was.

One of the older guardians, a narrow-faced man with neat white hair, spoke in a clipped voice. "We suspect Sebastian Shell may be censoring the text using illusions strong enough to imprint directly onto its magical substrate." His lips tightened. "Or worse, he has cast a specialized spell on the Grimoire itself, so it fails to record anything he does."

A flood of uncertain murmurs spread across the room. A few novices in the back exchanged worried looks, clearly out of their depth. Lila felt a pang of empathy for them.

She herself had been tossed into this chaos only a short while ago, a barista discovering her magical lineage late, and still learning how to keep illusions from knocking her flat.

Marcus cleared his throat, amplifying his voice with faint magic so it carried across the chamber. "I want full attention, guardians. We have verified that wards in multiple boroughs are deteriorating in real time. Patrol teams confirm illusions are slipping through every crack, sometimes scattered, sometimes concentrated on major thoroughfares. Meanwhile, our most informed text on magical surges, the Grimoire of Echoes, is going ominously blank. This is more than a coincidence."

Near the front row of seats, an older woman with iron-gray hair folded her arms with visible distress. "Surely the illusions themselves can't distort knowledge. We would have seen that phenomenon centuries ago in lesser forms." Her skeptical gaze landed on two younger guardians as though daring them to contradict her.

Lila pressed her lips together, resisting the urge to speak out of turn. She turned her head toward Caleb, who eyed the orbs with a contemplative frown. He waited until the older guardians finished their grumbling, then raised his hand to signal he wanted the floor.

Marcus offered a curt nod of permission.

"We do have historical references for illusions messing with wards—though not to this extent," Caleb began, his measured tone carrying an air of authority. "But illusions interfering with magical records is... unprecedented. He must be using advanced layering techniques to block the

Grimoire's insight. We shouldn't assume we can rely on its pages for warnings."

A few guardians around them nodded, but several more exchanged doubtful glances. The memory of Caleb's past with Sebastian weighed on the room. Lila could feel the tension spike whenever he spoke about this rogue warlock. Everyone knew the betrayal: Sebastian used to be Caleb's friend or at least a close ally in younger days.

A short, bearded guardian spoke up, voice heavy with suspicion. "And how exactly would you know about illusions on that scale, Blackwood? Maybe you overlooked your friend's talents once before. Perhaps there's more you're overlooking now."

Lila felt her cheeks burn. The insinuation was that Caleb's past blindness to Sebastian's dark practices still made him an unfit voice here, even as the illusions hammered at the city. Caleb's posture stiffened, though he spoke in a smooth voice.

"I can only offer my experience. I studied illusions with Sebastian. I know how he thinks. If he's focusing on large enclaves, we should look at the lesser-known corners of Manhattan. Those are unconsolidated spaces that the Council often leaves partially warded. If he's using illusions to distort knowledge, he must have smaller anchor points hidden away, out of immediate Council reach. We can start searching them."

A scatter of dissent rose at this suggestion. Someone said that it was too dangerous to send more guardians out. Another sneered that Caleb's impulses might lead them into illusions they couldn't handle. Lila glanced around, frustration rising in her throat with each word. It was absurd that, with illusions swallowing entire city blocks, they still hesitated based on old grudges.

She cleared her throat and stepped forward, letting her voice ring out. "This bickering helps no one. Have you all looked at that orb overhead? Look at these wards collapsing. Look at the confusion on the streets. We want to contain illusions, but while we stand around debating who is at fault, Sebastian is sabotaging the Grimoire of Echoes. Instead of waiting for the next meltdown, we need a plan right now."

Her outburst made the room go silent. Half of the guardians looked scandalized at her direct tone. Lila's heart pounded, but she held her ground. She had bruises on her arms from training spells that nearly backfired; she had illusions creeping into her own apartment. She was done waiting politely.

Caleb bowed his head slightly, as though grateful for her support. Marcus gave a decisive gesture. "Matthews has a point," he said, addressing the group with a steady gaze. "We can't keep pointing fingers. And yes, Caleb's history with Sebastian weighs on us. But that past may also be our best chance to anticipate Sebastian's moves."

A wiry guardian in a corner seat folded her arms with a scowl. "You keep saying what we should or shouldn't do, but we have no idea how illusions this strong can be anchored and hidden."

Another elder with a high collar frowned. "Maybe we should run deeper wards on the entire city, circle it with a protective barrier. That might at least stop illusions from spreading any further."

Marcus shook his head. "Do you have any idea how many novices would burn out just trying to hold that perimeter in place? We'd be left wide open once they collapsed in exhaustion." He exhaled and rubbed his forehead. "We need something more... unorthodox, as Matthews just said. A targeted approach. That means smaller teams, more specialized spells, and perhaps investigating enclaves we haven't systematically searched in decades."

The older guardians grew quiet. Caleb seized the moment to move closer to Marcus, voice firm. "I propose we send squads to verify each less-traveled nook. We know Sebastian's illusions need anchor points or catalysts. If we find those, we might unravel his hold on the Grimoire. Once we cut off the illusions feeding it, the text should show us truth again."

An older man with stooped shoulders narrowed his eyes. "You propose leading a rummage through ancient enclaves, rummage best left to guardians who are... unimpeachable."

Lila inhaled sharply. The jab was obvious. She wanted to toss out a choice remark, but she clamped her lips, noticing how Caleb tensed. She spotted guilt flicker across his face before he composed himself.

"I'll go with him," she said. Her words carried more weight in the hush than she expected. "I'm the novice here, but at least I'm not tied by old prejudices. If Sebastian is that determined to sabotage our every resource, let me serve as a second set of eyes. Caleb's illusions can counter Sebastian's illusions, while I can ground them with my earth-based spells."

Shock sparked in a few gazes. Some recognized her name from scattered gossip: the new Matthews witch who had a knack for earthen magic. Others eyed her suspiciously, as though she was stepping beyond her station. A few, though, reacted with cautious respect.

Marcus parted his lips, caught for an instant between discipline and relief, then nodded. "We'll formalize that plan. We have time to arrange squads—maybe two or three. One led by me, covering the known strongholds. A second infiltration squad for these lesser enclaves. If illusions are strangling the city's knowledge, we must move quickly."

"One last thing," a middle-aged warlock called from behind the row of seats. "How do we handle the potential that illusions target our own text? Sebastian could feed us anything, or hide entire truths if he's able to erase entries at will. We'll be flying blind."

Caleb nodded, jaw set. "We might have to rely on eyewitness accounts, and physical scrolls that predate the Grimoire's expansions. As for illusions in real time, we'll rely on wards. The reality is, we have to adapt. We'll get no perfect vantage unless we break Sebastian's hold on the Grimoire."

Silence stretched. Lila resisted the urge to rub her temples. They had no perfect vantage, indeed. But they couldn't remain paralyzed. One glance at the flickering orbs told her enough—magic across Manhattan was as fragile as a spiderweb scoring a broken window.

Marcus tapped the table for attention, effectively ending the big debate. "Get your instructions from the quartermasters in the next hour. We move out soon." His gaze flicked to Lila. "Matthews, you stay. Blackwood, you as well. The rest of you are dismissed."

A rustle of robes and muttered incantations circled the room as a handful of guardians hurried away. Some looked drawn and weary, others stiff with indignation over what they perceived as a rushed plan. Lila remained by Caleb's side, hyperaware of the tension that still radiated from him. She glimpsed the worry in his eyes, but she also saw gratitude.

Once the assembled guardians filed through the door, Marcus exhaled, leaning an elbow on the table. He lowered his voice. "I appreciate your willingness to stand up, Lila, but understand the risk. Sebastian's illusions are cunning, and we still can't confirm how he's censoring knowledge. If you notice anything suspicious in the field, do not try to handle it alone."

She swallowed the prickly sensation in her throat. "I won't. I promise." She felt the weight of the vow. Scenes of illusions unraveling wards hovered in her mind, fueling her resolve.

Marcus let his gaze rest on Caleb. "I'll speak to you both with more detail later. For now, gather your equipment. The infiltration squads must be ready by tomorrow evening. If the illusions keep strangling our records, we won't have much time to spare."

He offered Caleb a short, meaningful nod, then turned and left through a side corridor, conferring with two aides who hovered nearby. The lingering hush closed in, lit by the final flickers of orb-projected chaos in the sealed chamber. Lila slowly let out a breath. She felt like she'd aged a year in a single meeting. In the periphery, a swirl of faint illusions danced over the final orb. She saw the curve of a city block transform into a swirl of color, and then fade to black.

Caleb let his shoulders slump just enough to show relief that no one but Lila would notice. He pivoted to face her, eyes heavy with a complicated mix of regret and gratitude. "You didn't have to speak for me back there. That was bound to attract criticism."

Her pulse thudded at the quiet appreciation in his tone. She replied softly, "They were being ridiculous. We can't keep rehashing your past with Sebastian when illusions are wreaking havoc all over Manhattan."

He did not look away, expression struggling between apology and relief. "Thank you," he said, voice low. "I don't want to bring more trouble on you."

A faint smile tugged her lips. "I can handle it." She wanted to say more, that she trusted him, that despite the rumors swirling, she believed in his insight. But the rush of guardians bustling near the exit cut her off.

They made their way out into the corridor. The shift from the sealed chamber to the open hallway felt like surfacing from deep underwater. Torches mounted on the stone walls flickered with a more mundane glow, chasing away the gloom. Council novices hurried past, distributing small rune-laced charms for communication. Others discussed vantage points near the East River or the hidden catacombs stretching below Midtown.

Lila still fought the tremor in her limbs caused by frustration and worry. The illusions were building in scope. If the Grimoire of Echoes was compromised, they were truly on the back foot. She didn't know how large her role would become, but she knew she could not stand by and let illusions bend reality.

She sensed Caleb hover near her, close enough that the subtle tang of his cologne reached her. He seemed about to speak but then remained silent. A hush passed between them, not awkward, rather weighted with everything they had to do. She looked at him, noticing the tension in his jaw.

"Are you all right?" she asked quietly.

He nodded once, then let out a slow breath. "Better than I was after you spoke up." He brushed his fingertips near her elbow, the lightest touch. Though it lasted no more than a heartbeat, it sent a ripple of warmth through her chest. His expression softened. "It means a lot that you challenged them like that."

TWENTY-SIX

Night had given the footbridge a ghostly sheen, with moonlight reflecting off the restless water below. Though the path showed no mortal footprints, Lila could sense a gathering tension in the thick New York City night. She paused near the bridge's entrance and inhaled the damp air blowing off the water.

She spotted the first sign of magic when she rounded a dull metal railing. Wisps of green light flickered just beyond the footbridge. Purple flecks danced around the green, forming a strange, fluid pattern over the dark river. Her pulse kicked up a notch, and she glanced at Caleb, who stood at her side, jaw tight and eyes scanning the swirling aura.

They had come here after a tip about suspicious illusions. Though they found no physical culprit, the illusions were loud enough that Lila's own power thrummed in her chest, attuned to the magic swirling in the open air.

Caleb's lips formed a silent incantation, responding to the eerie flickers.

"Do you feel that buzz?" she asked in a low voice.

He nodded, stepping closer to her. "It's building from the far side of the water, but I can't sense a physical caster."

A wave of frustration flared in Lila. "Sebastian never misses a chance to rattle the city, but he sure knows how to stay out of sight."

Caleb gave her a quick, understanding tilt of his head. Shadows from the overhead lamp played over his sharp features. "Let's keep watch for a minute. If it's a stray conjuration, we should be able to unravel it."

They walked a few steps forward, the boards of the footbridge protesting gently underfoot. Beneath them, the green and purple lights twisted in a slow spiral, as though searching for something to latch onto. Wisps of magical residue tapped at Lila's senses, needling her to intervene.

Sure enough, a breeze gusted, carrying the flickers closer. She raised her palm instinctively, calling a faint thread of earthen magic. It coalesced around her fingertips, letting her sense the illusions more clearly. The swirling shapes looked like ephemeral vines, coiling and curling onto each other with no tangible anchor.

"Spiteful illusions," she muttered. "There's no reason for them to be here except to make people nervous."

Caleb's expression turned grim. "They might be meant as a distraction. I'd hate for random bystanders to stumble on these illusions at night. Let's handle them fast."

They positioned themselves at the midpoint of the footbridge, gazing down at the softly lit water. With a light touch, Lila closed her eyes and began to cast. She focused on centering her breath, picturing a calm sphere in her mind, just as Caleb had taught her. Through that quiet mental focus, she extended her magical sense outward. The illusions responded to the push of her power, rippling as if startled.

Caleb's voice cut in softly. "I'm weaving a mirror ward. Once I reflect these illusions back on themselves, you can ground them."

She felt the subtle shift of his magic, a careful incantation barely audible above the hush of water. Silver sparks glimmered at his fingertips. Lila waited, timing her own spell to match the rhythm of his illusions. The swirl of green and purple parted like smoke in a breeze, opening a path for her ground-based ward to settle. She let her breath guide her, imagining robust, earthen energy traveling from her chest, down her arms, through her hands, then outward into the water's surface.

A moment later, the illusions trembled. A swirl of color collapsed in on itself, dissipating into the night air with a soft hiss. The glimmer that had once twisted overhead faded gently, leaving only the ordinary reflection of moonlight rippling on the dark water.

For several seconds, neither of them spoke. Lila listened to her own heartbeat, loud in the quiet. Even the footbridge was silent, save for a mild creaking that signaled the end of the illusions. No one else seemed to be around. The tip they had followed was probably delivered by a worried local, or by some other mage trying to keep the city safe. Either way, the illusions were under control now.

"That's it," Caleb said with a hint of relief. "They're gone."

She exhaled, nodding. "No sign of Sebastian or anyone else, though."

Something in her tone trembled slightly, and Caleb slid his gaze over her face. She couldn't tell what he was thinking exactly, but she sensed a simultaneous concern and devotion in his eyes. It caused warmth to hover beneath her ribs, a tension that had nothing to do with illusions.

A few stray wisps of purple magic hung near the water's surface, too weak to be dangerous. Lila cast a final, gentle ward to dissolve them. Then she stepped back to Caleb's side, heart still thrumming with adrenaline. The illusions might have been minor, but the reminder that they could appear anywhere unsettled her.

She realized she was standing close enough to him that she could feel his body heat. The distinct smell of his coat brushed her senses: old wards, well-worn fabrics, and that subtle hint of his cologne. It felt intimate, standing here in the hush of a deserted walkway, the city's heartbeat pulsing in the distance.

"We should withdraw," she said softly. "The illusions have dissipated, and we don't want to linger if someone is watching."

Caleb agreed with a small nod. Without any rush, the two of them walked across the final planks of the footbridge and stepped onto a small open area at the water's edge. The night sky stretched over them, the lights of the city glittering beyond. Although it was quiet, Lila could almost taste the city's tension—like the echo of a chord that never fully relaxed.

When they reached the railing that overlooked the gentle flow of the river, she rested her forearms on the metal bar, hesitation tugging at her. Caleb stood only inches away, his shoulder brushing hers. The contact was barely there, but it sent a flicker of warmth through her. For weeks, they had been dancing around this newfound affection for each other. Their daily worry about illusions, the Council's demands, and the stress of near-constant vigilance had left them both on edge. But tonight, in this solitary moment, the strain broke free.

She turned her head just as he turned his. Their gazes locked, and heat spiraled through her chest. He had that quiet, intent look, the one that made her heart pick up speed all over again. There was no verbal agreement, only the awareness that they both recognized how fleeting life could be. Illusions could strike at any moment, and trust was rare in a city brimming with fear. Sometimes it felt like there was only the two of them, back to back against a shifting tide of magic.

Her breath caught when Caleb leaned closer, his mouth hovering near hers. She expected a soft, cautious moment, but the energy between them proved too urgent. His lips were gentle at first, then deepened with a sudden fervor that left her pulse hammering. All the tension and unspoken longing poured into that kiss, a heady wave of relief and hunger. She tasted the faint texture of coffee on him, mingled with the crisp night air. Her heartbeat thundered in her ears, drowning out every stray noise from the city.

He angled his head, pulling her closer. She felt his fingertips slide lightly along her jaw, anchoring her, and the warmth of his hand against her cheek spread tingles down her spine. She couldn't remember the last time something had felt this necessary. The water below them rippled in a quiet lull, as if acknowledging the moment.

When they finally broke apart, they hovered in that space of mingled breath, hearts pounding in unison. Lila swallowed and blinked up at him, the sidewalk lamps giving her just enough light to see the unreadable depth in his eyes.

"I—" she started, not sure how to continue. She closed her mouth again, uncertain if words could do justice to the swirl of feeling inside her. The threat of illusions, the weight of secrets, the comfort of his presence—everything coalesced.

He caressed the edge of her chin with his thumb. "I know," he murmured. "I feel it too."

She gave a shaky exhale, leaning her forehead against his for a moment. The tightness in her chest lessened, and the quiet hum of the city drifted around them both, reminding her that they couldn't sit idle. But for one fragile moment, she allowed herself to savor the safety in his arms.

Soon enough, they drew back from the railing. The swirling illusions were gone, and the footbridge was just an empty stretch of wood leading across the inky water. Caleb gestured for them to walk away. Lila nodded, keeping her hand tucked in his. In that small motion, she recognized how precious the contact was, how it steadied her frantic thoughts.

They slipped down the path and beyond the river's edge, choosing a vacant sidewalk that would bring them closer to her apartment. Shadows fell across the streets in faint lumps of darkness, but the tension from earlier had dissolved into a heady mixture of awareness and relief. She stole quick glances at Caleb's profile, noticing the set of his jaw and the fading concern around his eyes. He seemed more grounded now, possibly from that impulsive but long-awaited kiss.

By the time they reached her apartment building, her mind was buzzing with as many questions as answers: how to maintain control in a city of illusions, how to guard these new feelings, and how to face the Council without giving away everything. Yet right now, at her threshold, the only thing that mattered was the hush between them.

The apartment hallway was quiet. A faint yellow light flickered from an old overhead bulb. Caleb raised his open palm, tracing a warding rune across the doorframe. She watched him shape the magic with swift, meticulous gestures, an intricate pattern that glimmered like silver threads for just an instant. Then the light sank into the wood. She felt the pulse of the ward complete, ensuring no illusions would sneak in behind them.

His eyes met hers when he finished. "All set," he said quietly.

She reached for the door handle, and he raised his hand to hers. She squeezed his fingers gently, then turned the key. With a soft click, the door swung open. Her apartment lights were off, leaving the interior in shadow. Normally, the place felt cramped and too mundane for the swirl of magic in her life. Tonight, she welcomed its privacy.

Stepping inside, she pushed the door ajar just wide enough for them both. Her entire body still carried the aftershocks of that kiss on the footbridge. Every inch of her skin felt electrified, brimming with anticipation and longing.

Caleb followed, letting the door rest against his shoulder as he turned back to secure the lock. She watched him close it, heart drumming loud in her ears. She thought she might speak, but no words surfaced. In the low light, his face was half in shadow, yet she could see the tension in his posture. Tension and something else, a flicker of unguarded desire that matched her own.

Their gazes locked, and she caught her breath all over again. With slow, deliberate steps, he came closer, leaving only a whisper of space between them. She felt the soft brush of his clothes and the warmth of his breath against her cheek. Everything about this moment felt charged.

He lifted a hand to the back of her neck. "Lila," he murmured, voice hushed and intent. The way he said her name made goosebumps skim across her arms. Despite their mutual caution, the magnetic pull was too strong to ignore.

She rose on her toes and curved a hand around his shoulder, drawing him in until her lips found his. The doorframe pressed against her spine, but she hardly noticed. Their shared kiss turned fervent, heated by days —perhaps weeks—of pent-up longing. No illusions hovered around them, no urgent alarms. They had a few hours to claim something just for themselves.

Warmth flooded from his mouth to hers, radiating through her core. She tugged him closer, and he responded by wrapping an arm around her waist, holding her as though determined never to let go. Her heart thundered, an echo of the city's pulse, but in this enclosed space, it felt like they were the only two points of light in a kingdom of shadows.

She broke away just enough to catch a ragged breath. "Inside?" she whispered.

He answered with a single nod. Gently, he nudged the door shut, testing the handle to ensure the lock held. Lila's chest tightened at the finality of that soft click. Every muscle in her body quivered with anticipation. Her apartment had rarely witnessed a silence so thick with possibility.

The moment they stepped away from the door, their eyes met again in an unspoken agreement. She guided him deeper into the shadows, heart clenching with an ache that was equal parts need and relief. He gave a quiet laugh that vibrated with nerves and excitement, and his fingers curled through hers with sure intent.

As the door closed fully, the overhead light from the hallway vanished. She let the darkness cradle them, no illusions, no Council watchers, just the closeness of this moment and the promise it carried. Her pulse hammered louder, and she realized it wasn't fear. It was something far more potent: the knowledge that amidst the chaos of illusions and threats, they had each other, if only for tonight.

She stood on tiptoe and brushed her lips across his, electricity coursing through every touch. His hand settled at her waist, guiding her gently toward the welcoming shadows of her apartment.

Her back hit the wall just past the hallway, and his hands were already beneath her shirt, sliding up her sides, dragging heat in their wake. Lila gasped into his mouth, her fingers fumbling with the buttons of his shirt, eager to feel skin—warm, solid, alive.

He kissed her like a man starved, like he'd been holding back for far too long. One hand cradled the back of her head, the other gripped her thigh, hiking it around his hip with a growl that vibrated against her lips. She wrapped herself around him, breath catching at the friction where their bodies met. The ache inside her bloomed wild and sharp.

Her shirt was gone in seconds. His followed, tossed to the floor without ceremony. The press of his bare chest to hers sent a shockwave through her. She wanted to drown in the way he touched her—possessive but reverent, like he was memorizing her shape with every sweep of his hands.

"God, Lila," he rasped, dragging his mouth along her throat. "I've thought about this. About you. Every damn night."

"Then stop thinking," she whispered, tugging him toward the bedroom. "Show me."

They stumbled through the doorway, laughing between kisses that quickly turned breathless. He spun her gently, laying her back against the cool sheets, and then followed her down, all heat and muscle and barely restrained control.

His mouth worshipped her, lips tracing the curve of her breast, tongue teasing until she was arching beneath him, a soft moan escaping that made him curse under his breath. His hands were everywhere—firm on her hips, coaxing her legs around his waist, fingers splayed at her lower back as he pressed closer.

By the time he slid inside her, they were already undone. She met him with a sharp gasp, her nails biting into his shoulders. He moved slowly at first—deep, deliberate strokes that stole her breath—but the pace quickly grew frenzied, fueled by weeks of tension and the sheer impossibility of holding back.

They moved together in perfect rhythm, nothing between them but skin and truth. She clung to him as waves of pleasure crashed through her, her cry muffled against his throat. He followed moments later, his body shuddering with release as he buried his face in her neck, her name broken against her skin.

For a long while, they stayed that way—twined and breathless, the world outside forgotten.

Then Caleb pulled back just enough to see her face, brushing a damp strand of hair from her cheek. "I don't care what happens tomorrow," he said, voice still rough. "Tonight, you're mine."

She touched his lips with her fingers, heart pounding. "Then don't let go."

He didn't.

TWENTY-SEVEN

In the dim hush of the Council's secluded archive accessed through a warded door underneath the New York Public Library, Lila found herself crouched beside a splintered wooden shelf, gingerly lifting a heavy tome bound in a suede cover that smelled of dust and candle-wax. Her fingertips tingled where the old magic in the binding brushed against her senses, and she let out a quiet exhale. She paused to glance around the circular room, its towering shelves packed with books rumored to be older than the city itself. Small motes of glowing embers floated near the ceiling, each a remnant of an ancient enchantment meant to keep the atmosphere hushed and free of mortal ears.

Caleb crouched beside her, his shoulder nearly grazing hers. He held another leather-bound volume, smoothing one hand over its yellowed pages. The single enchanted lantern above them cast shifting shadows across his face, outlining the tension along his jaw. He had come here with her hours ago, and in that time, they had spoken little. They let the books do most of the talking. But she felt his presence keenly, like gentle pressure in the quiet.

She set her tome carefully on a low stone table. A small dust cloud puffed upward, making her eyes smart. "This one references illusions from the late 1700s," she said, running a hand over the archaic text. "It mentions wards shattering under repeated illusions, but nothing about them becoming truly real. Just illusions layered expertly enough to fool entire crowds."

Caleb nodded, settling the book in his hands on top of hers. "Yet the Prism can push illusions beyond that threshold. If it can make illusions linger longer than normal, or even take on some physical form, we face a threat the Council has never successfully contained." His voice was quiet, but she heard the strain behind each word. It shook her how deeply he felt the weight.

She watched him turn the page, eyes skating over the neat lines of script. Her gaze wandered across his features. He seemed older tonight, as if the tension pressing on them etched lines of doubt near his usually bright eyes. "You said Sebastian's illusions are advanced," she ventured, though the memory of that name left an ache in her chest. "But you've never really told me how he came to master them."

Caleb let out a low breath, shutting the volume gently. "He was always clever, fascinated with illusions that go beyond typical conjurations. At first, it seemed harmless—creative, even. We were younger, still learning together. Sebastian... thrived on pushing boundaries I never dared approach." He spoke evenly, yet the slight tremor in his fingers betrayed him. "I saw glimpses of his obsession when we were students, but I overlooked them. I told myself it was normal curiosity. I never realized how fixated he was on forbidden lore."

The flicker of the enchanted lantern made the shadows skate across the floor, pooling at their feet. Lila reached out, tentatively taking his hand where it rested on top of the closed book. She took in the warmth of his skin, the subtle clamp of tension in his knuckles. "You aren't responsible for Sebastian's choices," she said softly, though she suspected Caleb had been blaming himself for a long time.

He swallowed, his gaze dropping to their joined hands. "I keep wondering if I could have stopped him. I saw the sign of illusions layered too skillfully, illusions that trapped birds or altered small pockets of reality, and I said nothing when the Council might have intervened. It felt like betrayal to speak up. And that was my mistake." His tone turned rough with sharp regret. "He and I were... close. I turned a blind eye because I cared about him."

She laced her fingers with his, feeling an electric jolt move through her chest. Their bond had grown stronger over these last weeks, ever since they had spent that first night together. She had never imagined they would stand side by side in a secret library, discussing illusions that threatened to warp the entire city. But here they were, leaning on each other as though the rest of the Council—and the world—faded into the background.

She rubbed her thumb across the back of his hand.

"You weren't the only one who missed the warning signs. The Council should have paid more attention, too." Marcus had admitted, more than once, that the entire structure of their group tended to punish novices for mistakes rather than offer open dialogue, especially in older times. It was easy for trouble to fester in hidden corners. "Don't shoulder all of that guilt yourself," she said.

Caleb shifted closer, exhaling slowly. "It's easy to say, but not so easy to let it go. Every time we find a new report about illusions unraveling wards or seeping into corners of the city, I recall how Sebastian once joked about illusions rewriting the world's fabric." He tapped the spine of the old tome. "He wants to use the Prism for exactly that."

An uneasy chill gripped Lila as she imagined illusions creeping along Manhattan's busy streets, messing with unsuspecting mortals who had no clue a magical realm even existed under normal circumstances. The Prism's volatile energy, feeding illusions until they shaped reality itself, was a terrifying possibility.

She glanced around them. The archive was full of knowledge, crammed onto every shelf, yet they were short on answers that would truly stop Sebastian. She set her free hand on a page describing illusions that flickered in old London sewers centuries ago, wards that failed one by one as illusions gained momentum. It was a sobering account, ending with entire magical communities fleeing for fear of being exposed to mortals. "We need something that can turn illusions against themselves," she murmured.

He grunted softly. "Or at least disrupt them." Clearing his throat, he pointed to a short, cramped paragraph detailing illusions embedded into relics. "Here. This text claims illusions can't fully manifest if they lack a 'consistent anchor.' The Prism acts as that anchor now, boosting Sebastian's illusions. Severing that tie might collapse everything he conjures."

Lila nodded, though her heart panged with uncertainty. "None of these references say how to sever it. They only warn about catastrophic feedback if we just smash the source. The magic backfires on everything around it. We risk half the city if we get it wrong."

Caleb let out a bitter laugh. "That's the danger we face. The Council wants to keep illusions contained. But if Sebastian merges illusions with the Prism's power, they might become permanent. No one knows how deep that could go." He shut the book gently. "I've always specialized in illusions, but the scope we see now... it's beyond anything I was trained for. The moment illusions become self-sustaining, they're effectively real. People could be hurt."

She squeezed his hand, feeling his words resonate in her gut. She had seen illusions swirl over a quiet footbridge and stolen glimpses of illusions creeping into the city's wards. They had managed to banish pockets of that false reality, but it took all her focus, and she was still a novice by the Council's standards.

She inhaled a shaky breath. "My grandmother mentioned an amulet." Caleb's gaze sharpened, and she felt his hand tighten around hers. "She told me something about an old amulet in my family line. Supposedly, it can reverse or neutralize illusions. At least, that's what she hinted. We only spoke briefly, but she thinks it connects to the Matthews bloodline and how we've always used earthen magic to ground illusions."

He looked at her carefully, his expression serious. "An amulet that counters illusions?"

She nodded, letting the memory of her recent phone call with her grandmother fill the space between them. It had been a tense conversation, but Evelyn had sounded certain something within the family's relics might offer them a solution. "She suggested that, historically, illusions could be broken by anchoring them to earth-based spells. I think this lost amulet might help us sever the Prism's hold without causing a magical explosion. My grandmother wasn't entirely sure how, but she said it's older than half the relics the Council collects."

Caleb's eyes lit with a cautious glimmer of hope. "So your family line might have an artifact that counters the very illusions fueling Sebastian's plan." He paused, brushing the cover of the tome absentmindedly. "Have you pressed her for more details?"

Lila curled her fingers around his, feeling a flutter of reassurance. "We didn't get that far yet but she said she would look through her old journals. She said the last time the amulet was used was generations ago, when a different threat tried to slip illusions past wards."

His exhalation came as a soft hiss. "That's a long time for an item to remain hidden. But if it still exists..."

They both fell silent. She could hear the faint scratch

of distant quills on parchment, from scribes who were always somewhere in these never-ending corridors. A faint whiff of candle smoke drifted past, mixing with the cold stone scent that had settled into her senses since they arrived.

Caleb pulled his hand from hers, only to gently cup her fingers between his palms. She felt a rush of warmth bloom under his touch. It made her stomach flutter, the memory of how close they had gotten in the last few nights swirling at the edges of her mind. "You realize," he said softly, "that if this amulet works, you'll be the one crossing illusions with it. Earth magic is your strength, not mine. I can do illusions, run wards, but that artifact might respond only to Matthews blood."

She swallowed. The idea of being the final line of defense against illusions that could become real set her heart hammering. At the same time, a faint ember of pride curled in her chest. She had been terrified of her powers for so long, yet perhaps she was exactly what the city needed. "I know," she whispered. "And I'm ready. I just... need your help figuring out where it is. I won't do this alone."

His gaze softened, and she thought she saw relief. "You're not alone," he promised. "We'll study everything we can find about relic-based illusions. If your grandmother's old pages can guide us, we'll find the next step." A small tilt of a smile ghosted across his mouth. "And if the amulet is real, then maybe we have a shot at unraveling Sebastian's illusions before they break every ward in Manhattan."

Her heart lifted. She was surprised by how comforting it felt to share that moment of optimism, even in this claustrophobic place. Stacks of esoteric texts rose around them, many proclaiming doom where illusions were concerned. Yet here was a slender thread of possibility. She gently released his hands and placed her open palm on the table, pressing down on the dusty volumes. "Let's start by cross-referencing whatever your illusions knowledge can glean with the mention of my grandmother's artifact. At least that might show us if the amulet lines up with known relics."

Caleb leaned over, flipping the book in front of them to a section describing catalysts that could disrupt illusions. He pointed to a diagram labeled with obscure runes. "If your amulet is tied to earthen wards, then it might anchor illusions in place and dissolve them from within. This diagram suggests a principle like that, though the specifics are incomplete."

Lila scanned the intricate swirl of glyphs. Her breathing slowed as she pictured the scene: illusions surging through the city, only for the amulet's power to ground them like a lightning rod dissipating an approaching storm. The idea made her pulse quicken with cautious excitement. "We need to confirm it," she insisted. "My grandmother said some references in her old notes might mention an incantation. We can't rely on half-remembered rumors."

They both rose, books in hand, stepping around the table to a tall lectern that provided better light from the lantern overhead. Another wave of dust rose from the stone floor, and Lila coughed, stifling the sound against her sleeve. This archive was quiet, yes, but it was also old, full of half-forgotten secrets the Council seldom touched until crisis demanded it.

As she laid the tome on the slanted wooden surface, she felt the subtle press of Caleb by her side, nearly hip to hip. They fell into silent coverage of the text, scanning line after line for any mention of relic-based illusions or forcibly reversing illusions mid-manifestation.

After several minutes, Lila touched the corner of one page. "Look here. It references a 'keystone amulet' that harnesses an earthen base to anchor illusions. Says it was rumored to be used in some old city. The script is half smeared, though. I can't read the rest."

Caleb brushed his fingertips over the faint print. "It isn't conclusive, but it's a start." A faint smile tugged at his lips before it faded. "We'll compare it to your grandmother's journals. If they align, we might have just enough detail to attempt a reversal on the Prism's illusions."

She felt jubilation spark in her chest. "I'll contact her tomorrow and see how soon she can get me more information. She hinted that she has a box of older diaries and letters. That might be our best bet." She closed the tome with deliberate care, letting the hush settle over them again. Relief and new apprehension tumbled together inside her, fueling a cautious hope.

She turned fully toward him, the glow of the lantern dancing across both their faces. Her heart gave a traitorous flutter at how close he stood. The complicated warmth pulsed beneath her skin, the same pull she had felt each time they had stolen a moment away from the watchful eyes of the Council. His presence reassured her. It also made her vividly aware of how the quiet tension between them could heat at any second.

She cleared her throat, tilting her chin up. "I think we have a real chance of stopping Sebastian, or at least countering him, if we find that amulet. Will you... help me figure out how to use it?" She didn't want to assume anything. She needed him to say it.

His answer came without hesitation. "Always, Lila." Her name sounded like a promise. He reached for her hand again, then paused, as if waiting for permission. When she didn't pull away, he laced their fingers gently. "This is our best lead yet. Whatever it takes, we'll do it together."

His quiet conviction lit a small blaze of confidence in her. She squeezed his hand once more, savoring the moment. The Council's archive felt less oppressive now. With a purposeful inhale, she stepped back and gathered the dusty volumes they had set aside. "Then we should start learning," she said, voice firm, "and keep looking until we find exactly how to harness that amulet."

Caleb nodded, his eyes steady on hers. "But first, I need to have you in my bed. I seriously, can't think about saving the city until that happens."

She managed a small smile and gave him a long, sensuous kiss. "Agreed. Her kiss deepened as she tugged him closer, tasting the heat behind his words. When they finally broke apart, breathless, her voice was husky with desire. "Then let's stop wasting time."

Caleb didn't need to be told twice.

He pulled her against him, one arm wrapped tight around her waist as the other swept their scattered research off the table with a loud clatter. She gasped, half startled, half thrilled, and he smiled—wicked and unrepentant.

"You said my bed," she teased, threading her fingers through his hair as he kissed down her neck. "You're terrible at following directions."

"You're lucky I'm adaptable," he murmured, his lips brushing the edge of her jaw. "But if you insist—"

In the blink of a heartbeat, he lifted her, arms firm beneath her thighs. Lila let out a surprised laugh as he instantly transported them to his house. She clung to him, heart pounding with more than adrenaline.

When he set her down on the edge of his bed, he didn't move right away. He just looked at her—really looked. "You terrify me," he said quietly. "In the best way."

"Why?"

"Because I've never wanted something I couldn't afford to lose."

Her breath caught, emotion tightening her chest, but it was swept away the next second as his hands found her waist and his mouth claimed hers again—fierce and unrelenting.

They undressed each other slowly at first, savoring the unveiling. Fingers tugged at fastenings. Warm palms skimmed exposed skin. Her top slipped to the floor, followed by his shirt, and when their bare chests met, a moan slipped from her lips—low and unguarded.

He laid her back against the cool sheets, his body blanketing hers, all heat and promise. His kisses turned desperate, trailing down her throat, across her collarbone, pausing at the peak of her breast as his hand slid down her thigh and coaxed her hips to rise.

Lila arched into him, needing more—needing *him*. Her nails raked across his shoulders as he moved over her, between her, inside her, in a rhythm that felt ancient and new all at once.

They moved like they were chasing something just out of reach—each thrust a vow, each moan a surrender. He whispered her name like a spell against her skin, and when she shattered beneath him, she pulled him with her, both of them unraveling in the dark, tangled and trembling.

Afterward, their limbs still tangled, he traced lazy circles on her back, his breath warm against her temple.

"You know we're going to have to get up and actually *read* those books," she murmured.

"Eventually," he said, voice rough and satisfied. "But right now, I'm studying you."

And the way he said it made her wonder if she'd ever be able to look at a dusty old archive the same way again.

CHAPTER
TWENTY-EIGHT

Lila leaned against the metal pole inside the crowded subway car, trying to ignore how the rattling floor vibrated through her shoes. She was wedged between a businessman scrolling on his phone and an older woman holding a canvas tote, and her arms practically pinned at her sides. The overhead lights flickered, turning every reflection on the glass doors into momentary shapeshifts that made her heartbeat quicken. Ever since she had awakened to her magic, Lila found herself wary of every flicker around her—any subtle hint might be a stray illusion creeping toward her.

Glancing at the next stop on the subway's overhead map, she exhaled slowly. Not that she expected illusions on a random Tuesday evening, but the city hadn't exactly been predictable lately. In the past few days, she'd heard rumors among the Council watchers that illusions were flaring in unfamiliar patterns. A stolen glance at her phone told her that Caleb hadn't checked in since his earlier text about re-warding a section of midtown. He'd said every-thing was quiet so far, though perhaps he was simply trying not to worry her.

As the subway screeched to a halt, new riders shuffled on, pressing even closer together. Lila felt goosebumps prickle across her arms. For a second, she assumed it was just the unpleasant mustiness of the train, but then her stomach twisted with a different, more acute awareness: raw magic. It pulsed through the air, though no one else seemed to notice. An itch crawled down the back of her neck, making her breath stutter. She tried to calm her thoughts, cycling through the grounding techniques she had learned. One of her earliest mentors taught her that illusions often triggered subtle ripples of magic that brushed the senses like a static charge, and right now, static was definitely building in the train car.

Giving up on her original plan to take the subway to her usual stop, she squeezed her way to the door. In the tight space, it wasn't easy. A jolt of that unseen force rattled her bones, and she nearly slammed into a scowling teenager who mumbled a complaint under his breath. Lila apologized and pushed forward. The overhead announcer droned the name of the next station. She needed off, now.

She stepped onto the platform one stop early, breath unsteady. The wave of pressing bodies continued onward, but as soon as the train whooshed away, she was left listening to her own heartbeat in the comparatively still air. The magic was still present—pulsing, tugging at her attention like a half-heard melody. Lila looked down the platform and saw nothing overtly magical: just a few flickering overhead lights and some tired commuters checking their phones. Yet the sensation remained, urging her up the station's steps to the street level.

One flight, then two. She wove around a kiosk near the turnstiles, scanning for anything that glowed, sparked, or shimmered. Her goosebumps still prickled, and the adrenaline in her veins felt too sharp to ignore. Her breath quickened, the city's noises beating against her eardrums in a collage of horns, echoing footsteps, and distant chatter. When at last she reached the final step onto the sidewalk, Lila nearly lost her footing. The force of the magic buzzed so strongly that nausea scratched at her throat.

A swirl of tinted lights drew her gaze up the block. Thousands of neon reflections colored the midtown corridor, but a section of the street flickered with a strange, erratic glow she didn't recognize as any standard billboard. She stepped forward, weaving through the foot traffic of tourists and office workers, searching for the source. The evening bustle pressed around her: the smell of exhaust fumes, the chatter of pedestrians, and the hum of the city's perpetual motion.

She caught sight of the bizarre phenomenon hovering near a busy intersection. It sparkled in the air like broken fragments of a hologram, flashing in and out of sight. People paused to stare, wide-eyed, then scratched their heads and walked on. Some bystanders took photos with their phones, presumably thinking it was a new high-tech advertisement. But Lila recognized the tang of illusions. She breathed in, picking up faint magical residue that spiked her pulse.

Her stomach knotted. She forced her way closer to the flickering lights. The holograms took shape in front of a row of honking taxis, morphing from geometric patterns into what looked almost like strange silhouettes of tall, spindly figures. At first, the illusions appeared fleeting— barely there and certainly not an immediate threat. Yet with each second, their glow sharpened. She could sense the swirl of chaotic energy intensifying.

A horn blared. One of the illusions stretched across the lanes and momentarily dazzled a driver, causing him to swerve. The man cursed loudly out the window. A startled woman yelled in protest, hugging her coat around her as she sidestepped the sidewalk curb.

Lila's pulse pounded. She needed to stabilize this. The last thing the Council wanted was an entire block calling emergency services to report glowing apparitions in the middle of traffic. She discreetly lifted a hand, pressing it against the side of her coat as if checking a pocket. Under her breath, she whispered the starting lines of a ward incantation. Keeping her eyes on the illusions, she tried weaving a minimal barrier that would dull their brightness. Typically, illusions needed an anchor—a persistent flow of magic or an artifact fueling them. If she could pinpoint the anchor here, maybe she could sever it quickly. Easier said than done if Sebastian or one of his lackeys had set this up from a distance.

She inhaled, feeling the swirl of power channel through her veins. The illusions flickered, resisting her attempt to dampen them. Sparks crackled around the edges of the shapes, and for a moment, one elongated figure snapped its head—if it even had a head—toward her as though it sensed her interference. A chill shot down her spine.

This was too large for her to handle alone. The entire intersection sizzled with illusory static, and people were beginning to notice. Two passersby cracked jokes about "weird city experiments," but at least three others looked genuinely concerned, phones held high to record. Swallowing her pride, Lila mentally triggered the small protective charm she carried. Caleb helped her craft it, spelling it to emit a subtle flare he could detect. She didn't want to broadcast an alarm so widely that Council watchers would swarm in panic. Caleb, though, could hone in on it instantly.

She whispered, "Please pick it up," and renewed her attempts to ward away the illusions. Her energy slowed the flickering holograms by a fraction, but it felt like scooping water out of a sinking ship. The illusions pulsed even stronger, warping the city lights around them. A swirl of greenish sparks flew past her cheek, singeing a few strands of hair. She yelped softly, patting her hair and flattening against a lamppost to keep from stumbling into the busy avenue.

"Are you okay?" someone asked, voice thick with curiosity.

Lila forced a tight smile and nodded. "Fine, thanks," she lied, turning back to the illusions. She poured more effort into the grounding trick that she learned from Caleb. Earth-based magic often helped her stabilize illusions, drawing out the ephemeral energy. She closed her eyes, pictured the concrete beneath her, and tried to merge that sense of solidity with her own magic. The illusions hesitated for a beat, wavering like a neon mirage in a gust of wind.

Then a fresh spike of energy cut through the street, shutting down her progress. The illusions flared brighter, flickering in bizarre shapes that rose nearly to the second floor of a nearby building. People gasped. Someone let out a startled scream. Drivers honked wildly, trapped by traffic lights that blinked in erratic patterns. Lila's mouth went dry. Where was Caleb?

An urgent voice sounded behind her, and the press of a familiar presence touched her senses. Next thing she knew, Caleb Blackwood pushed through the crowd, eyes narrowed and crackling with adrenaline. Relief shimmered inside her, sparking alongside a rush of warmth she dared not linger on. Instead, she focused on the illusions. Having him here meant she had a chance to end this mess before calamity struck.

"Lila," he said, stepping up to her. "I caught your signal. You okay?"

"Been better," she answered breathlessly. A swirl of sparks drifted around them, making her eyes water. "It's strong. Feels like whoever set it up put a siphon right into midtown's energy. It's huge."

He slid a quick glance at the illusions twisting overhead. His jaw tightened. "We take it down together."

She swallowed, nodding. Their shoulders brushed—just enough to make her remember the last time they were side by side in the middle of sudden illusions. Back then, the tension had simmered into something that flung her heart into overdrive. Tonight, the chaotic swirl of magic left no time for self-conscious flutters, yet the charge between them still sang through her every nerve.

She inhaled, bracing herself as Caleb raised a hand. He spoke a low command word. Silver-white sparks gathered at his fingertips, forming an intricate net of illusions that he cast upward to meet the pulsing shapes. Lila recognized the strategy: illusions often fended off illusions if guided properly. They aimed to mirror the swirling patterns and neutralize them. While he spun that net overhead, Lila dove back into her earth-based wards, pressing her palm to the concrete sidewalk. She used the solidity beneath them as an anchor, driving the illusions to dissipate.

"Ease them down," Caleb muttered, voice taut with focus. "I'll reflect the shapes. You sever the feed from behind."

She nodded, concentrating. The illusions crackled in what felt almost like genuine hostility. Pedestrians, most of them gaping or fumbling with camera apps, started shouting at one another to get out of the intersection. A taxi squealed to a stop, tires screaming. The illusions shimmered, fracturing into dozens of smaller flickers. Lila clenched her jaw, pushing her magic outward. She felt the cold tingle rush through her chest, into her arms, and down into the pavement, where she pictured roots of energy tangling around the illusions like vines.

Caleb took a step closer, his arm practically brushing hers. She felt his breath near her temple as he whispered a string of words she couldn't quite catch. His illusions soared overhead, weaving an interlocking mesh that pinned the chaotic shapes in place. Sweat trickled down Lila's brow. The neon swirl flared, but this time, the combined force of her grounding and his mirror illusions forced them back. A final shriek of leftover magic crackled like sparks in a burned-out wire, and then the illusions began to fade. Their remnants fizzled in wavering arcs of color before they vanished completely. The night air settled around them, leaving only a faint hum of disturbed energy.

For several heartbeats, no one moved. Then a murmur rippled through the crowd. Pedestrians blinked, looking at one another and at the seemingly normal street. Lila's pulse hammered in her ears. She glanced at Caleb. His lips parted as though to speak, but instead he lifted a hand, hitching a subtle, final note of power into the air. She recognized that move: the damping charm. Within seconds, a hazy wave of confusion rolled over the watchers. They shook their heads, scrolled their phones, then wandered off. A few people frowned at their cameras, puzzled to find only shaky footage that looked like digital static.

A siren wailed in the distance, though it didn't come any closer. Caleb hissed through his teeth, finishing the charm. Lila exhaled and tried to steady her trembling arms. She hated using memory-blurring magic on unsuspecting civilians, but the alternative—widespread panic —posed a greater danger both for mortals and for the magical community.

"That should hold," he said, voice hushed. "They'll chalk it up to some glitchy ad or a short in the grid." His gaze slid from the dispersing crowd to Lila, concern flaring behind those intense blue eyes. "You sure you're not hurt?"

She wiped the sweat from her temple, feeling her heart slow. "Just singed my hair a bit. I'm okay." A wave of relief coursed through her, tempered by the knowledge that illusions like this were becoming more frequent. "Whoever's fueling these illusions is ramping up the risk. Do you think it's Sebastian?"

Caleb's expression darkened, frustration tightening the lines around his mouth. "Could be. Or it might be one of his loyalists. Either way, they're testing us."

She nodded grimly, scanning the street. Already, cars were crawling back into motion, and the earlier chaos was slipping from memory thanks to the charm. The city lights continued blinking overhead, all normal illusions of Manhattan's neon sprawl, but Lila no longer trusted that everything around them was mundane. Truthfully, she hadn't trusted that for a while.

He reached out, resting a hand gently on her elbow. That small contact made her breath hitch. Even with the echo of stress pounding behind her eyes, she felt the pull of him—how his presence steadied her, how their teamwork felt more natural now than ever. She almost let herself lean into him before remembering they stood in the middle of a bustling intersection, passersby swirling like a shifting tide.

She cleared her throat. "We might want to do a quick circle around the block. Make sure no stragglers are left."

His gaze flickered. "Agreed." Still, he didn't release her arm for a second. His attention lingered on her face, and she read the same awareness in his eyes that she felt radiating through her chest. The shared tension in that moment, the weight of illusions dissolving around them, made the city feel strangely muffled. She swallowed, softly pulling her arm free.

Together, they paced the perimeter of the intersection, scanning for any lingering flares of magic. They passed a small electronics store with flickering lights in the window; Caleb paused just long enough to verify those weren't illusions. Satisfied it was nothing more than faulty wiring, they moved on. Lila tested the sidewalk with a gentle pulse of earth-based power, but felt no further disturbance.

Eventually, they reconvened beneath a row of street-lamps. The city's normal hum surrounded them: impatient footsteps, the faint whoosh of a passing bus, a swirl of crisp night air. Even so, a remainder of adrenaline still coursed through Lila's veins, setting her nerves on edge. If illusions could manifest this strongly in a random midtown intersection, then the threat was far from contained. She thought back to smaller illusions that had spooked the Council in the past, and how they were nowhere near as blatant as this display.

Caleb seemed to read her thoughts. His shoulders tensed. "They're growing bolder," he said quietly. "We'll need more watchers on the streets. The Council doesn't want to cause alarm, but if illusions come up again this fast, we'll be scrambling."

She raked a hand through her hair, feeling the slightest grit that told her a few strands had indeed been singed. "I hate this," she whispered. "It isn't even the scale of illusions itself—it's how... random it feels. They're testing all corners of the city, making everyone jump."

He nodded. "We'll find answers." Then he glanced at the thinning crowd. "Let's wait until the last of them disperse. Maybe we can slip away and compare notes somewhere quieter."

She gave a tight smile. "Sure. If you don't mind a late dinner, I know an all-night soup place a few blocks over." Her attempt at a casual suggestion came out wobbly with leftover jitters, but the corners of Caleb's mouth curved in a mirror of her uneasy grin. He gave a nod, stepping aside to let a couple pass.

Then, before either of them could take another step, a faint sparkle of residual illusion flitted across their view. It scattered like glowing dust motes, just above a storm drain on the curb. They both froze, muscles tightening, but the sparkles dimmed and vanished in a heartbeat.

Exhaling, Lila exchanged a knowing look with him. The illusions might be gone for now, but traces of unnatural power lingered. Sebastian or one of his allies had definitely tested a new trick here. She caught the same wariness in Caleb's eyes and recognized that determined glint in his expression.

He lifted his fingers in a subtle gesture, weaving a final, gentle ward over the drain to lock down whatever lingering magic might remain. The air rippled faintly, then settled. The sound of a car horn snapped them back to reality, and they realized a curious bystander had slowed to watch. Lila shrugged innocently, and the bystander resumed walking, soon forgetting the moment entirely.

Caleb finished with a quiet breath. "Nothing more we can do here," he said. "Let's get going."

Lila nodded, feeling her heart pound a bit harder. She knew this incident was only a small glimpse of the madness that might erupt if illusions escalated across multiple neighborhoods. Adjusting the strap of her bag, she softened her gaze at him, grateful he had responded so quickly. Without him, she would have been overwhelmed. She opened her mouth to say something—thanks, relief, maybe a half-joke about her hair—but words stuck in her throat.

Instead, he raised an eyebrow, catching her hesitation. She gave a small nod, letting silent gratitude speak for her. The neon lights blurred overhead, and the city's movement swallowed them both until all the remains of the illusions vanished. Lila noticed how their shoulders remained close, the tension of uncertain possibilities fueling a spark of connection she couldn't quite define.

They made eye contact, sharing a moment of honest, unguarded relief. She knew that the illusions they had just faced were only the beginning, that tonight's display was a harbinger of something bigger stirring in the underground corners of Manhattan. Her chest tightened with the realization that she and Caleb would be called to the front lines again, possibly soon. Yet that grim awareness also underscored how necessary their alliance had become.

Finally, Caleb lifted his chin to gesture at the sidewalk ahead. "I'll walk with you. We can talk about a plan." He paused, lips pressed together in a faint smile. "And maybe check out that soup place—unless you'd prefer a different spot."

Lila's hands still trembled, but she forced a more relaxed breath. "Soup sounds fantastic right now." Her throat felt painfully dry, and the thought of curling her fingers around a warm bowl gave her comfort. Even so, neither of them sounded particularly enthused, too keyed up from the illusions.

They stepped off the curb, following the flow of foot traffic. The bright midtown lights gleamed on the pavement, painting everything in reflections of watery gold and pink. At a distance, a pair of police cruisers rumbled past, sirens silent, scanning for any sign of trouble. People hurried along, oblivious that minutes ago, illusions had nearly shaken the intersection into chaos. Caleb walked closely at Lila's side, and she realized how their partnership had evolved from reluctant teacher-and-student to something with deeper trust.

They paused under one final streetlamp, letting the crowd pass them. Caleb cast a watchful glance around. Determining they were alone, he said softly, "I'll file a quick sign to the Council so they can send watchers to check for leftover illusions. Then I think we deserve that break."

She let out a humorless laugh. "Yes. Definitely." Shoving her hands into her pockets, Lila turned toward him. "Caleb, we..."

He met her gaze, eyes glowing faintly from the magical residue that still surged in his blood. She recognized the same rush in her own veins. Their illusions might have dissipated from the street, but that charge of energy remained alive between them, undercut by raw adrenaline. They didn't need words to acknowledge it. She felt a surge of longing answered by caution, an unspoken push-pull that threatened to overshadow everything else.

Eventually, he nodded, the lines of his face drawn with seriousness. "We'll figure it out," he said, voice low. "Sebastian's illusions, your gif... all of it. One step at a time."

She exhaled, thankful that he understood. As they moved away from the glow of that streetlamp, her heart pulsed with fresh conviction. Whatever Sebastian attempted, they were determined to confront it together. The illusions had almost taken over a bustling midtown intersection, and right now, only a subtle warding charm and a few clouds of confusion magic had kept the incident from blowing up into a citywide crisis. Yet Lila suspected the illusions were far from done.

When they reached the corner, she paused, letting a wave of exhaustion settle over her limbs. This was just the beginning, she thought. Her gaze returned to the place where neon holograms had danced, the air now calm and unremarkable. An uneasy chill crept through her, and she flattened her bag against her hip, determined to stay vigilant. Caleb stood quietly at her side, tension rippling under his coat.

Only a few minutes ago, she had clung to her warding

spells, convinced she might fail in front of a street full of people. Now, the illusions were gone, yet a deep uncertainty lingered in her chest. Sebastian, or whoever was behind this, had truly tested her resolve. And she would not let them shatter it.

Caleb gently touched her elbow, his voice calm despite the roiling energy in his eyes. "Ready?"

She gave a single nod. "Ready." Her mind kept spinning, already imagining how they would write up a Council report, how they would explain the intensification of illusions in broad daylight. Part of her wanted to protest the secrecy, to let the world see what hydrant of magic simmered beneath Manhattan's pavement. But the rest of her knew better: illusions could cause chaos if they spilled beyond the city's wards.

As they left the intersection behind, warm city lights and normal chatter surrounded them once again. The adrenaline slowly ebbed, replaced by a rattled sense of caution. Neither of them spoke for several steps. Eventually, Lila saw him flash a covert sign with his fingertips, verifying that no illusions tracked them. She answered with a small sign of her own. Nothing lurked for the moment.

Their gazes met in a fragile moment of camaraderie, the weight of unspoken words lingering until Lila finally looked away, scanning the shops up ahead. In the hush of that loaded pause, their shoulders brushed again—an accidental contact that sent a new jolt through her, reminding her how closely intertwined danger and attraction had become in her life.

A final swirl of faint magical glow faded from the intersection behind them, evaporating into the night air. Lila caught a glimpse of it in her peripheral vision, and she knew at once that she and Caleb had barely scratched the surface of the havoc Sebastian could stir.

THE STORY CONTINUES

The Story continues in book two, *PROPHECY, coming soon to Amazon.*

EXCERPT FROM PROPHECY

Lila stood just inside the wide double doors of the Council's briefing chamber, the clang of metal locks echoing behind her. Soft orbs of magical light hovered overhead, illuminating the stone walls in a pale glow. The sight reminded her how far she had come from the cozy bustle of The Daily Grind. Now, every time she stepped inside these halls, she felt the weight of politics mingling with the pulsing undercurrent of raw magic. Anxiety rippled through her stomach, twisting as she caught sight of three rows of unyielding faces staring back at her.

Caleb stepped up beside her, his coat shifting over the shoulders he carried so stiffly. She sensed the tension clinging to him—the same tension that had crept between them for days, fed by endless illusions stalking the streets of Manhattan. Together, they walked deeper into the chamber, approaching the curved table where Marcus and several other Council elders sat. The quiet made Lila's pulse throb in her ears, each beat a reminder of her own inexperience. Yet she refused to let her nerves swallow her. She was here as much out of necessity as duty.

Marcus cleared his throat, his voice reverberating across the marble. "You're all aware we've experienced multiple disruptions to wards around the city," he began. "Tonight, we address an even more troubling matter than illusions alone: sabotage targeting our core nexus points."

Murmurs rippled around the chamber. Council members on either side whispered behind their hands. The far edges of the room teemed with younger witches, many sporting the hollow-eyed look of those who had spent sleepless nights patching wards that illusions threatened to tear apart. Some novices wore scuffed jackets scented with burnt thread, proof of the random blasts of magic that had erupted in the last week.

A new figure stepped forward, tall and statuesque. Her heavy robes were embroidered with silvery crescents, each gleaming in the soft lamplight. The symbol of the moon— Lila had seen it in a few arcane texts, but never in such intricate detail. The newcomer exuded calm confidence, from the regal angle of her chin to the measured way she addressed the group.

"Allow me to introduce Keira Costa," Marcus said. "A Luna witch dedicated to safeguarding our city's nexus points."

Keira dipped her head in greeting. Her voice sounded low and resonant, like a lullaby woven through midnight fields. "My craft draws upon the moon's phases," she explained. "Luna witches work to harmonize magical flows, stabilizing them when they grow volatile. Over the years, I've routinely checked the main nexus points beneath Manhattan. Most remain intact. However"—she hesitated, allowing the weight of her words to sink in —"several sites have been tampered with. The sabotage disrupts not only our wards but the natural flow of magic. Tiny fractures in the lines can weaken illusions in some areas... and amplify them in others."

Caleb's lips parted in concern. Lila sensed a flicker of relief that someone with expertise was finally putting words to the growing unease. She too had felt that sense of imbalance in the city. Her recent attempts to ground illusions had become unpredictable; sometimes the illusions barely responded to her efforts, other times they imploded with unexpected force.

Keira's gaze swept slowly around the room. Lila guessed that calm empathy lay beneath her poise. The Luna witch's eyes held pity for everyone who had lost hours, if not days, fighting illusions that materialized in restaurant kitchens or subway cars.

A flurry of hushed conversation broke out among the elders. Council watchers exchanged dark glances, referencing rumors that a traitor lurked in their midst. Lila caught a snippet from one muttering guardian who refused to look at her: "Tampering from inside. Must be how Sebastian or his allies got so far." The mention of Sebastian twisted an old pain inside Lila's chest. She still bristled at how he targeted novices, how he hijacked illusions for personal gain.

Marcus raised his hand to quiet the chatter. "I want full cooperation," he declared. "Keira Costa has graciously offered her knowledge. Anyone with evidence of tampered wards must come forward."

At that, Keira nodded and let her robe's sleeves fall to her elbows, revealing swirling tattoos that undoubtedly corresponded to moon phases. "I'm here to unify our approach to illusions that spike around nexus points," she said gently. "We need to coordinate. If sabotage is weakening certain wards, we must isolate those cracks quickly."

Lila suppressed the urge to gulp. She hated feeling out of her depth, even though Marcus had specifically asked her to attend. She forced herself to speak. "We've seen illusions near public areas—like midtown intersections, footbridges—and some in quieter places around Greenwich Village," she said, careful to keep her voice steady. "What if we match those spots against Keira's map of nexus disruptions? Any overlap might tell us which illusions are fed by these tampered lines." She tried not to flinch at how loud she sounded in the hush.

A few Council elders frowned, though their expressions suggested they were truly listening. She caught Caleb's supportive glance from the corner of her eye. He looked almost proud.

A warlock with iron-gray hair tapped his notes. "Cross-referencing illusions with these sabotage sites... that would require Council cooperation with outposts across Manhattan. Can we handle that?"

"We can," Lila said firmly, surprising even herself. "If we share illusions reports from watchers on night patrols with Keira's data, we can highlight patterns. Then, we piece together whether a single group is behind it or if multiple factions are meddling."

A ripple of agreement brightened the room. Caleb's posture relaxed. A flare of warmth spread in Lila's chest, from the center of her ribcage to the tips of her fingers. It moved through her so swiftly that she reflexively held her breath.

Marcus shifted in his seat, gaze flicking over to Keira. "What is your view on that approach?"

Keira inclined her head in Lila's direction. "That's precisely what I hoped to do," she said, her voice calm but resolute. "I can share the precise points where I've recorded fluctuations. If illusions match even half of those sites, we'll know where to concentrate our wards. We can then isolate which sabotage might be random, and which might be deliberate."

A hush wrapped around them. The gravity of the infiltration weighed heavily in the air. Lila wondered if anyone else felt the swirl of conflicting emotions that churned in her mind: fear, anger, and a strained hope that perhaps, this time, they had a workable plan.

Marcus nodded grudgingly, still radiating that cautious stance he wore like a cloak. "Very well. We'll proceed with that plan. Provide Keira with the watchers' logs, cross-reference them, and see what emerges. We must act swiftly, before illusions escalate and cause mortals to become suspicious." His focus shifted to the novices ringing the back wall. "If anyone hears talk of traitors or sees suspicious magical tampering outside these designated areas, you'll report it. Understood?"

A chorus of murmured affirmatives followed. Keira dipped her head again, stepping to the side so that a Council scribe could hand her a battered ledger. She clutched it, glancing at Lila with a faint, appreciative smile.

The gathering began to break into smaller clumps, watchers scrolling through illusions data on flickering orbs, elders conferring about which relics to move to more secure vaults. The swirl of final instructions and hushed urgency thickened the atmosphere. Lila exhaled slowly and pivoted toward the main doors, her mind already racing with strategies to help Keira cross-reference the sabotage sites at the earliest opportunity.

Caleb drifted after her, weaving through the departing crowd. His voice brushed close to her ear. "That suggestion was brilliant," he said softly, though he still scanned the corridor for eavesdroppers. "I was worried the Council might discount you again."

Lila's pulse stuttered. She remembered not so long ago when she felt too intimidated to speak in these chambers, let alone propose an action plan. "I wasn't sure how Marcus would react," she admitted.

"I'd say you impressed him," Caleb replied. "He might not show it, but he listened."

She felt a lift in her chest, an odd spark of confidence pushing away the gloom that had shadowed them. They reached the side corridor, stepping aside so a pair of witches could hurry past, arms laden with stacks of notes.

As soon as they paused, Lila became acutely aware of Caleb's presence—the faint scuff of his shoe, the line of tension still in his shoulders. She recalled the look on his face when she first spoke up at the briefing, relief warming his features like dawn light. The memory set a flutter in her stomach, echoing with possibility. But she also noticed the bruise darkening a small patch of skin just below his collar. An old illusion accident, or a mishap from earlier in the day? She decided not to ask; they had enough burdens.

He turned to her. "You've hardly eaten all day, right? Believe me, I noticed how quickly you downed that last cup of coffee. I think we could both use a break." His eyes flicked toward the tall windows, where the glow of the city's neon spilled against the glass. Evening had descended, painting the halls in subdued light.

She hesitated, glancing over her shoulder at Keira, who was already surrounded by watchers demanding more details. Lila wanted to help, but she sensed that diving into new data right now meant working until dawn. Her body ached for a moment of normalcy, some reminder that life existed outside illusions and Council emergencies. She nodded. "You're right. Let's step out for a bit. Maybe talk about the next steps without a dozen ears listening in."

Caleb's mouth curved in a grin so subtle that only she would notice how pleased he seemed. "I know a place around the corner," he said. "They serve the best warm bread in the city."

"Then lead the way," Lila said, pushing aside the swirl of guilt that told her she should stay. The Council had a plan. For at least a couple of hours, she could trust them to coordinate with Keira, read logs, and raise flags if needed.

They slipped into the corridor leading to the exit, where a pair of robed guardians stood watch. The guardians dipped their heads in acknowledgment, letting Caleb and Lila step through the warded threshold. She felt a gentle tingle of magic over her arms, as if the wards scanned them for illusions before releasing them. Outside, the streets felt jarringly normal compared to the tension inside the Council. Taxi cabs, headlights, and the hum of city traffic rushing past reminded her that countless people just a block away had no idea illusions prowled the corners of their reality.

She followed Caleb down a side street illuminated by orange lampposts, passing rows of stylishly old apartments and restaurants with chalkboard menus. Her muscles gradually loosened as her eyes swept the sidewalks, searching for signs of illusions. Everything seemed normal for now. She hoped it stayed that way, at least until they discovered who or what was tampering with the nexus points.

At last, they arrived at a small restaurant with a rustic wooden door and a sign shaped like a crescent moon. Warm light spilled onto the sidewalk from within, carrying the smell of roasted garlic and herbs. A kindly host greeted them—an older woman who wore a welcoming smile and appeared blissfully unaware of wards or Council business. She offered them a quiet table near the back, and Lila followed Caleb across the restaurant's polished floor.

The instant they sat, candlelight dancing off the table's frosted glass surface, a hush settled around them. The warmth inside the restaurant seemed to soothe her frayed nerves far more than she had expected. She unzipped her jacket and sank into the cushioned seat, eyes drifting over artworks portraying city bridges lit by moonlight.

Caleb leaned forward slightly, elbows on the edge of the table. He studied her as though trying to read every flicker of emotion that crossed her features. "Are you all right?" he asked softly. "That was a lot of pressure in the meeting today."

She exhaled, letting herself melt into that question. "It was," she said, voice honest. "But I'm managing. It feels good to, I don't know, speak up. Especially when I spent so long thinking no one in the Council would listen."

His gaze warmed. "You did more than speak up. You steered the discussion. You've been training so hard these past weeks, but it felt different to see you in the middle of a briefing, telling them how to handle illusions." A trace of pride lingered on his lips.

Heat crept into her cheeks. She reached for the menu to hide her flustered expression. "Let's see," she murmured, scanning the list. Braised chicken, pasta, and a variety of vegetarian dishes caught her eye. She also needed to decide if she wanted a glass of wine. The notion of relaxing with a drink felt almost luxurious.

They ordered, settling on a rosemary flatbread to share, plus two hearty entrées that promised to fill the gnawing pit in Lila's stomach. When the server disappeared, Lila peered at Caleb through the low flicker of candlelight. She found herself studying the delicate slump of his shoulders and how the lines of worry at the corner of his eyes had softened.

"Thank you," she said, surprising herself with how gentle she sounded. "For believing in me back there, and for coaxing me out tonight. I might've stayed behind to compare notes for hours."

He traced an invisible pattern on the tablecloth. "You and I both know that would do more harm than good right now. We're not helping anyone if we collapse from exhaustion." He paused, then added, "I'm proud of how you handled everything with Keira. We need her input, but the Council can be defensive about outside expertise. You helped them see reason."

Lila felt a smile tugging at her lips. She recalled Keira's quiet bearing, that faint aura of empathy. "She's unlike anyone I've met," Lila said. "There's something so... centered about her. Like she's used to watching the city from a distance."

Caleb's gaze flicked to the passing server balancing two glasses of water. "Luna witches often focus on older forms of magic. Their rituals revolve around moon phases —a kind of cyclical approach that keeps them grounded even when city magic goes haywire. Keira's calm stems from that tradition. Plus, you can guess she's seen sabotage before if she's dealt with unscrupulous witches tampering with nexus lines."

Lila nodded. Another swirl of guilt teased the base of her spine. She wondered if she was stepping into deeper

Council matters than she was prepared for. But the thought of illusions swirling around unsuspecting neighborhoods, fueled by sabotage, hardened her resolve. "We'll handle it," she whispered, mostly to herself.

A short silence stretched between them. Candlelight flickered against the curve of Caleb's cheek, casting shadows that softened—and she realized how close they sat. The tension between them felt like a quietly thrumming wire. Past heartbreak, Council stress, and illusions had forced them together so often that it felt natural to share a moment like this. And yet, the gentle hush, free of immediate crisis, made Lila's heart flutter with unexpected intensity.

"How are you?" she asked him softly, forcing herself to meet his gaze. She saw the ghost of old guilt flicker there —Sebastian's betrayal, illusions creeping through the city. He had never quite shaken the blame he carried.

He let out a thoughtful breath, fingertips grazing the table. "I'm managing too," he said, echoing her earlier words. "Improvement doesn't happen overnight. I've come to accept that I can't fix everything on my own. Seeing you step up and help the Council... it eases some of the weight. Reminds me there's a real team now."

A pleased shiver lit her insides. For a second, she wished the illusions and sabotage didn't exist, so she could fully enjoy leaning into the warmth of his presence. But this was enough—a quiet meal, a respite from swirling illusions, and the hope that they might finally learn who was tampering with the nexus points.

Moments later, their bread arrived, steaming with the

aroma of rosemary and olive oil. Lila liberated a piece, and the crisp exterior crackled under her fingertips. She closed her eyes to savor the first bite, letting the flavors chase away the lingering scraps of tension that clung to her. Though the memory of sabotage and illusions loomed, she allowed herself a small measure of peace. Here, in the hush of a dimly lit restaurant, with Caleb across from her, she found a glimmer that maybe, just maybe, they had turned a corner.

He poured her a small glass of red wine and lifted his own glass in a muted toast. "To following through with that plan," he said. "To better days, and to a little break from all the mess."

She nodded, gently tapping her glass to his. The soft chime eased an unspoken knot in her chest. "To trusting our instincts," she added, voice quiet but steady. "And to finishing a meal without illusions barging in."

They shared a laugh, the rest of the restaurant oblivious to how that single laugh represented a fragile hope for both of them. For a brief time, Lila allowed herself to live in the moment. The idea of illusions creeping along an abandoned subway or the memory of sabotage behind prized wards hovered at the edges of her thoughts, but the calm hush of the dinner lulled her to focus on the now. She looked at Caleb and found solace, knowing this might be the first real break they had taken in a long time.

Ultimately, this was the difference: they weren't just partners facing illusions or Council politics. They were two people who, against all odds, had discovered how to navigate chaos together. And as they shared a real meal—

no wards firing off, no illusions bristling around them—they both wondered if this was how normal life might feel, once the city stopped trembling under Sebastian's shadow and sabotage stopped haunting the wards.

They kept talking: about new ideas for systematically reviewing sabotage logs with Keira, about potential leads the watchers might bring in later that night, about small comforts like coffee or hot showers that waited for them once this tidal wave of illusions rolled back. With every word, the closeness between them grew in hushed confidence, each glance charged with the resonance of a bond far deeper than a mentor and novice's alliance.

Their entrées arrived soon after, plates filled with savory sauces that mingled with herbed vegetables. Lila relished every bite, conscious that they might be called away as soon as the next magical emergency flared. But for now, she quieted that anxious notion, determined to enjoy one evening of calm. This was, after all, the first time they had allowed themselves to share a dinner beyond the walls of either the Council or Caleb's private sanctum.

Halfway through the meal, Lila set down her fork and let her gaze roam over Caleb's face. "Thank you," she said softly, repeating her earlier gratitude as a wave of affection pressed at her heart. She remembered how uncertain she had been the day she scribbled her name in the Council's Book of Oaths. Life had changed drastically, but it led her here.

He slid his hand across the table, brushing his fingertips against hers. The slightest touch ignited a subtle tingle, reminding her that magic wasn't the only energy crackling between them. "You've changed everything," he said. "In a good way."

A gentle hush settled, substituting tension for something warmer and steady. Outside, the city lights glowed through the windows, and somewhere beyond the walls, illusions might still fester amid sabotage. But here in a candlelit booth, they found sanctuary. Lila felt that if she had to step back into the raging tide of sabotage and illusions in an hour, at least she would do so with the silent echo of this moment in mind. Tomorrow they could chase the leads Keira Costa uncovered, cross-reference illusions with tampered nexus points, and chase down traitors. Tonight was theirs.

She reached for another piece of rosemary bread, heart stirring at the possibility of a tomorrow shaped by hope rather than fear. They shared quiet conversation until plates were half-empty and the server discreetly cleared away crumbs. As the faint notes of jazz drifted from overhead speakers, they lingered, unwilling to let the night slip away too soon.

In that small, hidden corner of Manhattan's chaos, Lila recognized that her life had truly shifted. She wasn't just a barista or a stumbling novice anymore. She was part of something bigger—and as she and Caleb shared a smile across the soft glow of the table, she realized she no longer faced it alone.

They breathed in unison, letting the restaurant's ambience envelop them. When the last of their dinner disappeared, they quietly agreed that this was exactly what they had needed. A small moment to ward off the heavier weight of illusions and sabotage, if only for an evening.

It was, in every sense, their first dinner together in a world that refused to pause for magic. Yet they took that pause anyway, forging a memory that might guide them through the tests waiting beyond the restaurant door.

OTHER FLORID ROMANCE BOOKS

To be notified of new releases and special promotions from Florid Romance, please join our email list:

https://floridromance.lmbpn.com/about/sign-up-for-our-newsletter/

For a complete list of books published by Florid Romance please visit our website:

https://floridromance.lmbpn.com/

BOOKS BY KELLI ROBYNS

The Enchanted Orchard
The Orchard (Book 1)
Family Curse (Book 2)
Crystal Heart (Book 3)

The Charmed City
Spellbound (Book 1)
Prophecy (Book 2)

BOOKS BY MICHAEL ANDERLE

Sign up for the LMBPN email list to be notified of new releases and special deals!

https://lmbpn.com/email/

For a complete list of books by Michael Anderle, please visit:

www.lmbpn.com/ma-books/

CONNECT WITH MICHAEL ANDERLE

Connect with Michael Anderle

Website: http://lmbpn.com

Email List: https://michael.beehiiv.com/

https://www.facebook.com/LMBPNPublishing

https://twitter.com/MichaelAnderle

https://www.instagram.com/lmbpn_publishing/

https://www.bookbub.com/authors/michael-anderle